WOLF'S LAIR

WOLF'S LAIR

A NOVEL BY

ROGER ELWOOD

WORD PUBLISHING
Dallas · London · Vancouver · Melbourne

WOLF'S LAIR

Copyright © 1993 by Roger Paul Elwood. All rights reserved. No portion of this book may be reproduced in any form, except for brief quotations in reviews, without written permission from the publisher.

Scripture quotations used in this book are from the King James Version of the Bible.

Library of Congress Cataloging-in-Publication Data

Elwood, Roger
Wolf's lair / by Roger Elwood
p. cm.
ISBN 0-8499-3386-2 (trade paper)
1. World War, 1939-1945—Germany—Fiction. 2. Heydrich, Reinhard, 1904-1942—Assassination—Fiction. I. Title.
PS3555.L85W65 1993
813'.54—dc20 92-44970
CIP

Printed in the United States of America

3 4 5 6 7 9 LB 9 8 7 6 5 4 3 2 1

Courage is resistance to fear, mastery of fear—not absence of fear. Except a man be part coward, it is not a compliment to say he is brave.

Mark Twain

I

Below the sleek black-painted airplane, its engines especially muffled, was an isolated section of dense Bavarian forest, at night just an anonymous jumble of vague shapes. Allied intelligence reports declared it was a largely uninhabited region. And no Nazi patrols had been detected any closer than two dozen miles or so.

"Godspeed, sir," the husky-looking British captain named Harrison Cowles told him. "I hope you're able to plug that monster!"

Tall, sandy-haired, with the frame of a long-time athlete, Stephen Bartlett smiled with the ease of a man not lacking in self-confidence. He had learned nothing but appreciation for Cowles, a gregarious individual who seemed courageous enough to storm the gates of hell itself if called upon to do so.

I wish Casey, de Gaulle, and the others had sent him along with me on this mission, Bartlett thought. *I don't see how the Nazis could ever intimidate someone like Cowles!*

"Plugging Adolf Hitler and his henchmen is my wish exactly, Captain," he said out loud. "And when that's done, I'm heading straight for home."

"And a fine wife and son you have, sir," Cowles added spiritedly. "Like you, I'd be proud to call those two my own. You can be sure I shall personally check in on them in your absence."

"I hope you do," Bartlett assured him. "My son Andrew will become an instant fan of yours."

Captain Cowles blushed as they shook hands, then Bartlett turned to his right and glanced at the other man standing beside him just then.

"Are you ready, Kleist?" he asked, looking at the tall, thin, blond-haired German who chose not to speak during the flight, nor had he said much back at the base in England, exuding stern competence but nothing else, including little of what could be called personality.

"We now liberate the fatherland!" Kleist declared finally, his voice firm but with an edge that Bartlett found rather curious.

"It *will* be done," Bartlett assured him, "because it *must* be done."

The two men snapped a ten-foot-long section of thin rawhide to their belts so they wouldn't drift apart when they jumped. They hesitated beside the gaping hatch just long enough to return Cowles's farewell salute; then they jumped out of the plane and into the bleak and intimidating darkness, the captain's hearty "God guide and protect you!" following them into the night sky.

Stephen Bartlett had parachuted often over the years. Each time he enjoyed the rush of adrenaline as it swept over him, nerve ends tingling, heart beating faster, stomach tight. Each time a pervasive and exhilarating sense of utter freedom mixed with danger grabbed hold of him.

Andy, Andy, Bartlett thought. *Someday, son, you and I will make our first jump together.*

His wife and their son would remain in England, well cared for by the United States and British governments, protection vitally necessary because if his identity were ever uncovered by the Gestapo, their undercover agents were certain to seek out his family with maniacal determination and deal with them harshly in retribution.

His thoughts were jarred back to reality as the canopy opened and the lines of his parachute tightened, jerking him upward, then slowing his fall.

Without warning, something tightened around his throat, digging into the soft skin. Oxygen was quickly being cut off from his lungs.

Briefly, he glimpsed the face of Kleist, someone who supposedly was driven by such an intense hatred of the Nazi leaders that he would face the dangerous task of attempting to assassinate them. As the two men struggled in midair, Bartlett heard words as though these came from the opposite end of a very long tunnel.

"Piano wire can serve so *many* purposes," Kleist said, a gleeful laugh tearing past his lips. "And a helpful wind along with it. Now I don't have to wait to do this on the ground."

As warm liquid trickled down his neck, Bartlett knew he probably would be dead in a few seconds. He had only one chance to save himself.

A knife in a holster strapped to his left side!

With his right hand Bartlett clutched at Kleist, trying to break the traitor's grip on the wire that grew ever tighter around his neck. With the other hand he desperately groped for the knife and missed; then his fingers closed quickly around the metal-rimmed, polished-wood handle. In one fumbling move he retrieved the knife and jabbed out blindly with it.

A groan. Again he struck. And again. The constriction around his throat ended abruptly, and the knife fell from his grip. He felt a tug on his belt as Kleist's inert body floated away, tightening the tether. Bartlett unsnapped the rawhide line and Kleist's limp form was carried away by a gust of chill Bavarian wind, wind that made the tree branches below seem like a single swaying mass.

Before Stephen Bartlett made contact with the thick branches that were winter-bare except for a covering of fresh snow, an image of his wife Natalie and their son Andrew, their arms outstretched, flashed across his mind. Then a dark and total abyss closed around him, and he surrendered to it.

Bartlett felt something wet against his cheek. Every muscle in his body tensed. There was an odor he couldn't quite place, thick and unpleasant.

Movement. The sound of snow being crunched lightly underfoot. And then pain as something tore into his wrist.

His eyes shot open.

Wolves.

He had fallen past the branches and landed on the hard, snow-packed ground. Perhaps an hour later, the pack found him while he was regaining consciousness. One had clamped its mouth over his wrist, which was covered by a heavy glove. The others seemed to be waiting. He sensed that they didn't know what he was. His winter clothing was so thick that they got no definable scent from his body, one reason why that particular material had been chosen.

Only his face was exposed.

They're going to go for it! The thought terrorized him.

Five wolves, the one dropping his wrist, then backing up as it sensed some response from him.

He tried not to breathe, to move in any way but he couldn't help himself. Air came out from his nostrils in white bursts. The closest wolf froze for a moment, studying Bartlett through blood-red eyes, its mouth half-open, a low growl beginning deep within its body, not unlike the warning of a rattlesnake.

He rolled over and over, as rapidly as he could. The wolves were now snarling and snapping at him, tearing at his clothes, trying to keep such a scarce meal from getting away. One of them locked its teeth on his ankle. He stifled a cry of pain, knowing that sound would only make them more frenzied.

He stopped rolling. Dead. He wanted them to think he was dead.

If they can't draw blood, if they taste nothing that appeals to them, they might become bored and go away, he told himself, knowing this gambit was one of desperation and nothing more.

Five wolves, suddenly all headed for his face.

Bartlett was a former college football player and a weight-lifter, bench-pressing a minimum of five hundred pounds. Judging by weight alone, none of the wolves would be a problem. But he doubted he could handle the entire bunch of them at once.

Just that one, he thought. *It seems to be the leader. If I can—*

In one sudden movement he grabbed it around its neck and jumped to his feet. The other wolves stopped in midstride, proving themselves to be the timid creatures they were, acting more from some canine version of bluffing than from any real courage.

Bartlett gripped the top of the wolf's snout just below the eyes and clamped down his fingers while wrapping his other arm around its neck. Then he twisted the head a full 180 degrees. He heard bones suddenly snap and a sharp cry of pain, then the wolf fell lifeless in his arms. He threw the limp form straight at the remaining members of the pack. They yelped, and then ran off.

Bartlett's entire body was trembling. Part of his insulated suit had been shredded by the wolves, and the near-zero temperature now would more easily kill him if he didn't get to some warmth soon. The remaining untouched inner layer was not thick enough to withstand the cold for very long.

But he hesitated a moment or two before slowly walking over to the lifeless body.

"I wish it could have been different," he said out loud as he glanced at the gray-black coat of fur, stirred now by gusts of icy wind, while remembering the German shepherd he'd had as a boy. That truly fine childhood companion bore more than a passing resemblance to the wolf at his feet.

In the next instant, Bartlett noticed another body that made him feel even worse, despite the fact that he'd had to do what he did purely to save his own life. This one was a she-wolf, and her enlarged nipples testified to the fact that she was still nursing.

Usually the males do all of the hunting for the pack, he reminded himself guiltily. *This winter must be a desperate one for them, if the females have been forced to join in the hunting.*

He was turning away when some movement caught his eye in a nearby thicket of bushes. He approached the rustling branches cautiously, realizing that, instead, he should have been leaving that spot without fail.

Inside the thicket were two wolf cubs. One was quite healthy-looking, the other barely alive. Both bore fresh wounds. Something had attacked them before the mother and the rest of the pack could intervene. Their apparent age, judging by the size of their bodies, suggested that the nursing process was nearly over but they were not yet trained to hunt food on their own.

This is absurd, Bartlett told himself. *I'm here to help people, not animals!*

Shrugging his shoulders, he turned away, took out his compass, got his bearings, and then glanced at his watch.

He would have to hurry.

Members of the German Resistance Movement were due to pick him up in just seventeen hours, if he could make it to their scheduled meeting point in time. It was near a small waterfall at the base of a particularly remote section of the Bavarian Alps that had served as a spot for hardy, roughing-it tourists before the war broke out and was especially valued for its isolation.

But his pack must have been jammed among the tree branches as he hit them, for he could not find it anywhere on the ground. His chances for survival were greatly reduced without the pack. Inside it were bullets for the pistol strapped to his waist, along with flares, some canned food, water, and a small first-aid kit.

He finally saw it on a branch after he had climbed halfway up the nearest tree, trying for a better view.

Sitting on top of it was a large falcon that had started to investigate the contents. Even as he watched, the bird succeeded in pulling open one end of the pack, then started eating some biscuits wrapped in silver foil his wife had made for him.

Bartlett couldn't use his pistol this time any more safely than during his encounter with the wolves because he couldn't take the chance some Nazis might have decided to patrol the area for the first time in weeks and the sound of a gun being fired could easily lead them directly to him. He got the falcon's attention by waving his hands frenziedly, trying to scare it away. Instead of leaving, though, the bird simply stopped eating and studied Bartlett curiously.

Here I am, on a mission to kill a maniacal human monster, and I can't do anything because a big bird likes Natalie's biscuits! he exclaimed to himself, the irony making him chuckle a bit.

He decided that if he couldn't get the falcon off the pack, he would have to do something about the branch itself. So he backed down the one tree and started up the other where his pack had become entangled. In his outer garment he had a second knife, this one a pocketknife with a serrated edge; he used it to saw away at the bottom of the thick branch, glad (at least temporarily) that the pack weighed as much as it did, for this meant that, soon, the pressure on the branch would cause it to crack and fall.

In just a few minutes that was what happened, with everything going according to Bartlett's makeshift plan. Everything, that is, except one factor he hadn't counted on.

A startled falcon.

It flew directly at him, grabbing the front of his jacket with its sharp talons and attacking him with a strong beak capable of tearing flesh from the bone. It screeched terrifyingly at him while its wings pummeled Bartlett's body.

Bartlett tumbled again, his pack hitting the ground first. He landed on top of it, contact bringing sharp pain to his shoulders, back, and sides.

The falcon spiraled after him. He had just enough chance to reach for the knife at his side and swing it out and upward. The falcon squawked twice as it was impaled, dying less than a second later; he flung it to one side.

After wiping off the pocketknife in the snow and sliding it back in its holster, Bartlett stood without moving, feeling weak. Frozen blood was caking his cheeks and neck, which had become swollen and sore from the piano wire Kleist had used.

He could feel himself beginning to waver and was suddenly tempted to lie down in the snow and just go to sleep, a fatal move in such temperatures, when he saw something moving a few feet to his right, next to the dead she-wolf. One of the cubs had come out of the thicket and was nudging his mother, trying to get her to move a bit so he could get his mouth around a nipple.

Bartlett stood. He had so little time to travel what was a short distance in good weather but which became all the more chancy the longer he waited. Hurting from the latest fall more than the first one, his neck, and his face stinging from the torn skin, he grabbed the pack, lifted it back up, slung the strap over his shoulder, and sighed wearily as he considered the distance ahead of him.

Contact had been made with the leaders of the German Resistance Movement and arrangements were in place for Bartlett to assist them in any way he could. If nothing else his presence would indicate how supportive the Allies were of any effort directed toward such a mutual goal, whatever the short-term costs might be. Yet his experience as a crack undercover agent and munitions expert unquestionably would prove to be much more valuable than simple moral support!

It was critical that the partisans be treated as equals, for they were risking their lives as much as Bartlett himself or anyone else sent in by the Allies to cripple Germany's war effort from within. But despite their courage, they were not professional soldiers or spies or anything of the sort.

Emil Kleist would have put everyone in even greater jeopardy than they already are, he thought. *Undoubtedly he would have come up with some story about my death, and then insinuated himself in the resistance movement in my place, feeding their information straight to Berlin!*

Fortunately, Bartlett was the only one with all the details of the mission, a precaution taken by the Organization of Secret Service director William Casey. Yet Kleist had known that *something* was in progress. Prior to leaving on the mission, had he been able to get a cautionary message back to the Nazi high command?

Anyway, the traitor's dead now, Bartlett thought, *I don't have to worry about—*

He stopped himself, realizing that he had seen Kleist carried away on the wind, bleeding from his stab wounds, but there was no certainty of the man's death, none at all.

What if he survived and finds his way to a Nazi outpost?

Bartlett shivered but not from the cold. He started to walk, then noticed that the cub had crawled directly into his path. Other men would have simply kicked it aside and continued on.

But Bartlett stopped, glancing at his watch yet again.

"I can't help you," he said out loud. "I'm wondering how I'm going to help myself if I don't make it to the rendezvous point in time."

With a sigh, Bartlett slid the pack off his shoulders, reached down, and lifted the fragile little body, then took it back to the thicket, intending to place it near the other cub, thinking the two bodies could somehow succeed in warming one another.

But what good is that without food? Wolf cubs are amazingly resourceful but they need some help at the beginning . . .

Dead. The other cub was dead. Its mouth was open, tongue extended, eyes half-shut.

If I leave you here, you're going to join him in death before very long, I'm afraid, Bartlett thought as he realized the cub in his hand wasn't as strong as he had thought earlier; its infected wounds, worse than he had thought at first, were sending poisons throughout the little body.

He knew he couldn't leave the animal there. So he opened his insulated jacket and tucked all but the head inside . . .

Stephen Bartlett's mission had begun at No. 10 Downing Street.

In the rear of the prime minister's residence, a special large, rectangular room, reinforced with plain-white concrete-block walls and ceiling, had been designated for critical wartime meetings of the prime minister, various generals, and others such as William Casey who had founded the American OSS.

Churchill was giving a speech elsewhere on the day of the meeting in a neighborhood that, months before, suffered ghastly losses from the *blitzkrieg*. Its citizens now needed the sort of encouragement that only he could give to them.

Dressed in street clothes, Casey was joined by Charles de Gaulle, wearing a field military outfit, and various high-level aides at the meeting that resulted in Stephen Bartlett being sent on a mission that would eventually lead down the road to assassination.

"The resistance had other chances to get the devil," Casey was pointing out, "and they failed time after time after time. Remember the summer of 1938? They thought that getting a few psychiatrists together and having Hitler declared insane would do the job!"

He paused for effect, then added with a sarcastic chuckle, "So Adolf had the shrinks murdered. War can never be left to those who have not made the potential of war a lifetime preoccupation."

It was obvious that easy agreement with the American was an uncomfortable prospect for de Gaulle but, whatever his prickly personality facets, he was a man of surpassing integrity, and admitting the truth, however reluctantly, was inescapable as far as he was concerned.

"You are correct, William," he said with unexpected warmth. "Your cogency is appreciated."

Casey nodded condescendingly and continued: "The harsh truth, Charles, is that we cannot allow the various resistance movements to do any of this completely on their own. Starting with the GRM and then moving on to the Czechs, we must send in our best men to help them."

The incompetence of the German and Czechoslovakian resistance factions, the latter headed by the egocentric former Czech president Benes, was being proven again and again.

"Failure can no longer be permitted!" Casey said, nearly shouting as he recalled the past episodes associated with Benes. "There are many generals and others in the German military and in the government itself who would grab control away from Hitler's gang if he were no longer there to pull the strings. Their failure to cause his downfall in no way mitigates their value as leaders once that downfall has occurred. Such a precious opportunity must never be allowed to slip through our fingers again."

"But there is something else to consider or, rather, someone else," de Gaulle immediately suggested, perhaps consciously trying to change the group's general perception of him. "While I agree that Hitler should be top priority, the Führer is not, after all, the lone monster."

"Himmler?" Casey interjected. "Yes, he certainly should be dealt with as well."

"I am not thinking of Himmler or Goebbels or Bormann or Göring."

Just then a door to the room opened and Churchill entered, still wearing his insulated topcoat, necessary apparel against the chill London air and typical foggy dampness. As always, he carried with him not only the aura of his importance as prime minister of a besieged nation but also a touch of the proverbial bull in a china shop.

"It has to be Heydrich!" he announced, getting some pleasure in grabbing the spotlight from de Gaulle. "Am I not correct, gentlemen?"

"You indeed are correct," de Gaulle said, each word spoken in a toneless and deliberate manner. The leader-in-exile was barely able to talk at all out of resentment over the intrusion. "Himmler's protégé is known to be far worse than Himmler himself and very possibly even worse than Hitler."

"You say 'known to be'? What do you base that on?" Casey asked, knowing the answer but wanting de Gaulle to justify himself.

"Before leaving my country, I saw Heydrich stand in front of a family of four Jews and personally shoot each one in the head. I could see him smile as he did so," de Gaulle continued. "After he was finished, he noticed that one of the two children, a six-year-old girl, was still alive. He took out a knife, grabbed her hair, and lifted her up in front of him while he slit her throat; then he dumped her body back on the ground and went off with the SS officers gathered around him, presumably to take care of other business."

De Gaulle exerted an effort to keep his feelings from further exposure—but failed.

"They were laughing, those monsters!" he said. "They *enjoyed* that moment. I could see that it gave them considerable satisfaction. And Heydrich was laughing the most boisterously!"

He blinked half a dozen times in rapid succession.

"I wanted to storm from the woods and kill that beast!" he went on, trembling. "I cared not for myself, but any such move might have meant that the men with me also would be slaughtered. I had to think of the overall mission."

He looked from Churchill to Casey, seeking solace from them.

"I regret not doing what I had to fight against doing," he said. "It haunts me to this very moment."

For a short while de Gaulle stood silently in front of the concrete-slab table strewn with maps, his eyes closed, his tall body trembling.

"We should call this Bartlett fellow," Churchill offered, finally able to break the silence that lasted for several minutes. "I've gone through his dossier. I think he is the only choice worth considering."

The American had received the highest security clearing of any individual Casey had ever checked out, causing the OSS founder to joke, "He's a safer risk than I am." Bartlett, a superb espionage agent who had tipped off the Allies about forthcoming plans to institute Hitler's "Final Solution" against Jews and Gypsies in the conquered countries of Europe, was also the top munitions expert the Allies had. Especially interesting was his work toward foolhardy various explosive devices.

"Whatever explosives or weapons Stephen Bartlett designs or overhauls *will* work," Casey stated. "He must be the one we select. I am willing to risk my own reputation on this man. But he has another quality that is singularly important as well."

"And what is that?" de Gaulle asked, fascinated, but nevertheless trying to act in his usual detached manner.

"He is not an arrogant sort," Casey replied. "He can fit in with the partisans almost instantly. They will accept him as one of their own."

"You feel he can be entrusted with the full scope of WOLF'S LAIR?" de Gaulle asked.

"That, and anything else we ask of him. We have never before dealt with somebody of his caliber in the areas we want him to work. I am thinking not only of bombs but also of his espionage experience. I want Bartlett to make sure the partisans use the right explosives, yes, even if this means having him construct something new on the spot. But, in addition, while they are going after Heydrich himself, I want to see if Bartlett can successfully pose as a Gestapo agent and get inside the monster's house where, we are told, some extraordinary documents are being kept. If we can make WOLF'S LAIR a dual triumph, then it is worth whatever the cost might be."

WOLF'S LAIR . . .

More than just a code name, it was also an attempt to mislead the Nazis if indeed the plot to assassinate Heydrich happened to be uncovered by Gestapo operatives. Their immediate assumption would be that the Führer himself was the target, since they all were well aware of the fact that WOLF'S LAIR was the English translation for Rastenburg, the site of Hitler's principal headquarters outside Berlin itself.

"I agree this should be done," Churchill remarked. "And you, Charles?"

"I must say this Stephen Bartlett seems like an exceptional fellow," de Gaulle said slowly, with seeming reluctance, unaccustomed to praising anyone who wasn't French.

Even with that, de Gaulle was not quite finished. To the surprise of both Churchill and Casey, he added, after clearing his throat, "We should thank God we have this man."

2

Hours later the blizzard intensified, giving Bartlett more than a clue as to why that area had remained "largely uninhabited." Until then, he had been making reasonable progress, but the heavier snowfall forced him to slow down, and the bitter cold was beginning to make itself felt.

Finally, he could go no farther. Briefly he wondered if weather patterns had been considered, and why it wouldn't have been better to wait just a few weeks. Surely that was all it would have taken, unless the German Resistance Movement had given some hint that it planned to strike before summer and if the Allies wanted to help, they had better pitch in without delay.

Reinhard Heydrich was to be assassinated by a bomb!

This mandated that the bomb to be used *had* to be absolutely reliable. There could not be the slightest chance of it misfiring. And no one other than Stephen Bartlett had the knowledge that would make this possible. Which was why Casey and the others back in London were betting that Bartlett would come to be considered invaluable to the GRM and its Czech counterpart. He had spent much of his life studying munitions of every kind, and constructing not a few, fascinated by the power they embodied, though he sometimes wondered why—from childhood fireworks then sticks of dynamite to handmade bombs and other, more sophisticated and potent devices when he joined the OSS.

But constructing these devices was only one aspect of his usefulness during wartime. He was also uncommonly adept at defusing even the most complicated devices, including German bombs that had been dropped on London without detonating, sometimes landing on rooftops, where their weight often caused them to collapse through more than one floor. Or they sometimes fell without exploding and landed in the midst of parks such as Saint James and Hyde, as well as on side streets and main thoroughfares, confronting anyone—terrified motorists and pedestrians alike—who happened to venture there. But apart from all this, Bartlett was invaluable because he had proven himself to be one of the most adept espionage agents working for the Allies. It was rare that any man combined the skills that had become second nature to this American. That was why the partisans needed him but also why everyone in the Allied command center in London would have many sleepless nights waiting for him to return safely.

This mission is mandated because of the maniac I'm supposed to help take out, Bartlett told himself. *I hope I can fulfill—*

Just as that thought was born, Bartlett grew dizzy and sank to his knees, trying desperately to marshal some strength and get back up, get to his feet, anything but just rest there. He couldn't stay in one spot longer than a few minutes, couldn't lie down in the snow, not even with the kind of clothing he wore; he had no choice but to keep going, keep his blood pumping . . . or become as dead and frozen as the bleak landscape that stretched out before him in every direction.

But his strength was gone. Snow covered his still form in minutes. He thought about the wolf cub huddled close to him and how he had wanted to save its life, only to have it come to share death with him.

Growling . . . At first Bartlett thought it might have been part of a dream, a dream that already was impossible to remember clearly.

He heard shouts. Human voices.

"Don't shoot!" someone said in German. "If there's a patrol anywhere nearby, the Nazis will be on us like the vultures they are."

"But the wolves, Franz! They're all around us!" another yelled. "We're going to be torn apart!"

Bartlett opened his eyes to an astonishing sight: Three very tough-looking men dressed in soiled, well-worn sheepskin jackets were standing a few feet away. The snow had stopped falling. Nighttime darkness remained, with red eyes everywhere, dozens of pairs.

"Must be every last wolf in the whole region!" one of the men gasped. "All of them *here!*"

The growling had gotten louder. Bartlett tried to move, to say something, but what came out of his mouth was unintelligible. He was heard, though, understood or not. The shortest of the men ran to his side.

"I'm Franz Kallenborn," he said in heavily accented English. "We'll get you warm as soon as we can leave this spot and make it back to our haven. Frankly, Stephen, I've never seen this many wolves together before. Their packs usually aren't as large as this. They must be really hungry!"

Bartlett managed to unzip his coat a bit more.

"The . . . cub . . . I think . . . it's the cub," he said hoarsely.

The little creature poked its head out, looking sleepy and warm.

"Could it be they've come for one of their own?" Kallenborn said. "How is that possible?"

"Don't know," replied Bartlett weakly, his voice hoarse. "Give the cub . . . to them . . . *be careful!*"

Kallenborn pulled out the thin young body, carried it to where the wolves were standing, and placed it on the snow in front of them; then the three men hurried to Bartlett, bending down beside him.

"Hope that does it," Kallenborn commented. "You're in bad shape, Stephen. We need to get you treated right away. If the cub doesn't satisfy them, we'll have to shoot our way through. And that puts us in great danger of being detected by the very enemies who have been wrecking our country."

Bartlett suspected that being called by his first name was a sign of warm and ready acceptance by someone who looked as though he could topple a tree by gnawing bare-toothed at the bark.

One adult wolf appeared, then two others. They sniffed at the cub's body, one of them nudging it.

"Let's get out of here while they're ignoring us," whispered Kallenborn, frowning deeply.

The three men lifted Bartlett's body as carefully as they could.

"Fortunately, you were close. In fact you almost made it to our haven," remarked Kallenborn. "We're only a short distance away."

They had come on three low-slung, wooden toboggans fitted with metal skis. Bartlett was secured on top of one by well-worn but strong leather straps; Kallenborn stood directly behind it.

"You two go on ahead," he said. "My new friend and I will not be far behind you."

Bartlett glanced up at this man, a stranger, realizing that in the weeks ahead the two of them would depend upon one another for their very survival.

"Thank you," he said, his voice weak, nearly inaudible. "I owe you such a great deal already."

"If all goes as we have planned, *I* expect to owe *you* much more," the other replied. "So will all of this, my homeland!"

The haven was as great a monument to human ingenuity as anything Bartlett had encountered thus far in his career.

"We pray for the snow," Kallenborn told him in a gruffly honest manner. "It hides us even better."

What Bartlett witnessed was an extraordinary relic of sorts from World War I, a concealed bunker set deep within that section of the Bavarian Alps.

"When spring comes, we have only the trees and undergrowth to help keep this secret of ours," Kallenborn remarked. "That does the job, but we always feel a little more secure during blizzards."

And for good reason! The bunker was completely covered at that moment by a smooth blanket of snow. Even when it was not, the Germans a quarter of a century earlier had done such a fine job of concealing it that the portals, from the outside, looked like nothing more than small openings between the rocks.

"We have to be concerned about tracks betraying us," Kallenborn added, "so we always have one of our members assigned to eliminating them each and every time someone enters or leaves."

Bartlett only vaguely heard what the other man was saying. The warmth inside the bunker felt extraordinarily good, and he was beginning to doze off. He saw flashes of the interior and of men with rifles standing at attention as Kallenborn passed by; a pile of hand grenades covered the top of a long metal table. Finally, lifted off the toboggan as gently as possible, he was taken to a small room at the end of a short corridor.

"These are my quarters," Kallenborn told him. "You will sleep in my bed, and I will take a place elsewhere for this first night and however many more will be necessary."

After his clothes had been stripped off him, towels were dipped in hot water and applied to his body for short periods. Two men worked at the warming process, which included serving hot soup that Bartlett was certain was the most delicious he had ever tasted. After they were gone, Kallenborn stayed, talking nearly nonstop in an effort to keep Bartlett's mind off the pain that returned to his limbs and elsewhere.

"It is amazing, Stephen, what we encountered, you know, with those wolves," he told Bartlett. "We have never known them to be anything but creatures worthy of loathing and some fear."

"They could . . . have . . . attacked," Bartlett managed to croak.

"Yes, that *is* what my comrades and I had been fearing. But they seemed instead to be just waiting. I cannot explain that, you know. My rational Germanic mind finds it utterly perplexing, strange . . . "

"I think . . . they wanted the . . . cub, nothing more."

Bartlett's voice was giving out. Kallenborn noticed this and suggested that he try to get some rest. "I should grab some shuteye myself," he added. "It has been a very long night for both of us."

Kallenborn patted Bartlett on his bare shoulder and pulled the thick blanket closer around his neck.

"Sleep well, my friend," he said sympathetically. "We have some awful days ahead of us."

Bartlett spent the rest of that day and much of the next recuperating. His quarters were spartan, with just the bed he was on, two bare wooden chairs, and, between them, a single, small square table on which he saw a photograph of Kallenborn and a blonde-haired woman holding a blond-haired young boy.

"They're gone," Kallenborn had told him earlier when he saw Bartlett looking at the picture.

"Gone?" Bartlett asked. "You mean, they are being kept somewhere—"

"Dead, Stephen. Dead."

Clad in a faded red shirt, open at the neck, and freshly pressed gray slacks, Kallenborn had picked up the photo and held it in front of him.

"We were able to get passage on a train to Switzerland. The plan was for me to leave them there and then slip back into Germany. We were so close to the border, Stephen."

"The SS stopped you?"

"The SS blew up the entire train!"

He put the photo back on the table and faced Bartlett.

"Some of the passengers survived," he said, his eyes bloodshot. "I happened to be one of them."

A few minutes later Bartlett went back to sleep. He slept until midmorning of the next day, finally getting the rest he needed. Then began a long parade of one GRM member after another, each realizing that he represented Allied support in general but, more importantly, American participation specifically.

One area of early consultation with them was over their weapons stockpile, which was stored in a section of the bunker near his quarters. Kallenborn thought that surveying it would be interesting, but he assured Bartlett they could stop as soon as his energy wore down, then he could go back to bed.

"You are in very good shape with grenades," Bartlett complimented Kallenborn and the others in the small group that had accompanied him, and they were obviously pleased that he felt as he did.

Their supply was divided into three types: First were the pineapple grenades, each with an iron body scored so it would break into fragments—grenades used primarily for defensive purposes. A second type was can-shaped with a cardboard body containing a powerful charge, to be used for offense. The third was a phosphorous grenade, capable of laying down a foglike screen intended to conceal small troop movements.

"And now you will see our land mines," Kallenborn announced, smiling with totally justifiable pride. "We intercepted a shipment destined for Rommel's campaign in North Africa."

"Isn't Rommel sympathetic to your cause?" Bartlett asked.

"He is, he is . . . perhaps someday he will actually *join* us," Kallenborn replied, his tone more of wishful thinking than any real expectation that the brilliant general would come over to their side.

The American saw scores of brutally effective German Shu mines, each consisting of a half-pound of TNT in a wooden box topped by a lid that was propped open by a twig. When the twig was disturbed, the lid dropped and the TNT exploded.

"Ah, bouncing Betties!" Bartlett exclaimed.

The German couldn't help but be impressed. "You may be everything you are supposed to be!" he said, tongue-in-cheek.

Minutes later, as Kallenborn led Bartlett to yet another room, the largest one of the bunch, he commented, "Do you feel like seeing our rifles and pistols now? We could wait."

"I'd be happy to look at what you have," Bartlett agreed, then gasped as he glanced inside and saw the extent of the cache. "Enough to keep an army going!"

"We are indeed an army," the German told him. "We don't have the uniforms. There are no parades for us, not as yet anyway. We have no crushing bureaucracy with which to be concerned. We hit, then we run; we hit, then we run. We fight for honor, we fight for our families, we fight to take back this ancient land from the serpents who have overrun it."

"But some of those serpents were once your friends, your neighbors . . . " the American started to say.

"My mother," Kallenborn replied, "serves the Third Reich as one of Hitler's personal cooks."

"Perhaps she was forced into it."

"No . . . she volunteered! I protested and she disowned me, yet pledged not to turn me in to the Gestapo."

"And your father?"

"He's been dead a very long time. My mother blames the Jews."

"How could that be?"

"He committed suicide. She says the Jews drove him into bankruptcy. As a result, they got his clothing business for, as you Americans would say, ten cents on the dollar."

Bartlett hadn't known that.

"Franz," he said, "I am *very* sorry, my friend, so very sorry."

"It is something you either live with or it crushes you. If the Jews took advantage of my father for profit, and I'm not sure they did, then what does that make Hitler and his gangs for doing the same thing with Germany in the midst of *its* woes? Frankly I have no time for the Jews, but I cannot allow that feeling to bind *me* to the monsters who want to annihilate them."

Bartlett was deeply affected by the other man's candor. It had never occurred to him that there were Germans who distrusted Jews but who drew the line at sending them off to the death camps. He had fallen into the trap of assuming that if they were anti-Semitic, they were automatically Nazis.

"Germans will never totally accept Jews," Kallenborn offered. "We all can point to instances throughout our history where it has *seemed* that we were the victims and Jews the oppressors."

"But you would give your life to save them," Bartlett pointed out.

Kallenborn shrugged. He could see Bartlett was tired and suggested the American get some sleep before the evening meal.

"Fine," Bartlett answered. "That's just what I need now . . . a little rest."

Minutes later, as he was falling asleep, he couldn't help but see that the main problem with Kallenborn and the others wasn't their ignorance of firepower. Where they desperately needed assistance was with strategy. From what he had seen, they were surprisingly inept, in part because their sources of information were often erratic, but also because most had never had to function on a *military* basis before. They were farmers, lawyers, schoolteachers, policemen, and so on—the business of the battlefield once had seemed very distant to them. Yet now they had begun to think of themselves as qualified tacticians . . . just the sort of situation where an outsider's advice ran the greatest risk of damaging the most egos.

3

"You have been through so much in a short time," remarked Bruno Vetters, a short, hefty man in his mid-thirties, as they were eating dinner. "I am very glad to see you are feeling better."

"And anxious to get started," Bartlett replied. "Wars sometimes may be necessary but they hang on just a bit too long for my taste."

Vetters understood that Stephen Bartlett was a man of sometimes the most sardonic humor.

"I thought we Germans cornered the market on that sort of joke," he said, not without appreciation. Vetters stood and smiled as he asked, "If you've finished eating, would you feel like coming with me? It is dusk now; we sometimes sit outside after dinner to get some fresh air."

Bartlett would have been delighted to join him under any other circumstances, but the day had been a tiring one, and he thought he would fall asleep as soon as he made contact with the well-stuffed, comfortable pillow.

"May I go with you the *next* time?" he asked, concerned about offending the other man.

Vetters shrugged his shoulders.

"It is fine," he said. "I know how you must feel. Being a hero can take a great deal out of a man."

He shook Bartlett's hand.

"Perhaps next time, as you say," Vetters said kindly.

As they walked back to his quarters, Bartlett asked, "Do you feel you are totally safe here?"

"We are *totally* safe only in heaven," Vetters commented. "But, yes, this is as safe as any place in Hitler's domain can be."

They had reached the tiny room.

"Not what you are used to, I'm afraid," the German observed.

"Nor you, I imagine."

"That is true. I miss our large house in the middle of our farmland. I miss my loved ones." He shook hands with Bartlett and wished him a restful sleep.

"We are *very* grateful, my new American friend," Vetters said, genuine warmth coloring his voice.

"I hope I *can* help," replied Bartlett, "but I don't see myself as a dispenser of miracles, you know."

"You have already helped, Stephen, trust me on that; you have already helped in the way your presence here sends a signal to the men. You've come at exactly the right time, please believe that."

After a day of continuous activity that included passing on to the GRM members some badly needed advice about setting up explosives, Bartlett was too tired at first to sleep soundly but finally managed to drift off into a state of near-sleep when he heard a voice shouting.

"Wolves!" the voice said. "There are a dozen wolves outside."

Bartlett's eyes shot open. Before he could get out of bed to see what was happening, Franz Kallenborn had eased open the door to the small quarters.

"Thank God you *are* up already," he said. "I hated the idea of awakening you. We had a full day and you seemed so tired!"

"What's going on?"

"They brought it back," Kallenborn told him.

"The cub?" Bartlett blurted out.

"You guess correctly."

The bunker's small rear entrance was opened for them by one of the resistance's well-armed guards. As soon as they were outside they were confronted by an astonishing sight. A dozen pairs of red eyes pierced the evening darkness, and directly in front of the eyes was a hapless-looking cub.

"You are a bit weak. Can you walk forward a foot or two?" Kallenborn asked Bartlett. "Do you need help?"

Bartlett shook his head and obliged his friend.

The healthy adult wolves growled at the movement, then ceased, staring intently at him. Then the pack started to howl instead, the kind of howl that had readily identified their kind for centuries.

Kallenborn came up to Bartlett and whispered, "Has anyone here ever seen anything like this?"

In an instant the wolves were gone. Except for the cub.

Other men from the bunker had ventured outside and were busy muttering their amazement.

"We have a mascot now," one of them said happily, "at least we do if we can keep it alive."

"Him," Bartlett said as he bent weakly over the barely breathing body. "This is a male wolf."

He turned to ask someone to lift up the animal for him but Kallenborn had anticipated this and was already at the spot, starting to put his hands carefully around the pitiful little creature.

"They either left him to die," he said, "or they see you, Stephen, as someone to keep him alive."

"Should we do this, Franz?" Bartlett asked, surprised at himself for taking that side of the argument. "Can we afford the time, the energy, when everything must be concentrated on killing Heydrich?"

"Can we let our mission prevent us from being humane?" Kallenborn asked. "I'll let you decide, Stephen. I can drop him here now and he'll be dead by morning; then we can have all the time we want."

Bartlett glanced at the other men.

"A group project!" someone shouted. "We all will work to save the cub's life, yes? How can doing that hurt us? Hey, *can* we abandon the poor thing when we've witnessed what we just did?"

Bartlett nodded, sorry he had objected.

"You're right," he admitted to the others. "Maybe we can feed him a few Nazis now and then!"

Nursing the wolf cub to health proved to be a difficult task, one for which rough men assembled for purposes of destruction and killing were hardly well equipped.

"Wine!" one of the men suggested in all seriousness. "It could be part of his formula. Didn't Saint Paul write about a little wine for the sake of the stomach?"

"What is this you say?" a friend kidded him. "Your stomach must be upset all the time!"

At that point, the cub had been losing weight when he had so little to give up. But despite their skepticism, the combination of milk and wine seemed to accomplish one thing at least. It stopped the cub's moaning, which had been hard to take even for such steel-hearted men as the members of the resistance. The seemingly constant, pitiful little sounds coming from deep inside that frail body had been difficult for all of them.

Once, Bartlett happened upon Kallenborn holding the cub gently in his arms as he sat in a corner of the bunker's kitchen.

"He was in spasms," the man told him. "I couldn't let him go on like that without doing *something* about it. He seems to be drawing comfort from the warmth of my body."

Kallenborn smiled a bit, looking then not so much like a soldier fighting to take back his country from those who had usurped it but a boy who wanted very much to keep an animal friend alive.

"You're tired now, Franz, and it's late," Bartlett observed. "Let me take him for awhile."

Kallenborn hesitated, then stood and handed over the small body.

"Thank you, my brother," he said. "I do need some rest."

Bartlett took up a similar position, cradling the cub against his body. The cub seemed to be resting free of any pain. A few minutes later, the animal's eyes opened and he looked directly at the American before licking him once on the left hand, then falling asleep again.

Everyone in the bunker warmed to the little cub without reservation. Taking care of him and earning his affection added relief to the monotony and strain of their lives as they waited for the right moments to accomplish tasks they knew were unavoidable.

The wolf became nearly as much a part of their little settlement as any of the men. Each man seemed quite willing to appoint himself as the animal's protector or surrogate father. The only lingering difficulty was "house-training" him, but in time they were able to take him outside, wait patiently, then bring him in again as he learned why they were doing this. He made no move to bolt from any of them but seemed perfectly content to have their companionship.

It was again Stephen Bartlett's turn to be with the cub. They were outside the rear of the bunker. No fresh snow had fallen for a number of hours. Dusk had arrived. The glow of an especially crimson sunset spread over the ground, reflecting off the clear white covering. He remembered, as a child, scooping up some snow, running inside the Bartlett family house, and pouring vanilla syrup over it.

As good as any ice cream, he told himself, realizing how many years ago it had been and how far away he stood now, and what might lie ahead for him and for the others.

Bartlett brushed off the snow topping a large flat rock and sat down. After relieving himself the cub walked over to that spot and sat down, then stretched out in front of his human friend. Bartlett had become lost in other thoughts about his wife and son, wondering how they were coping, when he realized the cub was staring at him.

"What is it?" he asked.

There was something in the expression, a concern—at least that was how it looked to him. The cub somehow seemed to sense the loneliness that had just hit him as moments with his family had flashed across his mind.

Then wolves started to howl.

The cub immediately got to his feet, looking in one direction, then another, then finally, when the sounds were gone, he settled back down again. This time he was the one giving an impression of great loneliness in the way he held his head, his eyes darting from side to side, sporadic whimpers escaping from deep within his body.

"Go!" Bartlett said. "Go to your own kind. You're healthy now. Don't deprive yourself."

The animal looked up, and then, coincidentally or otherwise, shook his head several times.

"You've adopted us more completely than we could ever do with you," spoke Bartlett. "Having you with us doesn't go against our nature. But *staying* with us goes against yours!"

Bartlett decided to go back into the bunker. Careful as always, he waited until the cub was inside before he obscured the two sets of tracks. If there was no fresh snow by morning, men inside, with the specific duty of removing any footprints, would go to work with a vacuum-type machine that sucked snow from one area and threw it out somewhere else. In this case, it would cover the area where Bartlett and the wolf had been, eradicating any evidence of their presence.

This extra bit of work was essential. Energetic, vital men couldn't *stay* inside for months on end without their morale deteriorating. They had to get out, if only to suck the pure, cold air into their lungs. And yet no traces that they had been there could be allowed.

The trash cannot be thrown out or incinerated, Bartlett reminded himself. *The odor or the smoke or both could be detected by Nazi patrols on the ground or in the air. It has to be buried as deep into the ground as possible, and then the snow replaced on top. And all the while, someone has to be on watch, totally alert, searching for any clue of unwelcome intruders.*

The cub proved capable of absorbing the good moments experienced by his human benefactors as well as the very bad ones, such as when they heard planes overhead or Nazis driving by in tanks or jeeps or the sounds of distant gunfire. When they were nervous, so was he. When they were irritable, so he became, growling or snapping at them. Sometimes he went off by himself to some isolated corner of the bunker, where he tilted his head back and howled out his own feelings, sometimes in the middle of the night.

Yet nothing interrupted the bond that grew between the young wolf and the two dozen men who had taken him in. It would become deeper than any of them would ever suspect.

Weeks later, with some embarrassment, Bartlett, Kallenborn, and the others realized they hadn't named their adopted friend and were referring to him simply as the wolf or the cub although he was growing so rapidly the latter seemed more and more absurd.

Realizing this, the group took a break from more serious considerations and met about the matter with Kallenborn, Vetters, and a few others agreeing on the name Vulf, a German colloquialism derived from Wolfram, Wolfen, and others.

"Bloody appropriate I say!" declared Bruno Vetters. "Anybody here who will speak out against the use of Vulf?"

Two dozen GRM members were seated in the main hall at long tables still covered with the few remains of a remarkably hearty breakfast. No voices were raised in protest.

"Vulf it shall be then!" Vetters said as he stood.

"You look tired," another man said, raising his voice. "Up all night with the new addition? I would have given anything to see you nursing him!"

Laughter rumbled through the group.

"Yes, I was awake quite a bit," Vetters replied. "And I can tell you rascals that Vulf's a lot more alert now than any of you were at the grand age of just a few weeks of life."

"Did he wolf down his food?" someone added, followed by another wave of laughter.

"He gets goat's milk and raw rabbit meat now," Vetters said, not letting any irritation get to him. "Gestapo tidbits come later. I suggest that we should consider broiled tongue of Himmler or Goebbels. What say you all?"

They raised their coffee mugs and echoed hearty agreement.

"How about a Rosenberg liver paté?" another man suggested. "Or perhaps instead we should look at pickled stomach of Göring! No, no, that wouldn't be very good at all—too much lard!"

Bartlett was at Franz Kallenborn's table, next to the one where Vetters and several others were seated. He knew how refreshing it was for the men to be enjoying themselves just now.

What a good impact Vulf is having already, he thought.

That morning respite ended seconds later as the ground shook suddenly under them.

"Bombs!"

That common cry arose from man after man. Kallenborn stood and shouted them down.

"It *cannot* be!" he said, reassuring himself as much as his comrades. "We are safely hidden. This bunker is *undetectable!* Unless somebody here gets careless. Remember that! And *don't* let it happen."

"Or there's a Judas among us," rose a countering voice, causing everyone to fall silent.

Kallenborn hesitated, not wanting to admit this remotest of possibilities.

"As you say," he answered, "but if it's not a traitor posing as one of us, then it could only be some stupid act by one of us. With care, yes, we *are* safe."

Ironically, one of the men who had missed the breakfast gathering because of guard duty burst into the room.

"A plane has been shot down," he said, very much out of breath. "It landed a few kilometers from here. I could see it burst into flame as it slammed against the ground . . . But I saw something else. I . . . I . . . think the . . . the pilot may have saved himself by jumping . . . just a few seconds earlier."

Bruno Vetters, after tending to Vulf, volunteered to investigate, and two men at his table offered to go along with him.

Kallenborn agreed, and they left.

"If it's an Allied plane, we'll hope for a survivor," he said, watching the men leave. "If not, then we'll make sure the scum is soon in his coffin."

Bruno Vetters and two much larger men named Oskar Burgner and Wilhelm Gresse saw the wreckage within minutes of leaving the bunker. A cloud of black smoke made it easy to locate against the snow-covered ground and trees that had come to look like spun-crystal figurines.

They waited several minutes crouched around the perimeter of the site, making sure that unwelcome intruders had not also spotted it.

The plane had become a near-shapeless pile of twisted and scattered metal spotted with sputtering sections of flame.

"Could it be some sort of disguised Allied plane?" asked Burgner, twirling his mustache again.

"We can't rule that out," he said, "but it doesn't seem likely. I don't think they could have gotten their hands on either a Messerschmitt or a Focke Wulf, at least not one in flyable condition."

"It was obviously shot down," surmised Gresse.

"Don't depend on that, my friend," Vetters countered wisely. "Anything so obvious makes me very suspicious indeed."

Seeing no activity, the three men stood with great caution and walked closer to the wreckage. The engine was still sending forth occasional sparks but the smoke had begun to dissipate.

"Where could the pilot be?" Vetters asked, not able to spot him initially.

"If he *is* German?" Burgner asked.

"We kill him," Gresse said eagerly.

"Unless he had decided to desert and that's why he was shot down," Vetters reminded them.

"But how can we tell?" spoke up Burgner. "The Nazis have proven to be very adept liars."

"One thing at a—" Vetters said.

He saw a parachute at the far end of the plane, caught in tree branches. The pilot had wrenched loose, straps splitting, and was lying on the ground in a seemingly crumpled heap. The three men waited cautiously, then walked forward. As they came closer, they could hear him moaning.

Burgner, trained as a doctor, approached the body first. He died in an instant as shots were fired without warning from a concealed Walther nine-millimeter P-38 automatic.

Vetters and Gresse had Mauser M-96 pistols but these were older, less accurate weapons than the Walther, which had gone into production only the year before and represented state-of-the-art technology without excessive bulk.

They missed hitting the pilot, who had begun rolling over and over, making himself a difficult target. Yet *he* was able to fire accurately, catching Gresse in the chest and a second later, blowing apart Vetters's gun hand.

Only Vetters was still alive by the time the pilot was on his feet and approaching the prostrate bodies. He checked Burgner first, then Gresse, and finally stood before Vetters.

"Where is it?" he demanded with typical Hitlerian arrogance.

"Roast in hell!" Vetters snarled through the pain that had spread throughout his body.

Holding the barrel of his Walther inches away, the pilot demolished Vetters's other hand.

"It cannot be far," he said. "Kleist guessed right. Tell me *now*, swine—tell me *exactly* where!"

Vetters's blood seemed to freeze at the mention of that name. *So the traitor Kleist had not died after all!*

"You still have two feet," the pilot snapped.

"If you blow them away, I cannot lead you to where you want to go," Vetters said mockingly despite pain that set his brain afire.

"Wrong!" the pilot countered. "I can carry a weasel like you!"

He narrowed his eyes, leaving no doubt about his seriousness.

"Will you take me there?" he demanded.

"May the Führer spend eternity among the damned like yourself!" Vetters said, his voice wavering.

The gun barrel was aimed directly at his left foot.

"Dear Jesus, guard my path . . ." Vetters prayed.

Roaring with amusement, the pilot held his hand steady and closed his finger tightly around the trigger.

Without warning, except for a brief snarl an instant before it leapt, something large and black knocked the pilot to the ground, his weapon falling from his grip. Within the next few seconds, three wolves were on the man, methodically tearing him to pieces while Vetters, transfixed, watched in shock.

When they were done and the pilot was dead, one of them approached Vetters himself, stopped, and sniffed intently. Then the three wolves sat on their haunches, their snouts turned toward the sky, their mouths opening as a chorus of howling escaped into the chill air.

Vetters and the others had been gone for more than an hour. Kallenborn spoke to Bartlett as they stood just inside the bunker, near the main entrance.

"It is too long," the German remarked. "Time to worry."

"I agree," Bartlett told him.

"We can ill afford to lose such men."

"You are too valuable to send," stated Kallenborn. "I will go."

"But you are their leader."

"And *you,* Stephen Bartlett, are their hope."

Vulf was with Bartlett, standing by his feet.

"What would you think about taking our friend with you?" he asked with some reluctance.

"It might be good," Kallenborn agreed. "Upon my return, I will tell you how he behaved, yes?"

Bartlett nodded as he remarked, a trace of genuine sadness in his voice, "Vulf is a creature of the wild, Franz. It may be that someday our companion will want to leave us and return there."

He looked at the animal, now showing the full, beautiful coat of his kind, silvery-gray around the shoulders, much darker around the middle part of his body and back to the hind quarters.

"His mother was completely black," Bartlett remarked, the memory of the dead she-wolf still vivid.

"Vulf is special," Kallenborn told him, wistfulness in his voice. "He has the mark of a leader."

None of the men in the bunker were eager to let their friend-companion go back to his natural environment. Vulf had become more than a pet or a mascot. He was a cherished friend who slept in the same home and shared the same table with them.

"He might bolt," Bartlett observed.

"He might indeed," replied Kallenborn.

The two men glanced at one another, somewhat ashamed of themselves for feeling such concern for an *animal* in the midst of the savage *human* nightmare that had brought them together in the first place.

"Let's go, Vulf," Kallenborn said after a few moments.

They considered sending more than one man to see what had happened. But that idea was discarded because if trouble had developed with Vetters and the others, then stealth was more necessary than ever and it was easier for one man to stay hidden than for a group of burly GRM members to remain out of sight.

Vulf stayed with Kallenborn, who had thought that the animal might at least run ahead or to the side, but that was not the case.

Since no new snow had fallen for several hours, it was a fairly routine matter for Kallenborn to follow the tracks of the three men after he got beyond the area directly in front of the concealed bunker, which had been, as always, cleared of any such signs of habitation as soon as they had left. Remarkably, Vulf helped, sniffing the tracks as though he had been trained as a bloodhound.

A short while later, Kallenborn saw the wreckage of the plane and heard Vetters moaning. He sprawled next to the lifeless bodies of the two other men. With Vulf pacing beside him, Kallenborn rushed over to Vetters, who was barely moving, and saw that, for all intents and purposes, he had no hands left.

"Bruno!" he exclaimed. "I will get you back and we'll take care of—"

"They're both dead," a weak voice told him in raggedly whispered fragments. "It's . . . a . . . scheme, . . . I think, . . . Franz . . . When the pilot doesn't respond, the Gestapo will *know* he stumbled upon something. They'll come looking, Franz. . . . They'll find the bunker . . . We have to go elsewhere. We—"

Vetters blacked out, his eyes rolling up in their sockets, blood trickling out of the corners of his mouth, a single gasp escaping his lips.

"Bruno!" Kallenborn yelled with the gravest sense of apprehension as he tried frantically to find a pulse. He breathed a sigh of relief when he discovered his friend and colleague was not dead.

Kallenborn picked up his friend and started back along the same route he had just traveled. Vulf was in step with him. He was less than half a mile from the bunker when he heard the sound of military vehicles nearby.

They've tracked the pilot's whereabouts! he told himself. *They'll find us in a matter of minutes.*

Burdened by the weight of Vetters's body over his back, Kallenborn walked as fast as he could through the deep snowpack. He could see the mountain ahead, the familiar bulge at its base, looking like nothing more than a natural outcropping of rock.

Oh God, he prayed, *get me there before it's too late!*

The jeeps were closer. Kallenborn could hear harsh voices and expected to see soldiers any second. He stopped and slid his friend gently to the snow as he glimpsed a black-garbed figure moving between the trees.

The dreaded Schutzstaffel! Hitler's SS—his demonic avenging angels. The man coming toward him wasn't a simple soldier but a member of Hitler's proven elite guard.

And others like him! Half a dozen men followed along after the first. Initially they hadn't been able to spot Kallenborn and Vetters. Doing that took a few minutes.

"Look!" one shouted in German.

All of them brought out their Lugers and aimed them at the two men.

Kallenborn raised his hands, but Vulf dug his feet into the snow and started growling. Their attention suddenly on Vulf, the men seemed quite willing to shoot the animal if he sprang at them.

Lord, I beg you, Kallenborn prayed, *don't let our brave friends back there in the bunker do anything as foolish as try to help us! There may be many more than just this handful, waiting out of sight.*

The first of the uniformed SS intruders stopped not more than half a dozen feet away, as the others gathered next to him. He seemed to be examining every feature on Kallenborn's craggy face. Finally he turned to the other men with him and ordered them to reholster their weapons.

"We *have* found you!" he exclaimed triumphantly.

Vulf was about to spring. He gathered his rear legs together; his growling grew louder and his large teeth were visible as his lips pulled back.

"Stop him," the man pleaded. "We have no interest in harming either of you!"

Kallenborn's heart was beating so fast he half-suspected he might succumb to a massive stroke any moment. Dropping to his knees briefly next to Vulf, he whispered soothingly into the wolf's ear, calming him down. Then he stood again, with Vulf pressing tightly against his left leg.

"You *are* Franz Kallenborn, are you not?" the intruder asked as he stepped closer, squinting a bit while trying to confirm his initial identification. Part of his attention was on Vulf, who had resumed snarling.

Kallenborn opened his mouth, then clamped it shut, stunned by the apparently warm recognition from a stranger dressed in an SS uniform! His gaze darted left, his attention caught by movement in that direction. A lone figure walked toward them, apparently with the good judgment to wait until the others had had the situation under control. He was a tall, rather handsome figure, obviously accustomed to being in command, betraying a bit of a swagger to his steps as he strode toward them.

He approached Kallenborn without an instant of hesitation.

"I am Major General Henning von Tresckow," the German officer said solemnly, his thin, patrician face barely smiling. "It is good to see you, Franz. God has moved heaven and earth to bring us together this day."

4

The bodies of Oskar Burgner and Wilhelm Gresse were buried two hours after the Germans were welcomed into the bunker, and Bruno Vetters was given over to the care of the physician who had come with them. There were displays of grief as the partisans gathered outside but also a realization that many more deaths would occur before Germany and the other occupied countries were freed from Nazi domination. Two graves were dug laboriously in the hard, frozen ground, then, the shrouded bodies lowered in, the soil was replaced to give no hint of what had been done. Snow was piled with similar care on top. The Nazi pilot's body also was buried . . .

Later General Henning von Tresckow faced thirty-one men in the command center. The other SS soldiers had taken off their outer uniforms and mixed with the GRM members, though the latter seemed decidedly uncomfortable having six of Hitler's elite in such close quarters with them.

"There have been rumors circulating for weeks," von Tresckow said as he stood on a raised wooden platform in front of them. "The Gestapo suspected that you were in this general area."

"How could that be?" Kallenborn asked while sitting at one of the tables. "Do we have a double-agent here? Should we begin to examine—?"

Von Tresckow held out his hand to silence the other man.

"Nothing like that. The leak originated with someone at OSS headquarters in London."

"Emil Kleist?" Bartlett, next to Kallenborn, offered.

"Precisely, my American friend!" von Tresckow said appreciatively. "Emil Kleist was never told what was going on, as you know, but he knew *something* was happening. And he put, what is that expression—?"

"Two and two together," Bartlett added.

"Yes, he put two and two together, and got his suspicions into the proper hands—proper for us, not so proper for him. You see, his message happened to go through my office."

"You were the contact?" Kallenborn said in almost a shout.

"As God, not luck, would have it, yes."

"But the plane was sent anyway!"

"Franz, others were *aware* of the contents of Kleist's communique. I had to stage *something*. The matter couldn't be buried without arousing suspicion."

Kallenborn nodded and with a gesture of his left hand gave the floor back to von Tresckow.

"So I arranged for a pilot who was skilled as a tracker to fly over this area and see what he could find from the air. If there was nothing, he would land in a clearing a few miles away and proceed with an investigation on foot."

Von Tresckow betrayed the slightest of smiles.

"The fact that his plane crashed was certainly what could be called a fortunate happenstance."

For a moment, Bartlett couldn't read the other man's expression, then he realized what it meant.

"You sabotaged his plane!" Bartlett exclaimed.

Von Tresckow chuckled as he clapped his hands.

"The night before the scheduled takeoff . . ." he admitted. "Few questions are asked of major generals in a military force that worships rank."

"You slipped onto the airfield," a GRM member guessed, "and personally took care of the job?"

"That sort of thing has fascinated me for a long time," von Tresckow replied. "One of the answers to winning any war is how effectively the enemy can be devastated from the inside, would you not agree?"

One man started clapping, then another, and soon the entire group was on its feet, applauding him.

"Thank you," von Tresckow said, blushing a bit, "but there is more to discuss, my friends."

The resistance movement received much of its financing from funds arranged by von Tresckow and other military figures such as Ludwig Beck, Ulrich von Hassell, Wilhelm Canaris, Carl Goerdeler, and many more who pooled their finances, their most intimate relationships, and risked their own lives. Without such men, the resistance would be having an even more difficult time holding itself together.

Von Tresckow had brought new codes with him.

"The old codes may have been compromised," he said.

And he had a fresh set of maps.

"Additional installations were erected since the maps you have been using were drawn."

Kallenborn and the others studied the new materials as von Tresckow handed out sheet after sheet.

"My direct group is going to try something," he said finally.

"Against the Führer?" Bartlett asked.

"Indeed. Beck is ready to take over as chancellor if we succeed."

"Can you tell us anything?" one of the men asked.

"I cannot."

After the meeting was over, von Tresckow asked Stephen Bartlett to step aside. When everyone else, including Kallenborn, had left, the two of them sat down on the platform and the German unbuttoned his stiff collar.

"So you are going after Heydrich?" he said.

"I am," Bartlett admitted.

Von Tresckow grew especially somber as he said, "Reinhard Heydrich is Hitler without the insecurities, the maniacal excesses. He has no emotional reasons whatever for ridding the world of non-Aryans. You will never see him rant and rave over the deplorable nature of the Jewish race. He considers the Führer to be rather weak, in part because of those frequent outbursts of his, which some observers have often seen as bordering on the irrational."

"And when Heydrich becomes, in his own eyes, quite invincible, he will turn on everyone, including the Führer?"

"Yes, that is correct," von Tresckow said with a shudder. "Then we will have a man, if I must use that label at all, who, at the helm of this nation, could be capable of transforming a defeated Europe into a close approximation of what hell itself is surely like! Once he has done that, he will not stop. Europe alone is *not* his final goal!"

They did not speak for several minutes. A scratching sound at the closed door to the room interrupted their reverie. Bartlett walked over to the door and opened it. Pushing past him, Vulf headed for von Tresckow.

"Stephen?" the German said.

"Yes?" Bartlett asked.

As von Tresckow reached out and rubbed the top of Vulf's head he commented, "It is, I must say, a terrifying thought, but, my friend, this wild beast has more humanity than the man you will try to kill."

Von Tresckow soon was given some indication of just what Bartlett's value had proven to be.

"They placed great store in certain types of weapons," Bartlett told him as the two men sat in wooden folding chairs outside the back entrance to the bunker. They had been playing with Vulf, tossing a ball and having the now-large animal find and retrieve it. Von Tresckow enjoyed the diversion, and Bartlett admired him for being willing to step down from the role of major general and be just another man enjoying a sweet respite with two new friends, one human, the other very much like a pet dog back on his home estate.

"Several categories are necessary," von Tresckow agreed. "They need to realize that while handling heavy-duty firearms can be somewhat romantic, appealing to their masculinity in a powerful way, nothing can or should replace a simple revolver."

"I suspect that is part of their thinking now. It's one thing I've been able to impress upon Kallenborn and the others."

"And you Americans are manufacturing the most reliable handguns of all."

"You're right. If the channels of distribution can be kept open without the Gestapo or the SS interdicting them, I think we have a chance of supplementing whatever small supply they already have."

"I came here to see you," von Tresckow said after waiting a few seconds.

"I suspected so," the American admitted.

"You have to leave tomorrow for your rendezvous with the Czech parachutists who will attempt to assassinate Heydrich. I am not in touch with them directly. In fact, the men in this bunker are among the few in the movement who know where I stand. The two Czechs, Gabcik and Kubis, would be very surprised to learn about me."

"Why is this group so special?" Bartlett asked.

"Franz doesn't know this but I helped send the men here."

"You handpicked each one?"

"I did. And the final two most important choices were Franz himself and Bruno Vetters. I wanted this unit to be an example of how well partisans from different walks of life could function together."

Von Tresckow placed one hand on Bartlett's left arm and asked him, intently, "Are you through here, Stephen? Have you done enough? Are you satisfied? They needed to feel that you were here not to overpower them but to help. Have you been able to do that to your satisfaction?"

"I think so. They're in what amounts to a fortress. They can withstand a great deal."

"But that has been the case for some time. Has *your* mission here been accomplished?"

"Yes, it has. I expected at least a measure of animosity. I haven't gotten any of that."

"God has been blessing you, my friend."

"He has, Henning, that He has."

"I pray that you can help Josef Gabcik and Jan Kubis at least as much," von Tresckow said. "From what I hear, they are having terrible problems with the bomb they plan to use."

"The firing mechanism?"

"How in the world did you know that?" von Tresckow asked, his mouth dropping open in surprise.

Bartlett smiled, pleased with the German's willingness to let his emotions show.

"I was told they planned to use a cluster bomb. That type can cause much damage, in fact, it can splatter a man into a thousand pieces, but it is frequently unreliable because the firing mechanism is its Achilles heel. I nearly died a year ago for that reason. From then on, I have been making sure that cluster bombs were avoided whenever possible."

"It goes off too soon or too late, one or the other with no predictability, is that it?"

"Exactly!"

"What can be done?"

"It has to be entirely redesigned, piece by piece, and tested. If that doesn't do the trick, we'll have to switch to another type."

"Which do *you* favor?" von Tresckow asked.

"A fusion bomb. Far more dependable and just as deadly, in my opinion."

"I can see why you gained the reputation of being indispensable with any mission you are assigned. Churchill, Casey, even de Gaulle have indicated that they feel you are the single most important ingredient in what will happen over the next few weeks. The fact that you were able to stop here, to help these good men, is a very special kind of bonus."

The German was smiling.

"I hope we can be friends after the war," he said, his voice genuinely warm. "I would enjoy taking you and your family through Berlin, if anything is left of it by then."

Bartlett was ready to leave, with von Tresckow and the SS soldiers escorting him to a planned dropoff point. The route would take them east then north past Nurnberg and on to the border of Germany and Czechoslovakia.

"Once you get to the border, Prague is about 115 miles northeast," Kallenborn told Bartlett as they stood just inside the entrance to the bunker. "We have many outposts along the way."

"Are Gabcik and Kubis in Prague now?" the American asked.

"They are."

"Before you arrive there, if there are any problems, you can divert your travels to Plzen, Jihlava, or Ceske Budejovice. We have able resistance members or partisans in each place."

"How will I know where to contact them?" Bartlett asked logically.

"I have written everything down on a single sheet of paper," Kallenborn told him. "Memorize every word, then swallow the paper."

Another GRM member brought a backpack to them. Bartlett took it from him.

"Some food," Kallenborn pointed out, "some clothes, a Bible."

Von Tresckow was becoming anxious. "We cannot spend more time here. Long absences have to be explained, even by generals."

Kallenborn and Bartlett hugged one another.

"You have been here for some time, Stephen," the German commented, "you have learned a great deal. How do you feel?"

"As always . . . nervous," Bartlett admitted. "We have good plans, yes, but anything could go wrong."

"The partisans need you. They do not have your experience with munitions, Stephen. The bomb must be successful. If not, then even Heydrich, who in his arrogance scorns intensive personal security measures, would be compelled to build a thick wall of protection around himself."

"But Gabcik and Kubis *think* they know all that they must know."

"That is their greatest weakness," Kallenborn said, a perplexed expression on his rough-looking face. "If this mission succeeds, many will—"

He cut himself off for a moment, the pain of the previous night, when he had helped bury Burgner and Gresse, still lingering.

"Many will die," he went on, "but at least we will have gotten rid of a monster. If Heydrich survives, at least as many will be sacrificed but the monster will thrive, energized by a fresh surge of malevolence."

Vulf had joined them.

Bartlett bent down and fondled the animal's big ears.

"Our friend wishes he could go with you, Stephen," Kallenborn observed. "He has many of his kind out there whom he could summon to help you. The bond between wolves goes on for a lifetime, you know."

"If only that were possible," Bartlett agreed.

As Bartlett, Kallenborn, and von Tresckow joined the half-dozen SS soldiers who had preceded them, Vulf started to howl and kept on doing so for several minutes after Bartlett and his escort had departed.

Theresienstadt was a rather new camp.

"It is located in a quite beautiful spot," von Tresckow said as he and Bartlett sat in the backseat of the jeep while it and an accompanying military truck headed toward the Czech border.

"Wasn't that the camp Heydrich himself had constructed, part of it from a fort that had been built there two hundred years ago?"

"Indeed, Stephen. Ironically it had the reputation of being the most humane camp of them all."

"That doesn't jibe with what we know about Heydrich."

"No, not at first glance, that is. But we cannot ascribe that to any temporary outpouring of compassion from this man."

"Then why did he allow Theresienstadt to achieve that sort of image?"

"Sir, may I answer Mr. Bartlett?" the driver asked.

"Go right ahead," von Tresckow said, without a trace of irritation. "By the way, Stephen, this is Sergeant Otto Dietrich. He has quite a famous cousin."

"Marlene Dietrich, the entertainer?" Bartlett guessed. "Hitler wanted her to be his mistress but she refused and has chosen to remain in exile."

The sergeant was impressed.

"How did you know?" he asked.

"My wife and I love the theater. We keep up on such matters."

"Heydrich is sadistic," Dietrich went on. "This nature makes him quite different from Himmler, who is heartless and can order thousands murdered but gets no pleasure from it. To him it is nothing but a move on a chess board, and he is just as pleased if there is a less brutal alternative."

"*That* is news to me," Bartlett interjected.

"It makes Heinrich Himmler no less a monster; it means no less blood on his hands, but it *is* an interesting dimension to his warped outlook. But Heydrich *likes* the business of death. Whereas Himmler will stop when a prescribed purpose is achieved and go on to the next venture, Heydrich looks for reasons to continue if what he has been doing is especially bloody. This creature looks forward to murdering yet another Jew, another Gypsy, another Protestant."

"Is it true he's had some Jews skinned alive and their skin used for lamp shades?" Bartlett asked.

"Exactly, sir. He has several of these at his estate outside Prague. Once, it is said, he performed the loathsome 'operation' himself. But he was politely dissuaded from doing so again."

"Because it would hurt even Heydrich's image?"

"Not quite, sir," Dietrich replied. "He took too long. Concentration camps are on a schedule. Heydrich enjoyed the screams of that one dying Jew so much that he prolonged the woman's agony as long as he could before her heart gave out."

"Her?" Bartlett gasped. "He did this to a woman?"

"And got some sexual pleasure out of it, too, from what I hear."

Abruptly, von Tresckow tapped the sergeant on the shoulder. "Ahead, there's a bridge," he said. "Please, Otto, be very careful."

They were traveling through a region of the Bavarian Alps. Nearby was the Zugspitze, a peak of nearly ten thousand feet, with mountains of lesser height abounding.

Roads had been dug out of the hillsides, providing sometimes-precarious routes around the mountains while tunnels and bridges, often erected hastily by Nazis and partisans alike, provided the other means of travel . . . and one such bridge was directly ahead, a narrow one.

Bartlett gulped a couple of times as he saw *how* narrow.

"Not everything in Germany is constructed to last for centuries," von Tresckow said cryptically. "I don't trust this bridge."

The truck ahead had made it to the middle of the bridge, and their jeep had just rolled onto it when the first grenade was thrown, landing *under* the truck, and exploding in a shower of metal and flesh. A second grenade blew away the underpinnings at the far end of the bridge itself. They could hear a loud tearing, grinding sound as wood splintered and jagged ends scraped against rock. The collapse took the truck with it and whoever might have been left inside. Seconds later, flames shot up dozens of feet from the valley below as the gas tank exploded instantly upon impact.

The jeep was left on the remaining section that was somehow still supported by heavy beams.

"They couldn't know it's us," von Tresckow said.

"Why *couldn't* they?" Bartlett asked, obviously surprised.

"That is one of the problems we face. There is more than one group of partisans. Kallenborn doesn't head the only legitimate one."

Minutes passed. No more grenades.

"They can see we haven't been hit," Bartlett commented. "Why aren't they finishing the job?"

Except for the sounds of their own voices, there was only silence.

"A warning," von Tresckow reasoned. "Creating uncertainty can be a very effective tactic."

Dietrich turned and faced them.

"What do we do now?" he asked. "Wait for their next move?"

Just then, a groaning sound arose from beneath the jeep; they could feel the remaining section of the bridge tremble.

"I think that's it!" Bartlett said. "They can see the damage below but we can't. They know we won't be here much longer. They'll celebrate when they see us end up at the bottom along with your men."

"You can understand how they feel when you realize how many of their loved ones are in concentration camps because of men who wear a uniform that is quite identical to my own," von Tresckow reminded him. "They see this uniform and the swastika on the side of this jeep and they react by instinct, by the compelling hatred that is at the very center of their gut."

"Sir?" Dietrich said. "Let me climb out with a white flag and get back to the road. They don't know who we are. I'll convince them that we—"

"No!" von Tresckow spoke sharply. "Stay here for the moment, my good Otto. There's another possibility, you see."

"What are you talking about?" Bartlett asked.

"They might not be partisans after all," von Tresckow continued.

"Gestapo who are posing as—" Bartlett said as the same unsettling thought occurred to him.

"If that is the case, sir, how were they alerted?" Dietrich asked, fearful of the answer.

"There are traitors everywhere, Otto," von Tresckow reminded him. "The worst are those who consider themselves patriots."

The shattered wooden bridge trembled more violently, and they could see and feel the jeep slipping forward by inches.

"If this is being done by the partisans, they have what they believe is yet another successful strike against the Führer's puppets," von Tresckow added. "If our attackers are from the Gestapo, they will blame all this on the resistance movement, another alleged act of treachery that must be punished to maintain the honor and the defense of *Deutschland* against Jewish sabotage!"

"They get rid of you *and* have an excuse for more atrocities," Bartlett reasoned, admitting the devilish efficiency of such a scheme.

As von Tresckow drew a breath to reply, another grenade was thrown and the bridge fell out from under them.

Bartlett had no idea how long he was unconscious but he reasoned that no more than a few minutes had passed. As he opened his eyes, he saw the jeep a dozen feet away, flames consuming it. And climbing down the side of the mountain were four men carrying rifles over their shoulders.

Bartlett got to his feet and glanced around frantically, trying to spot von Tresckow and Dietrich.

In the jeep!

The sergeant somehow had been trapped inside, his charred form faintly visible among the flames, while von Tresckow was on the rocky ground to the right of the crumpled mass. He and Bartlett noticed each other at virtually the same time; he managed to stand a bit uncertainly.

"There!" Bartlett pointed to the four men who had made it halfway down.

"Do not delay! Go, Stephen!" von Tresckow shouted at him after looking in that direction.

"We go together," Bartlett insisted as he stumbled over to the other man.

"We do *not!*" the German argued. "You are far more valuable now than anyone like me who plans his intrigues behind closed doors, in a safe little office guarded by loyal SS members loyal to the Führer. You have a mission that *must* be completed!"

"But they're going to torture you; they're going to get details from you that could compromise the GRM and other groups. You *have* to go with me."

"They will never have the opportunity, Stephen. You see, I have learned one good thing from Heinrich Himmler."

Von Tresckow opened his mouth and pointed to a molar. "May God forgive me if it comes to that."

He reached out and rested both hands on the American's shoulders.

"They might be partisans, Stephen."

"But you yourself said they could be Gestapo posing as partisans. If that's the case, you would be offering them on a silver platter just what they want to know. Don't you see that?"

"I am not so naive, my friend," he said. "After all these years as a trusted officer of the Third Reich, you must not assume that I can be easily duped by those for whom I hold only contempt."

Bartlett hesitated, his emotions torn, not wanting to abandon such a remarkable man but also understanding the truth of his words.

"Whatever happens, Stephen Bartlett, our Lord is in charge," von Tresckow said. "Into His hands I commend my very soul."

He looked up at the four men who were nearly at the bottom of the ravine.

"Go!" von Tresckow demanded.

Bartlett ran, dizziness assailing him, then adrenaline forcing energy throughout a body craving it.

Bullets passed within inches of his head.

For a split second, he glanced back at von Tresckow. There was a struggle, and the German was knocked to the ground. The four men gathered around his body, having lost interest in anyone else.

Bartlett expected any moment to be shot in the back or to be given an order to "Halt!" But there was only the sound of his breath coming in labored spurts as he continued running.

The Bavarian Alps rose around him. There was no way for him to scale either side of the canyon, each no more than a smooth wall of rock offering nothing for his hands or feet.

If they have decided to follow me, I'll be trapped, Bartlett acknowledged to himself, feeling more endangered at that moment than when he had parachuted into the snowbound region weeks earlier.

Still running, he checked to see if any of his weapons had been left behind in the fall. The Colt 1911-A1 was still in a body-hugging holster at his armpit, a flat ax strapped to his leg, and a small knife tucked in a sleeve inside his left boot. He sighed with relief as he found they were still there, though he worried that the pistol had been damaged.

Abruptly, a few hundred feet farther on, the crevasse ended against a wall of dirt and rock. Bartlett noticed a mountain-hugging road directly above, probably a continuation of the one he and von Tresckow would have traveled if the bridge hadn't collapsed. With irregularly shaped rocks jutting out from that side of the mountain along with branches of long-dead trees and roots of others amidst pockets of earth, an ascent here was possible, unlike the rest of the crevasse.

Bartlett tested a long thick, musty-smelling root at the base to see if it could sustain his weight. Indeed, it seemed sufficiently strong to support him.

Directly above him was an outjutting section of flat stone, sufficiently large to support his body. After stuffing his gloves in the right pocket of the heavy lamb's-wool coat he had been wearing, Bartlett grabbed the root and started to pull himself up. He had nearly reached his goal when he could feel the gnarled growth wrenching loose from its mooring. He managed to swing himself over to the flat rock, frantically grabbing it first with his left hand, then an instant later with his right.

One of the edges proved especially sharp, like a crude stone ax; it dug into his right hand, which had been only slightly numbed by its brief exposure to the cold. He tried to hang on, even as he felt rock scrape cruelly against the bone in that hand, and he yelled out, instantly regretting it for his voice was loud enough to alert anyone nearby to his presence.

No one. Not the hint of a response.

Flesh tore more and more as he tried to will himself to make it the rest of the way.

I can't do it, I—

He felt as though he should just let go, give in to the pain, and refuse to endure it any longer.

Somewhere in the center of his being, where reality didn't exist but wistful thinking reigned, he went back to England, to his wife Natalie and his son Andrew, and saw them waiting for him as he ran up the pathway to their home. And he knew, he knew, he knew that that was how it had to be. It couldn't end somewhere in the Bavarian forest at the bottom of a forgotten ravine.

His left hand was slipping again and something hard and sharp was mercilessly striking bare bone.

"No!" he declared out loud. "I will *not* fail in this. *I will not!*"

Bartlett tried once again, the now-tortured cartilage in his right wrist protesting, and, using whatever strength remained he was able to swing himself up and over the edge.

5

William Casey seldom betrayed any anxiety to those around him, but in the presence of Churchill and de Gaulle he knew any subterfuge would be perceived.

"This is appalling!" he admitted. "Stephen Bartlett could end up being sacrificed to one man's ego."

Even de Gaulle allowed himself to show some emotion other than indignation.

"I agree that Benes must not be allowed to interfere," he said, beads of perspiration shining on his forehead. "I have spent some time with Bartlett and I must say that he seems almost—"

He stopped himself, his face reddening as the others secretly enjoyed every second of his embarrassment.

"Indeed," Churchill said, voice portentous as always, "Stephen Bartlett seems . . . almost French?"

De Gaulle's eyes widened as he reacted to such surprising transparency on the prime minister's part.

And then he laughed.

It was a rare moment of humor in the midst of otherwise unrelieved tension, tension that began as soon as they awakened each morning, as soon as their minds pulled away from sleep and wrapped around the reality of a war that already had left unimaginable devastation in its wake and which threatened to overwhelm Fortress Britain, as they privately called the once-safe British Isles. Finally, relieved by that respite, they continued discussing the latest crisis. This one involved not the Nazis per se but rather the exiled president of Czechoslovakia, Eduard Benes, who early on had demanded complete control over any attempt to "get" Reinhard Heydrich.

"He is murdering *my* people," Benes had forcefully reminded them weeks earlier. "*My* parachutists will be building the bomb as well as exploding it. And *I* am the president, duly elected, of a nation being ravaged by monsters. Why should *any* of you control what happens next?"

The Allied leaders felt strong rapport with the way the man felt. But Benes's patriotism had an edge of arrogance, and since he had been a radical as early as before World War I, when he was active in the movement that tried to gain independence from the Habsburg Empire, they knew he was capable of actions that, though brave, could prove disastrous in the long run.

"Benes cannot do it alone," Casey had said afterward, when they were planning what they would do to ensure the success of any mission against Heydrich. "Fanaticism in the pursuit of liberty is laudable, but it can also blind even an intelligent man, and we must never think of Benes as less than that . . . or more!"

Then Stephen Bartlett was brought in from his war-time home a bit over an hour's drive from London. Hearing their proposal, his only concern had been that his wife and son be protected in his absence.

"I must concentrate on this mission," he told them. "I cannot be distracted by concerns over their safety since we all know that if the SS finds out my true identity, they'll go after my family."

"Captain Harrison Cowles, who will accompany you on the flight to Bavaria, will be in charge upon his return," Churchill assured him. "Until then, Scotland Yard has been given the privilege."

"What about Eduard Benes?" Bartlett asked. "Those in the resistance who support him won't be very happy about this if and when they find out, and you can be sure they will."

"There *are* a number of factions," Casey interpolated. "Another group *could* take out Heydrich or at least make the attempt before any of us have the chance. But frankly I doubt that this will happen. To their credit, only Benes's group seems inclined to take such a dangerous step.

"We need to get you to Gabcik and Kubis. Those two men are essential. They are far more reasonable than Benes. They admit their limitations. And they are *in* the battle, not in some armchair command post hundreds of miles away. If you are careful to insinuate yourself in an advisory, as opposed to a dominant role, they should be quite eager to get your munitions experience on their side."

Casey had met Gabcik and Kubis when they were in England for training sessions with various bombs, trying to decide which one would be the most efficient to use. The device had to be powerful enough to blow up a building, if necessary, but light enough to be tossed at Heydrich's car if that proved to be the approach.

"It was just awful," Casey said, remembering the men's experience in the training sessions. "I don't fault their dedication but they just aren't as adept with explosive devices as they are supposed to be. Benes is proud of them because they are fellow Czechs, but nationalistic pride is no substitute for hard-headed skill. And you have more of that in *both* men!"

"Benes will assume we are trying to wrest control away from him and turn the spotlight elsewhere," Bartlett pointed out. "His ego will not be able to tolerate that. He will twist the truth to his own advantage by accusing us of a separate mission to get Heydrich."

Even de Gaulle was impressed.

"You have studied the matter, I see," he observed. Then, with sarcasm tinging his voice he added, "How refreshing!"

"When my life is at stake, when my loved ones are being put in jeopardy, when countless others could suffer from wrong decisions or actions on my part, General de Gaulle, what choice do I have but learn *every* detail humanly possible? For that, sir, I have no better model than yourself."

De Gaulle seemed frozen for a moment, then walked stiffly around the table to Bartlett, who rose from his seat as the Frenchman approached. The tall, regal general silently reached out his hand and Bartlett shook it heartily.

"On to Germany!" Casey declared, his face beaming.

Stephen Bartlett and Harrison Cowles spent some time together before they left for Bavaria.

They both enjoyed walking through Olde London. Even though Cowles had lived in the city for many years, he never lost his appreciation of it.

"The mood was so very different before the war started," he said as they stood on a walkway around the dome of Saint Paul Cathedral. "We were so jovial, isolated from the masses of Europe in our own island fortress. We never thought Hitler would go so far as to bring his bombers to our very doorsteps. But of course he did, and he added another element as well."

"What was that?"

"Spies, Stephen. They're like rats in this city."

"We have them too."

"But you keep spies out better than we do. Those oceans around the States are like gigantic moats around a fortress."

Cowles waved his hand in a sweeping gesture over the city surrounding them.

"They come from Germany, of course, but Hitler has conquered so many countries now it's not just Germans we have to be on the lookout for, you know. There are the Austrians, the Czechs, the Italians . . . in every neighborhood perhaps, funneling information back to Berlin and other nerve centers."

"And what about the fascist sympathizers," Bartlett pointed out, "the high-bred English who would like to see Hitler win because they think he will help maintain the purity of their aristocratic blood by getting rid of the foreigners, especially the blacks and naturally the Jews, but not only those races? They strike me as a potential fifth column right here in England's vulnerable gut."

Cowles was quiet for a moment, then spoke up. "The man on the street down there assumes even today that Chamberlain was a closet member, you know."

"I've heard that," Bartlett replied. "But, as I understand it, though he was friendly with many of them, his blunders resulted from stupidity and a curious kind of naiveté, not any seditionist tendencies."

"Indeed, I've heard that as well."

"But you're not so sure."

"There is very little in this life of which we can be sure, Stephen. We do things today that we would have found abhorrent a decade ago. You learn to trust no one. Why, it's possible in theory that even you are a double agent."

"Or you!" Bartlett shot back in jest, but still uncomfortable with the notion.

"That's quite right," Cowles acknowledged. "Any man can be bought. All men have a price. It *is* a cliché, I admit, but a wise one, and in wartime, it's never less than true. Some of those Nazis frying Jews in concentration camps used to be simple farmers. Now, in free moments, they turn to writing love letters back home, to wives and girl friends, and then put away their pens or pencils and sheets of paper and go outside to shove more bodies into mass graves or dig gold fillings from dead mouths!"

The Allied leaders realized the quandary in which they had embroiled themselves. Despite their best efforts at absolute secrecy,

Eduard Benes indeed had found out, perhaps from an unknown operative, conceivably someone he had managed to plant at the same base from which Stephen Bartlett finally took off with his partner.

"Are you our friends? Or another enemy?" Benes had ranted, making up in volume what he lacked in height as an attempt to intimidate the men he felt had betrayed him. "You *know* that now I cannot do anything to stop this madness. But if I had *known* before this moment—!"

Rather than strike back with verbal barrages of their own, the others remained quiet, largely because they knew, on one level, that Benes had every right to feel as he did.

He threw a sheet containing a coded message onto the same large table where they planned all the Allied war strategy.

De Gaulle grabbed it and tried to be indifferent to the contents, but failed.

"A message from Berlin to Prague was intercepted," he said, interpreting the message. "It warns of something going on but it is not specific. Hitler personally has pleaded with Heydrich to take on an armed guard. Heydrich did so, a very minimal one, wanting to placate the Führer but not wishing to seem as though he is running scared."

"What you are saying is that the SS has been alerted but Heydrich is not taking it altogether seriously," Casey interjected. "Nevertheless, we will find that it now will be somewhat more difficult to snuff out the monster."

"Somewhat?" Benes blurted out. "Charles, why don't you continue with the rest of the message?"

De Gaulle's eyelids were closed tightly together.

"Charles, what is it?" Winston Churchill asked in deep concern as he approached the other man.

"The SS has said that if it is true that Heydrich is a target," de Gaulle said, speaking with utmost gravity, "in retribution they will destroy the village of Lidice man by man, woman by woman, child by child."

He looked from Churchill to Casey to Benes, who seemed in genuine anguish.

"I have known they would do something drastic if anything were attempted," Benes interrupted. "All of us here understand *that* danger. But my people and I had been operating *in secrecy,* can you not understand that? Those who knew anything at all were kept to the barest possible minimum.

"Then you bring in this American, *and see what has happened!* Now we may lose those precious lives in that small village and have *nothing* to show for it because Heydrich could emerge from all this bungling very much alive, and more a devil than ever!

"Gabcik and Kubis will find vital lines of communication blocked that could have been kept open because people are going to be more scared than ever now that, in a brilliant move, Hitler's intentions have been announced *in advance!*"

"That warning is one we cannot heed now," Casey sighed, his face drained of color. "Stephen Bartlett is on the way . . . may God forgive us the outcome."

"God may do that," Benes said, disgusted, as he turned to walk from the room, "but do not count on the Czech people and me as their leader to follow in His footsteps!"

Benes slammed the large door behind him. As he stormed down the hallway lined with armed soldiers and on to the No. 10 Downing Street exit, he allowed himself the briefest of smiles.

You know that now I cannot do anything to stop this madness. It is beyond even my reach . . .

His face became a blank stone mask once again as his car pulled up in front and the driver got out and opened the passenger's door for him.

Contrary to what you believe, I have moved much faster than any of you would dare to imagine, he thought with characteristic smugness as he settled down inside for the familiar ride to his heavily guarded residence. *It was, after all, my man posing as one of yours who was able to go along with this Stephen Bartlett fellow . . . prepared to kill the American rather than let Lidice be devastated and my mission fail!*

He bowed his head for a moment, a single tear trickling down his cheek.

May our Almighty Father guide and protect you, Emil Kleist, brave soldier in our righteous cause . . .

6

Stephen saw a footpath through the Bavarian forest, presumably for hikers and tourists. His right hand was raw, the flesh torn away from two of the fingers. The extreme cold meant he had not lost a great deal of blood, but the relative lack of pain now also heralded another danger.

Frostbite. The open wounds were so severe that getting gloves over his hands was agonizing, as torn flesh protested. He walked unsteadily along the snow-covered path, half-expecting pursuers, and breathing easier when, after several minutes, none appeared.

In his left pocket was a compass.

"I have written everything down on a single sheet of paper. Memorize every word, then swallow the paper."

He was glad he had done as Kallenborn directed. He knew where to go for the first stop, at least he knew as far as directions were concerned from the Czech border. Far less certain, since he no longer was being driven there by one of the most powerful German generals, was reaching the border in the first place.

And how would he slip over it into Czechoslovakia without von Treskow's authority to protect him?

Bartlett stopped for a moment, years of training almost seeming useless just then. He was surrounded by trees turned completely white by their covering of snow, with no signs pointing the way. His hands sent a constant parade of pain to his brain. The scene started to spin around in his vision.

It cannot be here, Lord, he prayed. *It cannot be here while Reinhard Heydrich builds more concentration camps and slaughters more non-Aryans. He attends classical music concerts performed by the Prague Symphony while men, women, and children are marched naked into chambers he ordered to be pumped full of lethal gas. He goes for a vacation in the Bavarian Alps while—*

Fresh adrenaline began to surge, Bartlett's blood pressure accelerating his body heat along with it.

One foot at a time he walked forward, not quite knowing where the strength came from but determined to summon whatever he had left and go forward, always forward, as far as he could, as long as he could, before the cold dropped him and made him just another anonymous frozen corpse.

Ahead! He heard the barking of a dog. He stumbled, fell, got back to his feet, continued on. And came upon a large German shepherd surrounded by somewhat smaller wolves. The dog was ready to fight them, but was certain to die in the process.

As soon as the wolves and the dog saw him, they fell into immediate silence, startled by his presence, forgetting one another for a moment.

He stepped forward an inch or two. The apparent leader of the pack, the largest of the wolves, started to snarl at him, followed by the others.

Bartlett reached under his coat for a pistol strapped to his side and tried to retrieve it, but the pain in his hand was too great; he couldn't hold on to it for more than a few seconds and dropped it at his feet.

The dark red eyes of the lead wolf followed his every movement, studying him with chilling precision, its lips pulled back in that continuing snarl, its canine brain processing sights, sounds, odors, analyzing each one as dictated by long centuries of instinct.

Then, suddenly, it ran off into the woods, with the rest of the pack close behind.

Not quite believing what had just happened, Bartlett looked momentarily toward the German shepherd, then fell to his knees, his hands throbbing. The dog walked cautiously forward and, convinced he was not a threat, started wagging its tail as it stood directly in front of him.

"Where . . . is . . . your—?" Bartlett started to ask, but the trees and the ground and the image of the German shepherd swirled into a jumbled collage that became more and more blurry until he passed out altogether.

The welcome smell of warm honey. As a whiff of it crossed his nostrils, he reached for it from the darkness into which he had fallen. Bartlett's eyes opened slowly and he saw that he was stretched out on a comfortable bed. An old man was sitting beside him, lifting a cup to his lips.

"Honey diluted a bit by some hot tea," his benefactor told him.

Bartlett swallowed two mouthfuls, nodded, and tried to speak but couldn't.

He glanced at his right hand, which had been carefully wrapped in gauze, an odor of peppermint coming from the bandages. His left hand was covered by a thick mitten.

"It's an ancient recipe," the old man said, "that cleans and promotes healing."

Bartlett studied him for a moment. Though he seemed to be well over seventy years of age, he was quite strong-looking.

"I owe you my life. You had to carry me for quite some distance," Bartlett said weakly, hoping his voice conveyed the warmth of feeling he had for what the man had done.

"I would say that you are now in the shape I used to be," was the answer, "but without your poor damaged hand."

He offered more of the liquid but Bartlett shook his head.

"My name is Kurt Landwehr. What is yours?"

"Stephen . . . " he started to say Bartlett then caught himself and said instead, "Stephen Courtney."

"You almost died out there," Landwehr commented. "But you managed to defend my dog against the wolves."

"Defend, sir? I wouldn't call it that."

"Gunther had run ahead of me for some distance. As I was catching up, I saw him surrounded by those wolves. Then the whole pack scattered when you entered the scene. What would you call that, my young friend?"

Bartlett debated telling him some of the story involving Vulf, omitting certain details; he decided no harm could come of it.

"That *is* extraordinary," acknowledged Landwehr after hearing the story. "You think there is some pact between them?"

"If not, I can't be sure what the explanation is," Bartlett said. "I've never experienced anything like this before now."

The old man stood and walked around the bed to a window at the opposite end of the room.

"I hear them howling at night," he said. "At times they seem frightening, at other times melancholy, as though filled with the greatest sorrow."

Bartlett had studied what few details he could find about wolves in reference books at the bunker.

"I think you are right," he recalled. "Sometimes it's a mating call."

"Summoning the females!" Landwehr exclaimed, chuckling.

"But sometimes they are warning interlopers not to come any closer. On other occasions they have lost a mate and they are letting out their deep and quite awful loneliness as they howl."

"With wolves, it seems to be very much for a lifetime, this male-female bonding," Landwehr added. "I know that much about them. If only human beings could imitate their example . . ."

The old man had a large white moustache, which he was fingering as he turned from the window.

"You have survived because of me, Stephen Courtney, which I hope you understand this to be true," he said as he approached the foot of the bed. "What I figure is that you owe me a great deal."

"Oh, I agree," Bartlett replied, apprehensive over what Landwehr might be about to ask of him. "How do I start repaying you?"

"With the truth."

"I wouldn't have it any other way, Mr. Landwehr."

"Call me Kurt, please."

"Fine, Kurt, if you make it Stephen in my case."

"The truth, remember?"

Bartlett nodded.

"Are you with the Gestapo or some other group from the Führer's lair?"

Bartlett hesitated, realizing that anything revelatory on his part could place him in danger, even from someone who initially seemed as harmless as Kurt Landwehr.

"I am not one of their agents," he replied, taking that chance.

The old man's eyes seemed to burn directly into his own, past them, and into his brain, ostensibly able to ferret out truth as opposed to the lies to which every Nazi seemed inextricably devoted.

"I think I believe you," Landwehr went on. "Sad to say, but Hitler's puppets have made believing anyone about anything a luxury that could turn as deadly as one of those wolves. But there *is* something about you, Stephen Courtney."

"What is that?"

"Well, let me put it this way: If wolves can trust you, you must have something right in your heart. They despise anything that smells of the SS or the Gestapo."

"I don't understand."

"My Gunther reacts similarly. Yes, those monsters have their own dogs but those are dogs they've raised from puppies to be as brutal as they are. Gunther isn't like that. He was showered with love from the beginning. He is my friend, and he hates my enemies."

"But wolves are wild creatures. How would they know the difference between a Gestapo agent or a farmer such as yourself? You *are* a farmer, aren't you?"

"I am. It is a good question. I think the answer has to do with the smell of blood they have on their hands, the sense of evil about them."

"Is that it, Mr., er . . . Kurt?"

"Despite what they say about Jews being slovenly drunks most of the time, the truth is that most Gestapo agents are smokers and drinkers, and they sometimes indulge in drugs such as opium and others."

"To escape guilt?"

"A guess, but I suspect it's a good one. No man ever completely does away with his conscience."

"Heydrich may be one of the few."

"Indeed, Stephen. Anyway, the wolves smell the tobacco, the bourbon, the whiskey, the opium, and all the rest. It offends their nostrils. I also believe many animals have *senses* that we as human beings have no idea of. They *know* when people cannot be trusted, when people are cruel. But enough of this. You need rest. You cannot do much of anything until your right hand heals."

The old man left him.

Bartlett knew he could not linger indefinitely. Two or three days had to be the maximum, and even such a short stay made him uncomfortable, bringing with it the danger that he would be too late to provide any help for Gabcik and Kubis. Whatever the outcome of their attempt to assassinate Reinhard Heydrich, there was no doubt that hundreds of innocent people would die in retribution.

For the Butcher of Prague to escape death would make any such tragedy all the more loathsome!

The message Benes wrote in GRM code and sent to Emil Kleist was short and emphatic:

WOLF'S LAIR MUST BE TERMINATED.

He sank back against the heavily padded leather chair. He had gone to the study from the transmitter room at the other end of the country house the Brits had provided for him, the same location from which he had successfully blocked calls from No. 10 Downing Street to Gabcik and Kubis, this irony not at all lost on him.

I didn't want it to be like this, he thought. *I didn't want to be responsible for murdering someone like Stephen Bartlett.*

He had on his lap a file that told the story of this man.

And now he will be dead because . . . because—

He slammed his fist down on the arm of the chair, spilling papers onto the floor in the process.

A wife and a son await a return that will never happen, he told himself.

He jumped to his feet.

I have to see them, I have to get to know them, to provide for them after they learn that—

Stalking out into the hallway, he summoned an aide and told the young man where he wanted to go.

"And put those papers back into their folder," he said, pointing through the open doorway.

A car pulled up in front of the house less than a minute later. Benes slid into the backseat.

The trip took a bit over an hour. He had time to think about Lidice, imagining piles of bodies in an open field just near the center of the village—men, women, and children riddled with bullet holes, some with their eyes still open, expressions of sudden pain frozen on their pale faces. He knew that Churchill, de Gaulle, and Casey thought he was nothing more than a raving egotist bent on having his own way. He realized that, when they discovered what was happening, they would crucify him with their words.

My people slaughtered! That is the price that will have to be paid! How can I inflict what I must upon them and not destroy the very beast for whom they will have given up their lives?

After an hour, Benes could see the Bartletts' thatched-roof cottage that rested atop a small hill in the country some fifty miles from London.

If Stephen Bartlett is not stopped and WOLF'S LAIR *is uncovered, the SS will waste no time. They will surround Lidice with their tanks, their troops, their machine guns, and they will bury it. Nothing will be left to show that hundreds of people once lived their lives there, and generations before them, but no more . . .*

He had ordered someone to phone ahead that he was coming. As the car pulled onto the long driveway up to the house, he saw a woman and a young boy on the front porch, waiting for him. Standing next to them was a tall, rugged-looking man, as English in his appearance as anyone Benes had seen.

The car stopped and he got out. The woman walked up to him and shook his hand, and the boy did likewise. The man hung back for a moment, saying nothing.

"It is an honor for me that you want to spend some time here," she said. "My husband and I admire your patriotism and your courage."

She introduced the other man. "This is our protector, Captain Harrison Cowles. Churchill insisted he stay here."

Benes winced as the Englishman grabbed his hand in a hearty manner. As the four of them were walking up the half-dozen steps to the cottage, the woman glanced at him with some concern.

"Your eyes," she observed. "You have been crying. Is there anything I can do to help?"

"Nothing, dear lady," Benes said, his anguish barely concealed, "nothing at all, I'm afraid."

7

On the second day, just as the sun was coming up, with a rooster announcing the event, Stephen Bartlett, wearing a thick blue sweater and old slacks Kurt Landwehr had found in the attic, noticed that the old man had arisen even earlier and was trudging through the snow to a small building at the opposite end of his property.

Bartlett was about to turn away from the window when he noticed something on the roof of the small structure. Squinting for a moment, he saw what it was . . . a small antenna.

He decided to stay at the window, timing how long it took Landwehr to leave the other building.

Five minutes passed, and his benefactor was still inside. Ten minutes. Fifteen. Finally, after nearly twenty minutes had gone by, the old man stepped outside and headed back toward the house. Bartlett knew there was only one conclusion. Landwehr was using a shortwave radio.

But where were his messages headed or coming from? Was he with the Gestapo or one of the resistance groups? Neither Kallenborn or von Tresckow had mentioned him as a contact. But then, von Tresckow had said one of the problems was the existence of more than a single faction dedicated to overthrowing the Nazis, and there seemed the very real chance that they could end up nullifying one another's efforts.

After Landwehr came back in the house Bartlett tried to conduct himself in a normal manner, giving no hint of any suspicions. Apparently he was succeeding because the old man, after breakfast, told Bartlett he had to go into a hamlet some miles away to get some groceries and would take Gunther with him.

"Would you like to join us?" Landwehr asked.

"My hand's been throbbing a bit," Bartlett replied. "I think I would be better off staying here, and putting some more of that warm honey concoction on it."

"Fine . . ."

As Landwehr was opening the front door of his cottage he turned, and smiled as he said, "Stephen, I've enjoyed having you here. I wish it could be longer."

Bartlett returned the smile and wished the old man a safe trip.

Landwehr walked through the snow to a detached garage a short distance from the house and soon drove away in an ancient Citroen that noisily belched dark gray smoke, obviously not long for the world.

As Bartlett watched the vehicle pass from sight, he caught himself feeling some affection for Kurt Landwehr. They had spent many hours talking since he had been taken into the German's home. Landwehr said he had no one; his wife and two sons had been killed in an avalanche two years earlier.

"This cottage was built for them," he had said. "It's bigger than it looks, you know. We wanted our sons to grow up in the country, to respect nature, to be hearty and strong and—"

"How did it happen?" Bartlett asked. "You must be ready for avalanches here. How was it that they—?"

Landwehr flashed an angry look at him but it was not for what he said.

"The Nazis," he replied, trying to control himself. "They were conducting maneuvers. They told no one. My family was not the only one affected. We were angry. We protested but we knew that if we spoke too loudly, went on too long, we could end up in one of the camps with the Jews and Gypsies!"

He bowed his head.

"So we kept silent after that. We buried our dead and went on living."

Bartlett could not believe any of this was an act put on for his benefit. He had to accept the genuineness of Landwehr's apparent feelings.

But what about the building at the other end of the farm and that antenna on top?

Bartlett decided to investigate since the old man would be gone for several hours. He still had his pistol. After making sure it was fully loaded he slipped on his sheepskin jacket and went outside.

Skis! Someone had placed his skis just outside. Stephen was *sure* they hadn't been there earlier.

It took him a bit less than five minutes to reach the small building. Inside he heard the sound of an accented voice but could not make out the words themselves. Carefully he approached the only window. Seated at a table, and holding a microphone was a man of medium build and short blond hair, sitting with his back to the window.

Bartlett held his breath, listening to what the man was saying in German.

"He *is* here . . . yes, yes, that is correct . . . I will take care of him before the day is out, you can be sure of that. Of course, I agree. I would not have tried the first time if I didn't."

The head turned slightly and Bartlett could see the long, thin nose, the narrow lips, the cold eyes . . .

Emil Kleist!

Bartlett wanted to burst inside and empty the contents of his Colt into the man's head, chest, stomach, wherever he possibly could, and then stand over that dead body and feel totally triumphant. But then an image of Kurt Landwehr entered his mind and he knew old man must be involved also.

He must have alerted Kleist. That's what he was doing when I saw him go out and—

Bartlett caught a name that Kleist spoke as he was signing off.

"Thank you, sir . . . indeed . . . thank you, President Benes. And God protect you as well."

Eduard Benes was ordering Emil Kleist to complete the job of murdering me! Bartlett thought as those words from Kleist ripped across his mind.

He turned and looked around at his surroundings, momentarily panicked.

Alone. In a frozen and isolated place. Waiting back in England were a wife and a son who prayed daily for his safe return.

The leader of the people I'm trying to help . . . wants me dead!

He wondered, suddenly, crushingly, why he shouldn't just make his way back to the bunker, tell Franz Kallenborn what he had found out and get his friend's help in returning to England.

Kleist provided an answer.

A bullet shattered the window pane, then grazed his right ear. He yelled in pain, but more loudly than he felt, hoping to make the other man believe he had been seriously hurt; he pretended to collapse directly below the frame of the window. Then he scrambled around to the opposite side of the little structure, holding the Colt ready as he waited for Kleist to burst past the front door.

Inside, there was a noise, movement, then a sound like a cabinet slamming shut, but that was it.

Seconds more passed.

He poked his head around the side and saw that the front door was still closed. Then he got down on his stomach and crawled up the three steps leading to it. He waited for a moment, pressing his left ear against the door.

Quiet.

Bracing himself on one elbow, he reached up and turned the knob quickly, expecting Kleist to fire again, this time *through* the door; Bartlett reached for the knob still in a half-sitting position, he kicked the door open with his feet.

The interior of the structure was empty except for the shortwave set, the table on which it rested, and the chair that had held Kleist, now laying on its side.

As Bartlett walked forward, his foot kicked against something, and he glanced down at the floor.

A trapdoor! It had not completely closed.

Kleist could be on the other side, waiting to ambush him. As soon as he touched the door and started to lift it up, the German might open fire on him.

So he started firing first, bullets splintering the trapdoor in rapid succession. He reloaded, fired again, then reloaded a third time, and waited.

Silence. Nothing was moving. Either Kleist was dead or badly wounded, or he hadn't been there anyway.

Bartlett slowly pulled up the trapdoor with his good hand, staying as far back from the opening as he could manage and holding the pistol in the other, though continued pain rendered that hand useless for anything else, including pulling the trigger.

He managed to fling the door all the way back at the same time he shifted his weapon to his left hand.

Still no one.

He peered over the edge, saw the beginnings of a tunnel, and decided to investigate. A short flight of stairs, hinged to the trapdoor, had dropped to the floor below, and he walked cautiously down into the tunnel.

The initial section was packed with documents. He grabbed some of them and skimmed their contents.

Information about various GRM activities, members, and collaborators.

"What the—?" he said out loud.

He saw a separate list. Each of the names had a check mark next to it, with one exception. His heart began to beat considerably faster when he saw STEPHEN BARTLETT printed near the top of the alphabetical listing.

No check mark. His was the only name left unchecked.

He paused, looked toward the rest of the tunnel, then glanced back upstairs.

The transmitter!

He recalled the code name and message codes Kallenborn had given him to memorize. Again, he was glad that he had done his homework.

After going back up the stairs, he walked over to the table, righted the chair, and sat down before the transmitter.

Everything was still turned on.

Bartlett grabbed the microphone, reset some dials as he spoke the code name: WOLF'S LAIR. He tried transmitting, then waited for a response. Nothing. Nearly a minute passed. No response. He tried several other times.

Zero.

"I've got to reposition the antenna," he said out loud, having noticed it was on a swivel base for precisely that purpose.

But that meant going outside without knowing where Kleist was hiding.

Yet he had no other choice. And he could waste no time alerting Kallenborn and the other GRM members.

He paused at the front door, trying to find some hint of Kleist's position while wishing for a pair of binoculars.

No sign.

A ladder led to the antenna.

Expecting to face bullets any second, he climbed up to the roof as quickly as he could. When he reached it, finding that he didn't have his compass with him, he tried guessing by the position of the sun, which was partially hidden by a patch of clouds and turned the antenna carefully, hoping he would hit the right direction the first time.

As Bartlett went back down the ladder, and looked behind himself at the same time, he thought he saw the stray glint of sun off metal; he froze, reminding himself what a clear target he represented.

Gone . . .

It didn't occur again, perhaps because Kleist had been aware of this carelessness and was determined not to let it happen a second time.

When Bartlett was back inside, he stood quietly, trying to calm nerves rubbed raw. Then he sat back down at the transmitter and tried again. This time a coded reply came over it almost immediately.

FRANZ HERE . . . HEARING NOTHING MADE US ALL SO WORRIED YOU HAD GOTTEN INTO GREAT DIFFICULTY . . . OR WORSE.

Remembering they were to use first names only and speak in code, Bartlett told the other man how very glad he was to have made contact.

"Franz, it means so much to me to hear your voice as well, my friend . . . however imperfectly it comes across the mountains!"

The transmission was hampered by a surge of heavy static.

When it subsided Bartlett quickly read off the list of names he had found.

Kallenborn wasn't able to respond immediately. When he did, the pain and the weariness in his voice broke through even the poor transmission.

EVERY ONE OF THOSE INDIVIDUALS WAS ONCE AN ALLIED AGENT OR A PARTISAN . . .

Bartlett caught that word "once" and repeated it into the microphone.

DEAD . . . STEPHEN, ALL OF THEM ARE DEAD . . . YOU ARE NOW THE ONLY ONE FROM THAT GROUP WHO REMAINS ALIVE!

The signal weakened further and Bartlett could hear nothing else that was intelligible from Franz Kallenborn.

A few seconds later, the first grenade exploded just outside the little building.

Franz Kallenborn heard the sound of the explosion, then the connection ended. He tried again and again to reestablish it.

Dead.

Bruno Vetters was with him, his hands still covered by bandages.

"Franz, have we lost Stephen?" he asked.

"I don't know . . ." Kallenborn replied, distracted.

"Benes must be told."

"Benes is responsible for this!" Kallenborn screamed in anger. "He must always prove his superiority at being a modern-day Niccolò Machiavelli. Nothing matters to him but showing the world he is the consummate patriot of this age. He is willing to sacrifice anyone—you, me, everybody here—if that can accomplish what *he* feels needs to be done in order to throw out the oppressors."

"But that is how *they* operate, Franz; you know that. It was the whole basis behind their demonic grab for power more than a decade ago. Aryans were supermen in their view, and supermen operate by might, by brutal force, not by any sense of honor or decency or anything of the sort."

Kallenborn threw up his hands in despair.

"Then whom do we serve?" he asked, his voice trembling. "The one who asks us to overthrow the beast is a beast himself!"

"Treacherous and—and—" Vetters stuttered, his face showing the pain he was feeling from his wounded hands.

"Can I get you anything, Bruno?" Kallenborn asked.

"A nice coffin to bury me in."

Kallenborn could understand his friend's despair. A wave of it was washing over him as well.

We've given up so much to be here, he thought, *to be here all these months, hidden away like moles. And now, it seems, the man who inspired us may be willing to see any one of us terminated if it fits his grand plan.*

"Why has Benes done this?" Vetters's voice interrupted his brief reverie. "What could he be thinking of?"

"Remember, we ourselves are another group of partisans," Kallenborn said, forcing the words out. "It may be that Benes was alarmed that yet another entity, a Yank, on the battlefield would cause the war to be lost in a maze of confusion."

"Nice words, intelligent words, Franz, but hollow, quite hollow. You sound as though you don't believe anything of what you've said."

Kallenborn bowed his head as he replied, "I don't, my friend. God knows I don't. But how can I tell myself that Eduard Benes would resort to murder just because he is afraid of giving up some of the glory by letting the Americans instead of the Czechs succeed? Is the only victory that counts to be won by *his* countrymen?"

"Contact him," Vetters suggested. "Talk to him. Tell him what is bothering us. Tell him that we will have to publicly disavow this action of his."

"Any new transmission risks sudden interception. We must be careful. Only in an emergency should we—"

"Is this not an emergency of the first order?" Vetters pleaded. "Franz, you *must* talk directly to Benes. That list Stephen read off? Every other agent, every other partisan on it, has been murdered. Was Benes behind *those* as well? How could he justify *any* such acts of utter ruthlessness? Get him, Franz. Get him now!"

Realizing now the truth of the other man's argument, Kallenborn relented a bit.

The process of contacting Eduard Benes over a clandestine radio operation was tenuous. Yet after more than an hour, they succeeded. Again only code was used.

Benes was stunned by what they told him about the list.

I KNEW SOME WERE DEAD. BUT OTHERS . . . THERE WAS ONLY SILENCE, NO WAY OF TELLING . . .

"You didn't authorize killing them?" Kallenborn asked.

I DID NOT!

"But you *did* assign Emil Kleist to murder Stephen Bartlett."

Silence.

"Are you denying this, Eduard?" Kallenborn demanded.

NO . . . I THOUGHT KLEIST HAD SUCCEEDED. I DID NOT REALIZE THE AMERICAN ESCAPED.

"Only for the moment. As we were speaking, Kleist apparently had started lobbing grenades at the building Stephen was in."

"The same building the shortwave unit was found," interjected Vetters, "and that damnable list."

WHY WOULD EMIL HAVE SUCH A LIST?

"You cannot *imagine* the reason, Eduard?" Kallenborn commented, with an edge of sarcasm.

THAT WOULD MEAN—

The connection ended.

"He's cut us off!" Vetters exclaimed.

"I think you're right, Bruno. However, I could hardly have expected any other reaction."

"And you don't despise him for it?"

"I suppose I do not. The man is devastated, his ego in shreds. He has been shown that someone he trusted, someone he thought believed in the same cause, the liberation of the Czech people, is in fact—"

"A double agent," Vetters finished the sentence. "Kleist likely has worked for the Nazis from the start. Oh, Franz, what has he told the Gestapo? All those murdered men! What does he know about *us?*"

Suddenly, despite being inside the bunker and protected by its insulation, both men felt nearly as cold as though they were outdoors, in the ever-present snow of the harsh German winter.

Stephen Bartlett pulled out the Colt again and dropped flat on his stomach to brace himself for the next grenade. He could not tell what direction the first one had come from. The attack had been so sudden, the grenade landing short and shaking the structure without doing damage to it.

A minute passed. Another.

Natalie and Andrew are waiting for me, he thought. *They don't know where I am or what is happening. They can only pray and wait for the phone to ring or someone to knock on the front door.*

He shook that distracting image out of his mind, training all his senses on what a single dangerous individual might be doing next. Kleist was playing a game, trying to unhinge his opponent by the element of uncertainty, often the best possible weapon.

The German could be anywhere . . . in the front, at the rear, or at either side of the little building. Kleist was able to make basically whatever move he wanted, and Bartlett could do nothing but react.

Yet only an old tree, tall and gnarled, with a trunk just under six feet thick, provided Kleist any real shelter. It was roughly two-thirds of the way between Kurt Landwehr's home and the building where Bartlett was trapped. Otherwise, there was nothing to hide behind, no mounds of snow, no bushes.

I'll have a clear shot once he steps out—

Footsteps . . .

The roof! Kleist was on the roof.

Bartlett glanced immediately toward the tiny fireplace across from him.

Down the chimney! That's where he's going to drop the next one!

Aiming the Colt directly at the ceiling, Bartlett fired several times and heard a cry of pain and then something tumbling down the chimney, landing on the floor . . . a standard-grade gray grenade. Jumping to his feet, he swung open the front door and ran outside, not knowing if Kleist had been seriously hurt or was dead, but heeding the more immediate threat of the grenade as he headed for the ancient tree.

The grenade exploded.

The little building was not completely demolished. In fact, as he discovered later, only in the area around the fireplace was there any damage at all—a large hole had been torn through the side. That sort of thing was rare but it *had* happened before. Not every grenade functioned perfectly each time.

A heavy piece of stone hit Bartlett in the back of the head, knocking him off his feet less than three yards from the tree.

"You have no more bullets!" came a triumphant shout from behind him.

Bartlett rolled over on his back, the scene before him spinning for a moment then steadying.

Kleist stood between him and the little building. A splotch of blood stained the thick white woolen jacket the German was wearing.

"Ah, I have two more grenades and a fully loaded Luger, and you are *out* of ammunition," Kleist shouted at him.

"Why?" Bartlett yelled back at the man. "All those dead Allied agents and the partisans?"

"I am German . . . is that not answer enough?"

"But so are many members of the resistance movement. Not all are French or Czechs or Dutch. Hitler has raped—"

"The Führer has *liberated* my country! He has torn it loose from the filthy Jews who were enslaving everyone!"

"Not true, Kleist. You go from an imagined tyranny to one that is real, with the blood of Jew and German alike flowing in the streets."

"*Our* blood is pure, our noses are straight, our mission is noble."

"Are Himmler, Bormann, Heydrich nobility then?"

Kleist hesitated a moment. Bartlett saw he had reached a nerve.

"Can any noble cause succeed in the hands of barbarians, Emil? Can you assume that Heydrich is a man of *any* ethical—?"

The clattering sounds of an old motor and the odor of gasoline filled the air.

Kleist spun around on one heel and saw Landwehr's wreck of a car heading toward him. He smiled as he waited until it was within firing range.

Bartlett lunged toward Kleist, knocking him off his feet. The German took the barrel of his Luger and slammed it down hard against Bartlett's bandaged right hand. The American screamed in sudden, overwhelming pain.

Kleist, now on his feet, took careful aim at the Citroen. An already cracked windshield shattered as he fired, and Landwehr slumped forward against the steering wheel. But the car's momentum continued moving it straight for the tree. As it hit the thick, centuries-old trunk, the gasoline in its tank ignited. Kleist threw his head back, cackling over the tragic sight, then turned back toward Bartlett. After holstering the gun at his waist, he retrieved from an inside pocket of his jacket one of the two remaining grenades; he started to pull the plug slowly, increasing the pressure on the American.

Suddenly, they both heard the sound of loud barking.

Gunther! In the next instant, fur partially aflame, Landwehr's devoted friend leapt from the car and raced toward Kleist.

"No!" Bartlett shouted, trying to distract the animal by his voice, frantically waving his hands. "Stay away from—!"

Startled, the German fumbled the grenade, dropping it near his left foot. He had time only to turn but not to run before Gunther, with his last remaining strength, knocked him off his feet, the two of them falling onto the grenade as it exploded a split second later.

After seeing there was nothing he could do to help either Kurt Landwehr or Gunther, Bartlett walked wearily back to the house and tended to his reinjured hand. Despite what Kleist had done, Landwehr's stitches amazingly had held, though fresh bruises had already begun to appear. He wrapped the hand in fresh gauze and applied a new bandage over that, then fell asleep for an hour or so in a well-padded chair.

Toward evening he awoke, deciding to go back to the other building and try to get through to Kallenborn again on the radio. As he walked outside he glanced at the wrecked old car still sending out little trickles of smoke.

Kurt, Kurt, I thought you might have been a Gestapo agent as well. But you were tricked by Emil Kleist along with everyone else . . .

He reached the car, stood for a moment beside it, half-deciding he should bring the old man's body out and bury it, along with Gunther's. But Landwehr was surrounded by collapsed, smoldering metal. He could not pry the body loose with his one good hand.

You gave your life for me, and now I can't even—

He had to shut off the way he felt then, enter the little building and sit down before the transmitter, and do what he must in order to get help. Emotions could not be permitted to blind his judgment. Countless thousands of future victims would cry out from their common graves in accusation if he allowed this to happen and failed in his mission to get rid of the devil who surely would become their butcher.

After picking his way through the debris inside, Bartlett found the shortwave unit virtually unscathed and still receiving current from an operational generator on the floor. The initial transmission seemed shaky, however. Undoubtedly tubes inside the shortwave had been jarred by the exploding grenade, and he couldn't be sure his signal was strong enough as it went out. Minutes passed. Finally he heard the first faint voice, barely audible, then gradually stronger.

PRAISE GOD, YOU ESCAPED, STEPHEN . . . I FEEL BADLY ABOUT THE OLD MAN, THOUGH.

Bartlett could hear Bruno Vetters in the background, saying, "Tell him, Franz. You know you're dying to . . . *go ahead!*"

Kallenborn's voice came through the transmitter again.

BENES GOT THROUGH TO US NOT MORE THAN TWO HOURS AGO.

"What changed him?" Bartlett asked.

BEING BETRAYED BY EMIL KLEIST.

"A house divided against itself . . ." Bartlett muttered into the microphone.

THIS IS EXACTLY WHAT BENES SAID . . . THE CZECHS WILL SEND SOMEONE TO GET YOU AS SOON AS WE KNOW WHERE YOU ARE. CAN YOU HELP US AT ALL WITH THAT, STEPHEN?

He did as well as he could.

CHECK IN WITH US EVERY SIX HOURS UNTIL WE ADVISE YOU WHEN TO EXPECT SOMEONE. I MUST END THIS NOW. GOD PROTECT YOU . . .

Bartlett signed off, then sat quietly in the near-darkness, still holding the microphone while hearing in his imagination a woman's soft, tender voice and feeling a young boy's little hand around his thumb, holding tight.

Bartlett split his time waiting either at the little building, looking over records that had been stashed there or in the house, going through Kurt Landwehr's belongings. Some of the files indicated that Kleist had actually performed *for* the partisans more than once.

Clever, Bartlett thought. *Sabotage a few buildings, blow up some tanks, kill some expendable German soldiers, and you create an image of someone loyal to the resistance movement while you are, at the same time, a kind of cancer eating away at it, dispatching key Allied agents and others one by one . . .*

Bartlett shivered as he considered such a cold, efficient, altogether brutal scheme, not entirely from the genius of it, although that was unsettling in itself, but as an admission as dark and as cruel as its source.

We're doing the same thing, practicing the same awful deceit!

He knew that the Gestapo didn't have some kind of corner on Machiavellian intrigue. Two years of war and missions apart from the current one had taught him that, and more.

It turns my stomach, what Kleist had been doing, but, for every individual like him, there is surely a counterpart on our side . . .

And caught in the middle had been someone like Kurt Landwehr.

Bartlett glanced out the window at the blackened wreck, then at the pile of what was left of Emil Kleist and Gunther.

I can't even lift a shovel. Otherwise Landwehr and Gunther would have been buried by now.

He found bits and pieces of the old man's life as he looked through whatever he could find in dresser drawers and closets. The contents of a shoebox proved especially unnerving: A note from Roland Freisler of the *Volksgericht,* or People's Court . . . appointed earlier that year, Freisler had soon gained a reputation as the "hanging judge." The letter congratulated Landwehr on being "helpful." Another letter was from Landwehr's son Otto. Otto Landwehr . . . a guard at Gross-Rosen, a small camp that, in the few months since it had been open, had become a center for prisoners who were being selected for medical experimentation.

Landwehr said he had no one. He told me his wife and two sons were killed in an avalanche two years earlier.

Another lie! He had only one son, still alive, and that son had written to him more than once, telling proudly of his work at a death camp. Bartlett leaned against the wall in the old man's bedroom. Lie after lie! Was it possible that, in wartime, *all* truth was a casualty? Yet why had Kleist gotten such obvious pleasure from fatally shooting Landwehr? Since both apparently were working for the Third Reich, what made the old man attempt to kill Kleist in the first place?

Finally, Bartlett felt burned out after going through letters from other Nazis—Himmler, Goebbels, Rosenberg, and others—all of which complimented someone they esteemed for his nationalism, and who also had been awarded a number of medals for his bravery during the First World War. In addition, there were newspaper clippings in several scrapbooks . . . reports of Landwehr's wartime exploits, family photographs, including quite a few of Otto Landwehr posing in his military uniform in and around Gross-Rosen and—

Bartlett trembled, close to nausea, as he came to shots of the son holding a lampshade that had been fashioned of human skin, Jewish or Gypsy. But the photo that made him finally put away that last scrapbook was of the younger Landwehr, smiling broadly, beside one of the camp's ovens, the heavy iron door ajar, some small bones visible amidst piles of gray-white ash. At the bottom a hand-written caption proclaimed: "Where all Jew babies should go . . . Love, Otto."

In the bedroom, Bartlett found medals and certificates awarded to Kurt Landwehr, frame after frame of them attached to black velvet and covered by clear glass, each recognizing the old man yet again as a valiant defender of the fatherland.

He fell asleep on Kurt Landwehr's bed with that image surging in his mind, a vivid contrast to everything else he had found, creating a puzzle that he finally felt too weary to try to analyze any longer.

The man who stood in the doorway seemed somehow familiar though Bartlett was sure the two of them had never met. The man was of medium height with narrow shoulders; he had a round face with perpetually drooping eyelids, topped by thinning brown hair.

"Stephen Bartlett, I trust," the other man said, his manner suggesting a coiled-spring personality, always on the alert, his nervousness betrayed by a slight twitch at his left cheek.

"Are you—?" Bartlett started to say, then realized how careless that would have been.

"Code name WOLF'S LAIR, am I correct?" the visitor asked.

Bartlett felt apprehensive. Perhaps this had something to do with the fact that he was half-asleep, that pounding on the front door having awakened him from a surprisingly sound sleep.

He studied the other man, trying to place him, trying to remember—and suddenly doing just that.

"Josef Gabcik!" Bartlett said.

He was greeted by a slight smile.

"I look different from any photos you may have seen, isn't that so?"

Bartlett had to admit that he did—older, paler, wrinkled, any fragile semblance of youth gone.

"May I come in?" Gabcik asked.

Bartlett stepped aside and let him enter.

"Most people are shocked when they see me," Gabcik said as he stood for a moment in the center of the living room. "Living nearly six months under the conditions Jan and I have endured would change anyone. I have lost what some would call the perennial virgin look, or as you Americans might say, my baby face!"

He started laughing, and Bartlett joined in, with Gabcik *enjoying* the humor in what he had said.

"I was saddened by the news of what happened to Kurt Landwehr," he remarked.

Bartlett was startled by that statement.

"What makes you say that?" he asked. "The old man has at least one letter of commendation from every top Nazi in Hitler's inner circle and more German medals than any of *us* will ever see. Why in the world would you be saddened that such a man is gone?"

Gabcik seemed to be studying him, saying nothing for a bit.

"You don't know the full story, my comrade," he replied. "We have to hurry but taking only a few minutes to tell you now should cause no difficulty. May I do that?"

Bartlett agreed to listen.

"But first, I must get something from his bedroom."

"I've seen everything in there and also in the tunnel beneath the transmitter building."

"You have not," Gabcik said in a somewhat scolding manner. "He had a place where he hid something that was very important to him."

Gabcik turned and walked toward the bedroom. Bartlett could hear furniture being moved then the sound of something being ripped away. A minute or so later, Gabcik returned, an envelope in his hand.

"I will show you the contents, but first sit down," he said. "You need to hear what *this* is all about."

They sat beside one another on the wood-framed sofa.

"Kurt Landwehr was all you might suspect of him until roughly a year ago," Gabcik began. "That was when his son began serving as a guard in one of the concentration camps."

"Yes, Gross-Rosen," Bartlett interjected.

"Not at first, my comrade," Gabcik corrected him. "Otto Landwehr started out at Maidanek."

"One of the worst of the camps, according to all the reports I have seen."

"Very definitely, Stephen. Oh . . . may I call you Stephen?"

"Surely. Is Josef okay?"

Gabcik nodded as he continued, "He was put in charge of Zyklon-B. It became his job to make sure the camp had a consistent supply. At first he was under the impression that it was nothing more than a disinfectant, which indeed was its original use. Then IG Farben, the manufacturer, found out about its toxic capabilities and informed Himmler and others. With just some slight changes, it became the poison gas they are now using."

"How did Otto Landwehr react when he found out?" Bartlett asked.

"Very little."

"He was not shocked?"

"His father never had any real evidence that he was surprised. Otto had been transformed by his months of working inside the camp. He had learned to turn off his emotions, to purge himself of any conscience. When he saw what was being done with Zyklon-B, which was almost immediately after the first shipments, he *volunteered* to help with the gas chambers to make sure everything was functioning properly."

"What did the old man do when he found out?"

"Kurt Landwehr was devastated. Each time he received a letter from his son, the contents contained some new boast about how many Jews he had seen die because of his work. Then, when he was transferred to Gross-Rosen, he was put in charge of the ovens."

Gabcik's face flushed red.

"Sometimes the men, women, and children being shoved inside were not dead. Otto Landwehr undoubtedly could have saved any number of them. But he did not. He stood by while they screamed and screamed and screamed!"

Gabcik turned away.

"Kurt saw what his son had become. He saw what national socialism had done to the only child his wife and he had ever had."

"What about Mrs. Landwehr?" Bartlett asked.

"It was hopeless for her," Gabcik replied as he turned to face the American again.

"Hopeless? Why?"

"She was a Jew. Otto Landwehr turned her in," Gabcik said. "She was taken from this house, and sent to Maidanek more than a year ago."

"When her son was a guard there?"

"He stood at the gas chamber door as she was being herded inside. She recognized him and he her, and she reached out for him, but he brushed her hand aside, and the heavy door shut behind her."

"He watched?" Bartlett asked, the words bitter on his tongue as he spoke them.

"*Yes!* He saw her drop to the floor, presumably dead. He stood there with no emotion at all on his face, and when they all were dead, Stephen, he accompanied the bodies to the ovens. He—"

Gabcik brought the back of his hand to his mouth, unable to speak for a moment.

"Otto Landwehr personally loaded his mother's body onto the conveyor belt and saw that she was still breathing. According to all that we have been able to find out, he did not hesitate *for a single moment!* Not an instant, Stephen . . . before he released her to go on into the oven!"

Both men were shaken.

"So Kurt Landwehr saw that the political system into which he had put so much trust, the Führer whom he served with mind, body, and soul," Bartlett said, "had made a monster out of his son and he could do nothing except seek its downfall?"

"Precisely. Kurt was the best subversive we could have hoped for. He asked us just one promise of us in return."

"What was that?"

"That we not touch his son until after his death."

"But why?"

"The reason is in here," Gabcik said, holding the white envelope out in front of him. "It seems an appropriate moment now for me to open it."

As he did so, pulling out the single sheet of paper, his hand shook momentarily, then he proceeded to read the contents:

> *I was, until this moment, my son's father. While I am alive, I must see that he is protected, no matter what he has done. But after I am gone, he is on his own. He will either pay for his crimes or he will escape. I can do nothing henceforth to determine the outcome. For he is no longer under my care. He is no longer my son.*

"Otto Landwehr will be dead by the end of the year," Gabcik said.

"If you can kill him so easily, why not go after Ivan the Terrible and others?" Bartlett asked.

"Too few resources. We can take on only special cases. Some Nazis have better protection than others. To the government, Otto Landwehr is insignificant. But to us, he is every bit a symbol of the corruption of national socialism. Having him dead will send a fresh surge of determination through every partisan!"

"There's more, though, isn't that so?" Bartlett probed.

Gabcik chuckled as he nodded.

"You saw through me," he admitted. "Yes, there *is* more. Emil Kleist saw to it that every resistance member, every Allied agent he betrayed who was caught alive, was sent to Maidanek. Kleist arranged for Otto Landwehr to be paid a bonus for each one he gave 'special attention' to."

"A pusher giving his addict more of the drug!"

"Exactly, Stephen."

"And I wondered why!"

"I don't understand, my comrade."

Bartlett hugged himself as he told Gabcik what he meant.

"There is no longer a puzzle then?" Gabcik said wisely.

"None," Bartlett replied. "Let's go."

They left the house. Bartlett saw a jeep outside. As they walked toward it, Gabcik paused, looking at the wreckage.

"Kurt cannot remain in there like that," he said. "We've got to bury him."

His eyes rested on the American's gauze-wrapped hand.

"Help as much as you can," he added.

First, the Czech had to dig through the snow to the frozen ground, which was rock-hard.

"It can't be done," he acknowledged wearily. "We can only pack the snow around him, nothing more. May he forgive us for that. When spring comes—"

After they were finished, Bartlett using his good hand to pack the snow around and over the body, the two men paused for a few moments, bowed their heads, and prayed silently.

A makeshift cross from two scraps of wood tied together marked the site. It would remain standing only as long as the snow stayed packed around it.

"Farewell," Stephen Bartlett whispered. "Farewell . . . dear friends."

Minutes after they left, headed across the border into Czechoslovakia, two explosions occurred at Kurt Landwehr's small home. Makeshift bombs Bartlett had made quickly reduced to scattered piles of rubble the transmitter building along with the old house where Landwehr had lived for much of his life. A single old music box with a lacquered mother-of-pearl lid somehow remained intact and was jarred into playing "Lili Marleen" over and over until it, too, was quite silent, quite dead. Then the stillness was broken periodically by the distant howling of wolves.

"We gave up everything to be here," Josef Gabcik remarked as they made their way in the jeep through a narrow, often partially overgrown path in the forest. "Yes, Jan and I surely did that."

"So it was with me," Stephen Bartlett replied earnestly. "My wife and my son remain behind, near London. I miss them so much."

"Anyone we love is in the midst of the most compelling danger now."

Bartlett felt as comfortable with Josef Gabcik as anyone he had met before.

"Everyone back in London thought you and Kubis would resent help from an American," he pointed out. "Benes wasn't the only one."

"They must have based their thinking on whatever reactions Eduard Benes seemed likely to have, not on the response they expected from Kubis or me."

"So you never expressed your disapproval to Benes?"

"Never, Stephen! The Führer has plunged all of us into this nightmare. The Nazis will *win* if it turns out they have unity while we are in ragged disarray. Think of a world dominated by that gang of monsters and you will see why none of us must ever react the way Benes has made Churchill, de Gaulle, even Casey, who should know better, *think* we would."

"But there *are* several resistance groups under different leaders. Doesn't that lead to inevitable confusion?"

"There is confusion from time to time even under a *unified* command. So you see, the situation with us is no better, no worse. Whatever the case, it is a reality that we must live with, do you not agree?"

Bartlett saw a bridge ahead like the one he and von Tresckow had approached only days earlier.

Gabcik noticed that the American reacted with a sudden, fleeting jolt.

"What disturbs you, Stephen?" he asked.

"It's so similar to one I saw not long ago."

"A bridge is a bridge, my friend. We blow them up all the time."

Bartlett jerked his head in the other man's direction.

"Four days ago, did you demolish a bridge not far from here?" he asked with urgency in his voice.

Gabcik rubbed his head for a moment.

"I believe we did," he replied. "Yes, that's right."

"What did you do with the German general named von Tresckow?"

"I only put together the explosives," Gabcik recalled. "Four partisans took him away. I have no idea where he is now. I heard no name mentioned. I would hope they killed the bastard!"

"How can we find out?"

"Find out?"

"Yes!" Bartlett said with exasperation. "He wants Hitler and Heydrich and the others dead as much as you and I do."

Gabcik braked the jeep, then turned and looked at the American.

"But I heard that he refused to say very much."

"He couldn't be sure, right away, whether you were partisans or Gestapo double-agents!"

"I'm sorry this worked out as it did but we mustn't be sidetracked."

"We can't let anything happen to that man. He's a part of the inner circle in Berlin. He may be our biggest asset."

"But he could be anywh—" Gabcik's eyes widened.

"You know something, don't you?" Bartlett said.

"Yes . . ."

"What is it?"

"It will have to wait until we get to the shortwave unit Jan and I brought with us when we parachuted in just after Christmas."

He could see the skeptical expression on Bartlett's face.

"Truly, Stephen, this is *not* some clever gambit on my part to get you to Prague without a detour."

He decided there was no reason not to trust a man willing to sacrifice life itself not only for the Czech people but for Jews and others across Europe who were being slaughtered in greater and greater numbers by the Nazis.

"I pray they haven't already killed him."

Gabcik could see starkly then the depth and the urgency of Bartlett's concern, and he was moved by it. He hesitated a moment before putting the jeep in gear and starting across the bridge.

When they reached the other side, he stopped again.

"What's wrong?" Bartlett asked.

Gabcik was struggling. The Butcher of Prague had to die; no mission was ever more righteous. But having the help of someone of the position and the caliber of the German general might prove to be nearly as significant for the cause of liberation in the long run. If Heydrich, then Hitler, and possibly others in the Nazi high command were eliminated, von Tresckow might be the one to take over the government and bring the war to an end within days, perhaps even hours.

"I think we should not wait, Stephen," Gabcik said. "I think we should try to make contact."

"But I thought you had no idea where von Tresckow might be."

"I don't. But others might."

Gabcik chuckled, more with embarrassment than with any real humor.

"It was only a slight, eh, deception, my friend Stephen," he said awkwardly. "Can you forgive me for that?"

Bartlett smiled and the men shook hands heartily.

They approached a hamlet, a collection of small houses made out of aging, rough-hewn stone, and with thatched roofs.

"Not the smallest change in hundreds of years," noted Gabcik as he brought the jeep to a halt. "Even the Nazis have ignored spots like this. Thank God for that! It is where the partisans gather and plan, in villages like this, out of the way, beyond the scrutiny of this nation's plunderers."

An old woman, bent, walked slowly across the street in front of them. A minute or so later, they saw a funeral procession start down the ancient street, with not one or two coffins but a dozen.

"God in heaven!" Bartlett said prayerfully.

"God is in heaven, Stephen, but Satan reigns supreme here," remarked Gabcik mournfully.

"What could have happened? Are these war dead?"

"Yes, war dead but not in the way you mean. The souls once in those bodies will come back to accuse Heydrich on the Day of Judgment."

"This is part of a broader nightmare, an extermination plan Heydrich spoke of in a private meeting with Hitler on October second of last year."

"Have you passed this information to Benes?"

"Only days ago. I have a good idea of how he's reacting . . . probably going nearly mad with shock and grief."

"Could *that* be why he is no longer standing in the way of WOLF'S LAIR, and not so much the betrayals by Kleist after all, however devastating they were?"

Gabcik paused briefly, pondering that one.

"I think it is both. Benes must have been hit with those revelations hours or days apart. Either would have unnerved and greatly upset him. But, ah, the two together! Eduard Benes today must be a man suffocating in the midst of the worst despair of his life. I recoil from his ego at the same time I want to take some of his pain on *my* shoulders!"

They drove down the cobblestone main street and onto a small bridge over a creek. Just ahead was the farm, which looked as though it had not had occupants for many months, if not years.

"We should park in front of the coops," Gabcik told him, referring to what remained of the farm's chicken coops, now a pile of rotting, loose boards.

He stopped the jeep and both men got out with slow, deliberate movements, then stood quietly for a moment.

"We do this so they have time to recognize me," Gabcik said finally, "and realize I wouldn't bring anyone along who was, in the slightest degree, a question mark."

Bartlett nodded, appreciating the good sense of what the other man had said.

Then Gabcik started walking toward the run-down farmhouse. When they reached the front door, the Czech waited.

Footsteps sounded inside.

"Josef?" a whispered voice asked.

"It is. May we enter?"

The door opened slowly. Bartlett saw the outline of a pistol gripped in a small rather pale hand. He and Gabcik stepped inside and for a minute or two stood in darkness, all windows boarded up, letting in no light whatever.

"Hello, Josef," a gruff voice said. "It is good to see you again."

"It is good to hear your voice, Max."

He turned to Bartlett.

"Stephen, this is Max Brunner," he said. "Max, this is Stephen Bartlett. The OSS has sent him to help us. He is the Allies' top munitions expert."

"We need him," Brunner remarked. "The bombs keep malfunctioning and we cannot always fix them. That is why we started using more grenades."

"But they aren't necessarily any more reliable," Bartlett added quickly. "I could have been killed by a grenade several days ago . . . if it had gone off as it should have. But it didn't. There was a malfunction of whatever sort. It didn't pack nearly the explosive power it should have."

"Whatever the case, we're glad you're here, and we welcome desperately your experience."

Letting out a yelp of pain as he banged his knee against something, Brunner found a light and turned it on.

"Needless precaution in the middle of the day," he told them, smiling amiably.

Max Brunner was barely five feet nine inches tall and quite thin, with eyes that seemed perpetually bloodshot and a complexion lighter than any Bartlett had seen before, giving his skin something of the look of porcelain.

"You seem startled at my appearance. Perhaps you have never seen a true albino before?" he said, enjoying the moment. "Indeed I am a pygmy among the giants you associate with our movement, men like yourself and Gabcik here, even Kubis."

"Sorry . . ." Bartlett said lamely.

"Everyone reacts in the same manner," Brunner admitted. "I am here because it would mean my death to be captured by the Nazis and experimented upon."

"Forgive me for being so direct, Max, but do you have General Henning von Tresckow here or know where he is?" Gabcik interjected impatiently.

"So *that* is who we have stumbled upon!" Brunner said, his eyes widening in genuine surprise. "Now I understand everything."

Obviously trying to cope with knowledge that affected him greatly, Brunner managed to mumble, "Would you like to see him?"

"Has he been harmed?" Bartlett asked expectantly.

"Harmed?" replied Brunner, getting himself under control by then. "Don't you suppose he deserves something more than that?"

"But you apparently didn't know who he was until I identified him a moment ago. Are you saying that Henning von Tresckow has been killed? Somebody didn't stop at beating him up, torturing him?"

"See for yourself."

Brunner asked them to follow him upstairs. He stopped before a door at the end of the corridor.

"The general is in there," he said without emotion, opening the door and stepping aside. "I must tell you that neither of you may be prepared for what you see."

Bartlett gritted his teeth, not knowing what to expect. He could see Gabcik doing the same thing.

The room was just as dark as the rest of the house had been when they first entered. Gabcik turned around toward Brunner, who remained in the hallway.

"Can we have some light?" he asked.

"He's been in there for two days with only darkness around him. I wouldn't recommend it."

"Must we stoop to the same brutality the Nazis are inflicting?" Gabcik spoke in a stern tone.

"Before you have a heart attack, Josef, or make me into some sadist that I am not, why don't you just listen?" Brunner replied.

"Listen?"

"Yes!" Brunner blurted, showing his exasperation.

"I don't hear—"

He stopped himself.

Someone was speaking so low his voice was hardly audible. Only a few words were distinguishable.

"Holy Father . . . this Thy unworthy servant . . . give me the strength . . . the wisdom . . ."

Bartlett could see the vague outline of a man at the opposite end of the room.

"Go ahead, Stephen," Gabcik whispered. "I'll stay here."

Bartlett approached the man, knelt beside him.

As his eyes adjusted, the American could see that von Tresckow was nearly naked, with only a towel wrapped around his waist, the odor of heavy perspiration coming from him.

"Henning! Henning, are you all right?" he asked with as much tenderness as he could muster.

Immediately, von Tresckow jerked his head around.

"Stephen! It *is* you. Thank God, my friend! Stephen, what I have learned is so awful. I never knew. I never knew any of it. So many of us have been kept in the darkness," von Tresckow said. "Heydrich plans to murder hundreds of thousands of Czechs and it doesn't concern him how many are not Jews!

"But he won't stop there, not this one! If millions are wiped out, it matters not at all to such a devil as he. Heydrich calls it his scorched-earth policy. He has said he doesn't care if one man, one woman, one child is left by the time he is finished. Extermination requires getting rid of *all* vermin!"

"But you have done nothing to be ashamed of," Bartlett told him.

"I once opposed those who went to war to fight fascism, to stop the worst imaginable crimes against humanity," the German went on. "I convinced myself at the very beginning that I was simply being a good patriot. Yet now there is only infamy, and I see that I have contributed to it."

"Not so, Henning. You learned the truth and you changed, and now you are one of the greatest hopes we have."

"My hands, Stephen," he said, holding them out in front of him. "Can I be like Pilate and wash my hands of the blood of the innocent?"

Von Tresckow lapsed into silence briefly, his head bowed, his body swaying gently back and forth.

Bartlett waited patiently, saying nothing.

"Stephen . . ."

"Yes, my friend?"

"You say *my friend*. Can you truly mean that? When we first met, I wore a uniform that has become a symbol of death to millions. That is why you see me as you do. I could no longer endure having it around me."

"But you must put it on again."

"*No!* I cannot. You must not ask that of me."

"You have no choice."

"Oh, but I do. I *have* chosen, Stephen. I have chosen to cast it aside as the filthy symbol it is."

Bartlett saw some photographs near von Tresckow's leg. Reaching over, he picked them up. It was almost impossible to see in the darkness, though his eyes were beginning to adjust a bit, but he saw enough to realize that the horrible images of men, women, and children lying in pools of blood were the images that had induced the German's current state.

"You have seen war before at its worst," he said. "Why—?"

"The worst, Stephen, is *not* a battlefield piled high with bodies," von Tresckow told him, his voice rising with emotion. "*That* I have seen again and again."

He turned abruptly toward Brunner, standing in the doorway.

"The lights," he said. "Please turn on the lights."

It was done.

Both men closed their eyes, then opened them slowly to the light.

"Here, Stephen," von Tresckow said as he picked up a photos. "That, I say, is by far the worst!"

A little girl, barely beyond crib age, clutching a doll in one hand, a Bible in another, her eyes closed in death, lay under the point of a bayonet.

"They had shot her already," von Tresckow said, his face reddening. "She was gone. But that wouldn't satisfy them."

He handed Bartlett a second photo.

"Look, Stephen, look at why I cannot wear ever again the uniform you are asking me to wear."

The lifeless child was stuck on the end of the bayonet as a German officer held the rifle out in front of him.

"He's smiling!" von Tresckow pointed out, nearly overcome. "He had to *ask* for that rifle. Officers do not carry these as their standard weapons. He had to *take* it away from someone and do what he did. He *wanted* to commit this awful act, Stephen. He seems glad, oh, see how glad he is! *Look at his face!*"

Both sat there for a very long time, saying nothing. Gabcik and Brunner soon left them alone and went back downstairs.

Nearly an hour passed.

"Stephen . . ."

"Yes."

"Is it possible that God still speaks to us?"

"I think it is."

"In words?"

"If not words, then in what we might call a conviction of the heart, the soul perhaps."

"It may have happened a few minutes ago, Stephen."

"What did he say?"

"That I must not quit, that I must put that hated uniform back on, that I must act as—"

"Salt?"

"Yes! How could you know?"

"If He says something, it is not always to just one person."

"Stephen, Stephen, how can this be?"

"Salt retards spoilage."

"But this country, this land of my birth is already spoiled!"

"No, Henning, it isn't *completely* so. You're still here, along with Beck, von Stauffenberg, and others. If *you* retreat, what will happen to *their* determination? If you *all* give up, toss away your uniforms and leave, that makes a statement, yes; but Hitler will surely order your execution. He may not get every last man but he will get most. Then whatever hope there could be of toppling the regime from *within* has vanished."

"*Can* I face another day of pretense? Again, as before, I will be in frequent contact with Himmler, Göring, and the rest. And that raving Rosenberg and his pseudo-intellectual babbling . . . I suspect even Goebbels tires of him.

"These are the lunatics whose asylum I must share while pretending to be a fellow inmate. The difference is that they run the country and can vent their pathological delusions on the German people!"

"There will be more little children on bayonets if you leave."

Bartlett shook the photograph in front of him.

"If you need a reason to *continue,* not an excuse to leave, think of *her!* Think of a child stuck through with steel, yes, or turning bright red as her flesh ignites, or dying as poisonous fumes fill up her lungs. Think of her weeping as she is torn from her mother, her father . . . think of her as she watches while they are shot in the back of the head and dumped into a ditch, and lime poured over their bodies."

Bartlett could feel himself becoming quite ill, reacting much as von Tresckow had.

"Think of that little girl coming to you in your dreams in the middle of the night, Henning, standing before your bed and asking, 'Sir, why did you desert the others like me who are still alive? You can do nothing about me but you could have tried to save them, yet now I hear their footsteps behind me, one by one, rising from their unmarked graves, from the ashes of Nazi ovens and—'"

Von Tresckow reached out to slap the American hard across the face but Bartlett caught his hand and stopped it in midair.

"Not at me, my friend. Keep that anger. Keep it within your gut and use it to strike back at *them!* Do what you must *to stop the madness!"*

Bartlett let go. The German held his hand there for a moment, trembling, as he tried to bring himself under control. Veins stood up across his forehead and on his cheeks.

"Stephen, I would appreciate it if you would leave me with my Lord for a little while now," von Tresckow requested.

"Take whatever time you need, Henning," Bartlett told him as he patted a bare shoulder. "I'll be downstairs."

Bartlett walked to the doorway. As he closed the door behind him, he heard the sound of a man sobbing from the depths of his soul.

"What happened?" Bartlett asked as they sat in a dusty kitchen, drinking strong coffee at midnight.

"He was very quiet," Brunner said. "We could get nothing out of him."

"Did you beat him at all? I saw no marks on him."

"There are ways of inflicting pain that offer no evidence, you know." Brunner shook his head in an exaggerated manner as he spoke. "Forgive me. That was cold. I sounded like one of *them!*"

"I have to agree, Max."

"It's the life we lead. We move from building to building, hamlet to village to town, back to another hamlet, and on and on. Some of us become careless and are caught and executed or sent to Treblinka or one of the other camps. We cannot take our families with us. Yet our loved ones cannot remain behind. They have to be sent to Switzerland or into Sweden or across the channel to the Brits. We fight against oppression but become oppressed in other ways. Our spirits shrivel up somehow, Stephen. We think only in violent terms, in terms of deceit, and in clever ways to undermine the enemy. In doing so, we become a little like those we loathe because we have to think like they do in order to outguess and outrun them."

Brunner looked toward the doorway as he commented, "I hear movement upstairs."

"I heard it, too," Bartlett added.

Gabcik only nodded, looking apprehensively at his watch and wondering how much longer it would be before they were on their way to Prague, or *Praha,* as it was called in the Slovak language.

"Von Tresckow said nothing until we brought him here and showed him those photos," Brunner continued. "A true Nazi would have been able to look at them and either react with dispassion, his heart thoroughly hardened over the past few years, or else try to fake an emotional response that we would see through in an instant."

"You believe his response was genuine then?"

"Oh, Stephen, you have no idea! It was as though *his* child was on the end of that bayonet. I feared for his heart, his mind."

"But you still didn't know who he was at that point," Bartlett pointed out.

"Anyone who had such feeling, such outrage left in him . . . it didn't matter. This was obviously not someone we should torture, then kill."

"He had no papers on him?"

"None . . . they must have been lost when the jeep burst into flame."

"Why did you show him the photos in the first place?" Bartlett asked.

"This . . ." Brunner responded, taking something out of his pocket.

A small Bible.

"We figured he either confiscated it and hadn't disposed of it yet. Or that it was his own."

"When he reacted the way he did, you were convinced this was indeed one unusual German?"

"Very unusual, yes. Later, we tried to feed him, but he refused to eat anything, though we managed to get some water down him."

More sounds from upstairs. And then someone speaking.

"Stephen, I think we should plan on getting me to an SS station tomorrow morning. I cannot explain an absence that lasts any longer," the now-familiar voice said. "Is that all right with you?"

"Yes," Bartlett assured him, raising his voice just a bit.

"I'm going to go to sleep now. Please awaken me when you think it best."

A pause.

"Stephen?"

"Yes, Henning?"

"I shall need to ask one of you to do something tomorrow that you will *not* want to do, my friend. But it is going to be very necessary that you follow my wishes."

"Whatever you say . . ."

"Good, good."

Footsteps. Then the rattle of a door, shutting.

The three men looked at another, having no hint of what it was that Henning von Tresckow had in mind.

10

The nearest SS station was thirty miles away. Minutes before reaching it, von Tresckow had Gabcik turn the jeep off the dirt road into a grove of small evergreens.

"Now there is something you *must* do," he said, glancing first at Bartlett then at Gabcik and Brunner, his patrician face quite solemn, deep blue eyes cold-looking, a heavy frown on his forehead. His words came as though each one meant some awful burst of personal anguish.

"What is it?" Bartlett asked, apprehensive over the German's manner.

"One of you must come very close to killing me."

Bartlett, Gabcik, and Brunner gasped in near unison.

"There is no alternative," von Tresckow insisted. "I *have* to look as though I've been nearly murdered. Otherwise, even a general can run out of excuses—and people willing to accept these. By doing this, by beating me badly, you save my life. You see the irony in that, surely."

They looked at one another, then back at von Tresckow.

"But how can it be one of us?" Bartlett asked. "We know what you stand for, what you're trying to achieve. One day, I pray it's soon, you may even lead this country."

"It has to be him, I think," von Tresckow said, ignoring Bartlett's words and pointing to Gabcik. "Brunner isn't strong enough. You, Stephen, don't have it in you to do this to a friend because you have not suffered under the uniform worn by that friend."

Gabcik threw up his hands in protest.

"Why is it that you judge me as you do?" he asked. "I now know the man beneath the uniform. I could not—"

Von Tresckow walked over to him and placed a hand on each shoulder.

"You have left your loved ones behind," he said with some tenderness.

"I did, yes, and so have Brunner and Bartlett," Gabcik replied.

"Leave the friend you think me to be, the friend I *am,* leave that friend behind, dear Josef, and think of me once again only as your enemy."

Von Tresckow suddenly slapped the other man hard across the cheek.

"Are you a man?" he taunted. "Do you still have a backbone, or is it that months of running and hiding have made you nothing but a weakling?"

He slapped Gabcik again with even more force and was about to do it a third time when the Czech grabbed his wrist, stopping him.

"Break it!" von Tresckow demanded. "Bend it back and break it, Josef!"

"No!" Gabcik said. "I cannot do any of this. I cannot become an animal like the rest of them."

"But you *are* an animal," von Tresckow said. "I suspected long ago that all Czechs were beasts. Now you are proving it right before my eyes. You know, I wonder if Heydrich should be executed or applauded. After all, if he lives, there will be less garbage like your kind to pollute—"

Gabcik snapped. He lunged for von Tresckow, knocking him off his feet. Bartlett started to run to both men and separate them, but Brunner grabbed his arm.

"Von Tresckow's right," he whispered. "Let this happen . . . for the sake of all of us."

Gabcik, though shorter and lighter than von Tresckow, was more muscular. The German put up a fight but only to spur the other man on. In a short while von Tresckow's nose was broken, two ribs were dislocated, and several teeth had been knocked out.

Gabcik was shaking by the time he managed to get himself under some kind of control.

"Not enough," von Tresckow gasped. "Listen to me! Think of fields of flowers, beautiful flowers . . . of what is underneath them, feeding their roots. Think of the bodies of helpless children buried there, think of—"

Abruptly, Brunner strode over to von Tresckow, taking out a nine-millimeter Browning pistol he had stolen from a cache of weapons the Germans themselves had confiscated from Czech soldiers.

He swung the barrel, breaking von Tresckow's jaw. The general fell to the ground, unconscious.

"Let's drag him as close as we can get to the station without risking their spotting us, and leave him in the middle of the road," Brunner said. "As we're pulling away, I'll fire twice. When they come to investigate they will find his body in no time!"

Bartlett looked back once as he was climbing into the jeep and saw von Tresckow lying face down on the snow, a trickle of blood forming a stark pool against the white. He could hear groans coming from the suddenly helpless body.

His gaze met Brunner's and Gabcik's. That image lingering in their minds, none of them could talk as the jeep headed back to the farmhouse.

WOLF'S LAIR . . .

Reinhard Heydrich looked at the coded communique a second time then crumpled it and threw it to one side, missing the wastebucket but not caring since an aide, eager to please him, undoubtedly would soon spot it and dispose of it properly.

"They truly think they can get to the Führer without their plot being uncovered," he said out loud. "Yet how sloppy they are in protecting their transmissions!"

He chuckled as he thought, *and at Rastenburg of all places! Non-Aryans indeed are inferior mentally. Now that the truth is known, the guard around Hitler will be made stronger than ever.*

The phone on his hand-carved desk rang . . . it was Himmler, Heydrich's secretary announced.

My superior beckons, he told himself, holding the receiver a quarter-inch from his ear, his eyes narrowed with disdain, his lips pressed so tightly together that they almost disappeared altogether.

After finishing the conversation, which lasted a bit less than five minutes, Heydrich slammed the receiver back on its cradle and leaned back in the hand-stitched, high-back leather chair, his entire tall, thin frame trembling with contempt.

So he thinks I, too, may be in danger . . .

Heydrich considered that to be a near-impossibility because he had instilled so much fear in the Czech and Slovak peoples.

They know what will happen if they even try anything, let alone succeed!

His eyes shifted to the lamp at the left corner of his desk and he reached out, touching the yellowish, near-transparent shade.

I hope they do, he chuckled. *I could use more of these . . .*

The plot to assassinate Hitler had been authenticated; confirming evidence had been passed to them by their courier in England.

Stephen Bartlett . . .

He repeated the name from the communique, along with information provided about the man from Nazi intelligence sources. Bartlett was tall, good-looking, with an exceptionally muscular build. He had oversized blue eyes, large cheekbones, thick, flat lips, and a protruding, dimpled chin. When he wasn't speaking German, which he did fluently with no trace of anything other than a middle-class German accent, he reverted to speech that betrayed a bit of what the Americans called a southern twang.

Finally he forced his attention away from the photograph to read about the American's compelling knowledge of munitions. One report said Bartlett was so good he could make something quite deadly out of two twigs and some olive oil!

Heydrich chuckled a bit at that one, but realized that Bartlett was not a laughing matter if the rest of what was contained in the file was accurate. The Nazis had always considered the various resistance movements to be ineffectual in terms of their use of explosives and such. They could shoot their handguns, perhaps, and use their knives and bayonets with some skill, but that was the limit of their expertise, though any bomb, no matter how inept the one who threw it happened to be, could cause some damage.

They're having a terrible time keeping their weapons in good repair, he thought happily, *with rust setting in and—*

But Bartlett could change all that. If he encountered explosive devices that failed to work, he was more than capable of reconstructing them so they would work properly or else he could come up with something new altogether. If he could get to enough partisans and teach them just a fraction of what he knew, and they in turn could pass this on to others—!

Springing forward, he picked up the phone and got through to SS headquarters after less than a minute had passed.

Himmler had already left. Cursing, Heydrich turned his attention to Martin Bormann.

"I want this man caught and executed!" he demanded with bellowing vehemence. "And I must have more SS agents to ferret out any others like him!!"

Bormann agreed these orders would be sent.

"And I want to retaliate against his family," Heydrich ranted on. "Where are they?"

When Bormann told him Bartlett's wife and son presently resided just outside London, Heydrich let out a loud, coarse laugh.

"We already have a very dependable man there," he reminded master plotter Bormann. "You know who I mean. We bought him mind, body, and soul a long time ago. He must be given this assignment. I suspect he may enjoy it. After all, he was the operative who uncovered this plot in the first place."

Heydrich spoke under the guise of indignation over anyone being stupid enough to hatch an attempt to kill the Führer. But there was also something else in what Himmler had told him that spurred him on.

"It seems a bit strange, Reinhard. We came upon this too easily," Himmler had said. Then he had paused and added an unusually sympathetic admonition. "Please, my friend, be careful. It could be a gambit to deceive us."

That was when he spoke of Heydrich himself possibly being the target instead of Hitler. Himmler had begged him to increase security around himself.

In response, Heydrich had reminded his mentor that he had issued a directive promising the total destruction of Lidice if any kind of plot were uncovered against Hitler or any other top-ranked officer of the *Schutzstaffel*.

"You have the proof," Heydrich had said. "I should like to start the extermination immediately."

Himmler vacillated, wanting more confirmation. What the SS already had in hand was reason enough to heighten security, yes, but it was not enough to massacre hundreds of Czechs. He seemed more worried about international reaction than about letting Heydrich have his way.

"The original intent was to intimidate any conspirators. You must remember that, Reinhard, and not be so anxious to spill more blood. You see, there is yet another possibility in the midst of all of this."

Heydrich had demanded to know what that was.

"Consider this, Reinhard: Consider for a moment that the Allies might be willing to sacrifice Lidice in order to have more concrete evidence of the so-called barbaric designs and methods of the Third Reich. They could use this as a propaganda tool to give impetus to partisan resistance movements all over Europe."

Heydrich was not placated, reminding Himmler of the camps that *he,* Himmler, had been responsible for constructing.

"You are soon going to assign Mengele to Auschwitz and you talk to me about a few hundred bodies from a village that is inconsequential?" he said with growing anger. "Mengele will dispose of twice that number in a day and then send a handful of survivors to his laboratories. Heinrich, Heinrich, you must let me commence *now!* Delay will imply that the SS has been bluffing, and if in this case, in what others as well? I want merely to *execute* the scum. A single bullet or two will do the job, and then it's over. However, what if the international community finds out about Mengele and Eichmann and the rest? The destruction of Lidice will seem almost humanitarian in comparison!"

"By then there will be no international community worth anything to oppose us," Himmler had answered. "We will have extended the borders of the Third Reich to the very shores of Britain itself. Russia will be annexed . . ."

Heydrich got nowhere with the man who had been his benefactor. That was when the conversation ended.

Someday, Heydrich thought, *I will not have to be obsequious in your shadow. Someday you may be enveloped by my own.*

He stood, bored, and strode to the door of the large, antique-filled room that had become his office.

He threw it open, startling his secretary by demanding, "When will the rest of those lamp shades be here? If more skin is needed, I shall be only too happy to issue an immediate directive. See to it now!"

Heydrich was about to shut the door when something Himmler had mentioned resurfaced.

Consider this, Reinhard: Consider for a moment that the Allies might be willing to sacrifice Lidice in order to have more concrete evidence of the so-called barbaric designs and methods of the Third Reich . . .

He smiled as he licked his lips.

"Not if I turn their own weapon against them . . ." Heydrich mulled over that possibility out loud.

His secretary, not realizing he was talking to himself and not to her, did not hear clearly since he spoke in a low voice; she seemed fearful of earning his displeasure by asking Heydrich to repeat himself, so she kept quiet, waiting patiently for him to elaborate.

He had bowed his head for a few seconds, his mind working over the details of a sudden plan.

Abruptly, Heydrich looked straight at her and said, "Erika, get Heinrich Müller on the phone. Tell him I need to start a rumor within the resistance movement. And I want this done *without delay!*"

They drove on back roads past Strakonice and Pisek, then across a small bridge over the Vltava River and on through Tabor, then on a northerly route toward Benesov, their destination, approximately forty miles from Prague.

Bartlett noticed the abundant fertile farmlands that characterized that region of Czechoslovakia and the villages dating as far back as the Middle Ages. The lifestyle of the citizens had remained little different despite four or five hundred years of history since they were first constructed; much of the population lived without automobiles or machinery, plowing their fields with the same hand tools and horses, and socializing in each village's *hospodas* or *krcmas,* as some called the ancient taverns.

"The Nazis want to get rid of us and put in their own kind, repopulating the entire country," Gabcik told him. "How can they rationalize that on any level, even an intellectual one? The heritage in this nation is *ours!* It dates back so very far. Does their Aryan supremacy know no limits whatever?"

"I doubt that it does, in *their* minds," Bartlett replied. "The very basis of what they believe is that there is no wrong *on their part* because they are supermen, and being above all other men, they are not bound by the petty moral, ethical, spiritual, or geographical boundaries of their neighbors."

He found that to be the most chilling aspect of confronting the Nazis. In some respects, it placed the Allies at a strategic disadvantage unless they acted in a similarly unscrupulous manner.

"We cannot win unless we prove to be every bit as vicious as they are," Bartlett said, "and use many of the same tactics."

"That is true," Gabcik agreed regretfully. "Whole towns might be bombed out of existence sometime during this war. I suspect that Dresden one day will be an Allied target. Frankfurt must be on the list as well. And certainly Berlin. Can any of us suppose that only *military* personnel will be killed? Innocent men, women, and children inevitably will die or be maimed for the rest of their lives."

Gabcik knew he was in an untenable position, railing against the depravity of war while being an instrument of the very mind-set he was deploring.

"Call me a hypocrite," he said. "I wear that mantle knowingly, oh, I do that, but sadly, very sadly. All this talk of sudden death in the short term buying us quicker victory sooner over the long haul happens to be true in this instance, my friend. Heydrich cannot be allowed one second more of life than is necessary."

"Is the bomb ready?" Bartlett asked.

"Not quite. We are having trouble with the firing mechanism. That is why you may have heard that grenades are a standby possibility."

"That I have. But I don't trust them any more than a hand-tooled bomb. In fact, I trust the bomb more, because I can open it up and work with it, correcting any deficiency that shows up. Grenades don't offer that advantage. They work or they don't. And you never know until it's too late."

Gabcik smiled, his expression a genuinely warm one.

"Praise God you are here, Stephen," he said, with gusto. "Praise God you have been able to get through to help us!"

They stopped at an inn midway between Tabor and their destination and slept well through the night, then left at dawn.

"Jan Kubis will be so glad to see you," Gabcik told him after reaching Benesov. They approached a several-hundred-year-old, red-roofed, white-fronted, two-story structure that served as a partisan headquarters for that region.

A plump Slovak woman wearing a bright red-and-white polka dress came rushing out to greet them.

"My name is Katrina Hrdlicka," she said as she embraced Gabcik and then Bartlett, nearly crushing them in the process. "If you had been another minute, I don't know how I could have stood it!"

"What is wrong, dear one?" Gabcik asked, concerned that she was even more excitable than usual.

"This!" she exclaimed as she thrust a small sheet of paper into his hand.

He read it quickly and handed it to Bartlett.

"I don't believe it," the American said at first. "It's a not-so-clever lie designed to spread disillusionment among the partisans."

"I think it is partly what you say," Gabcik replied. "Whoever leaked that information hopes to shatter our will but I am not as sure as you that it is *concocted.*"

Bartlett reread the brief note:

> *The Nazis have said Lidice will be destroyed if a plot against Hitler or the SS leaders is uncovered, but the Allies have already written off the village as a necessary consequence of this war. It may even prove, in their eyes, to be a valuable propaganda tool.*

Anger flushed his cheeks red.

"A propaganda tool!" he repeated. "That sounds like something out of Josef Goebbels's office."

"It's too obvious for that, Stephen. He would be more clever than that if he were actually trying to deceive us."

"You think *this* might be genuine?"

"That is the only other—"

Katrina interrupted him.

"No more talk," she said with great impatience. "You must go to Jan. You must talk with him."

"Is he here?" Gabcik asked.

"No, no," she told him. "Lidice . . . he's there. I don't know why but he just took off, shouting back to me where he was heading. Please, you must go to this good man. He needs someone right now. He needs someone bad!"

Lidice was thirty-seven miles northwest of Benesov. But unlike the other places they had passed through, this village was in an area of heavy SS and Gestapo activity near Prague, the nation's capital.

Both Bartlett and Gabcik possessed the requisite forged identity papers, but each time they approached another SS checkpoint they endured several tense moments until they were waved on past. The closer they got to Lidice, the more the scrutiny to which they were subjected.

Finally, though, it seemed no more troopers were immediately apparent. Katrina hadn't known where Kubis would be, so when they made it into the town limits, they resigned themselves to a hit-or-miss afternoon of trying to find him, not daring to make any actual inquiries for fear of drawing attention to him or to themselves.

"How many of them know what is hanging over their heads?" Gabcik spoke softly after they had parked the jeep and stood in the town square.

"They seem happy enough," Bartlett observed, adding quickly, "as happy as anyone can be when their country is being occupied by monsters. Maybe they don't know."

"I think it's something else, Stephen," remarked Gabcik with sadness. "They have learned to treasure each moment alive with a roof over their heads and loved ones by their side, knowing all this could be snatched away in an instant by evil men in dark uniforms; so it all seems that much more precious to them."

A little girl passing by noticed them and handed a flower to each from the assortment she grasped in one hand.

"She's so pretty, so innocent," Bartlett said when she was out of earshot. "I try to persuade myself that even Heydrich could not go so far as to kill such a child, nor could the ones following him if we are soon successful."

"You are quite wrong," Gabcik remarked. "Those photos Brunner showed to von Tresckow? Heydrich, like that trooper, would not stop at such an infamy."

Bartlett remembered the photos all too well.

Suddenly, Gabcik seemed to freeze. In reaction, Bartlett did the same thing, neither man breathing for a moment. The Czech was staring straight ahead.

"Kubis . . ." he muttered.

"Where?"

"Straight ahead, being shoved into the backseat of that black Mercedes."

Bartlett saw the little vignette: two large men in black-leather trench coats were dumping another man, much shorter, into the waiting automobile.

"He's been caught," Bartlett said a bit lamely.

"Yes, and we can't let that happen. We must follow them and find an opportunity to pry Jan loose."

"They're Gestapo, apparently . . . well-armed."

"But they don't know the countryside like I do. They don't know the shortcuts. I think they will take the main road out of town and stay on it."

"We'll ambush?"

"Any way we can, Stephen. We must bar nothing. They will get *everything* out of Jan if given a chance."

Bartlett knew this was no reflection on Jan Kubis's valor. The Gestapo possessed drugs and other methods that had been used for years and had been perfected since the war began. No man or woman could withstand them indefinitely.

He and Gabcik walked as casually as possible back to the jeep. As they were getting into it, the Mercedes drove past them.

"This is going to be what I suppose you will call a wild ride," Gabcik warned him. "There is a shortcut through a dense patch of forest with fallen trees and thick undergrowth. If we are fortunate enough to cut through all that without complications, we should be able to come out just ahead of their car, but believe me, we'll have only seconds, at most, to take our positions."

Both men checked their pistols, then reholstered them.

Gabcik swung the jeep around and headed in the opposite direction out of Lidice.

"The Nazis are big on main roads," he said. "They care little about narrow, unpaved back roads."

"But why?" Bartlett asked. "That seems too obviously careless. What could they be thinking of?"

"All *good* Nazis are trained to fear nothing less than a battalion, even though they tell themselves it is more respect than fear. They are convinced that they can easily handle one or two or half a dozen men or more with great ease, given their superior Aryan conditioning.

"Hold on to your seat!" Gabcik said as they entered the woods.

Even the rugged jeep groaned and creaked as they bounced over exposed roots of the old large trees. Ahead the trees gave way to more farmland.

"The main road takes a sharp turn near here," Gabcik told the American as they stopped beside the highway. "Even the Mercedes will have to slow down to negotiate the curve. That is when we take out the tires."

"Kubis could be injured," Bartlett reminded him.

"Jan will be dead and the rest of us destined to follow, if we don't get him away from the Gestapo!"

The two men were in place when the black Mercedes approached the turn. Gabcik was on one side of the road, Bartlett on the opposite. As soon as the front wheels had entered the curve, both men opened fire with silencers on their pistols.

First the tires on the driver's side went, then on the passenger's side. Bare wheel rims caused sparks as brakes were applied and the Mercedes lurched left, then right, careening off a mileage marker set in a high stone base. Then it slipped over the edge of the road and into the ditch beside it, tumbling over once, then twice, ending up on its roof, its wheels still spinning by momentum, the odor of leaking gasoline strong.

Bartlett and Gabcik waited seconds. No movement.

"We've got to get him out!" Gabcik started to say, but was interrupted by the sight of a man frantically trying to crawl out of the backseat through the now-empty window frame on the car's side.

"It's Jan!" Gabcik shouted, his voice exultant.

He jumped to his feet and rushed forward. Kubis heard him and looked up. When Gabcik reached the car, the two clasped hands with great passion. Then Kubis clutched the other man's upper torso while Gabcik grabbed his sides as gently as possible and pulled. Neither noticed the burly Gestapo agent who poked his head through the other door frame on that side.

Still not quite at the car, Bartlett saw the agent immediately and raised his pistol to fire.

Too close. If he missed, he would hit either Kubis or Gabcik.

He reholstered the pistol and sprinted forward, leaping up and over the side of the Mercedes. He seized the agent around the neck. By this time, Gabcik and Kubis were sprawled in the ditch. The Gestapo agent was stronger than Bartlett could have imagined, and Bartlett felt himself being pulled into the Mercedes. The odor of gasoline seemed more intense than ever. He flailed out with his fists, hitting the agent's chin and hearing bones snap in response. He tried to turn himself around and up, but a second pair of hands suddenly began pulling him back down. A third pair grabbed his neck—at least one other agent was still alive!

Distantly Bartlett heard the sound of flames, sputtering at first, then stronger. Soon he felt heat and heard someone screaming in pain inches from his ear. Then, in his skewed vision, a single hand reached down and a strong voice yelled, "Reach up, Stephen, reach up! I'll pull you out!"

He reached for the hand as he braced his free arm against the roof of the car and pushed upward, perspiration making him slippery. But finally, seconds later, he was out of the fire-engulfed Mercedes, its metal turning red, the burning flesh of others strong in his nostrils.

11

You three look like you've been traveling with the damned!" Katrina exclaimed as the bedraggled trio walked unsteadily to her front door.

"In some respects we have," Gabcik remarked wearily.

"Jan!" she went on, settling her attention on Kubis, who had been blessed or cursed with a baby-faced look that made him seem then like a hapless child who had tangled with the worst town bully imaginable and sported the most awful cuts and bruises as a result. "What can I do to help? Please tell me!"

"A hot bath for each of us and a stiff shot of the strongest medicine you can find," he told her, followed by a forced chuckle.

Later, after baths and a relaxing tea she had concocted herself, they sat on stiff oak chairs in Katrina Hrdlicka's small dining room as she served them a full meal including steaming, butter-covered cornbread muffins and hot soup made from vegetables she herself had grown, along with ground-lamb patties that tasted like filet mignon to her hungry guests.

Gabcik told her what had happened.

"Mother of God!" she blurted, then blushed. "Sorry . . . You all are blessed. You're here, alive, stomachs full. How wonderful our Lord is!"

"But I wonder how we will feel a week from now," remarked Kubis.

"A week?" Katrina repeated, confused, with hands on her quite ample hips. "What is happening—?"

She saw the dour expression on their faces.

"Mother of—!" she started to say again but caught herself this time.

During the frantic ride back to Lidice, they decided they would have to strike at Reinhard Heydrich within the next week or risk another incident like the one they had just undergone.

"Every additional day brings with it the potential for unforeseen disaster," Gabcik observed.

At first Kubis had been rather quiet, his small frame curled up almost in a fetal position in the backseat of the jeep. With that remark, he had become more alert, his eyes flashing with emotion.

"And another day of life for the people of Lidice," he said. "But then that shouldn't matter to the Allies, should it? This atrocity becomes part of a propaganda trap for the Nazis. Think of it! A few words for world opinion in exchange for hundreds of lives! What a deal that is, wouldn't you say?"

Bartlett and Gabcik didn't react against his bitterness, for they shared it themselves. But they also realized another truth.

"Martyrs," Gabcik remarked. "Yes, I know, it *is* hellish when this happens. But in war—"

"Shove that rationalization crap," Kubis interrupted. "Martyrs are people who *choose* to be martyrs. They *willingly* throw down their lives for a cause. But who's giving the citizens of Lidice such a choice?

"I don't think any of the victims *know* what is about to happen. They see a few more SS troopers arriving daily and they suspect something is in the air but they have no idea what it's all about."

Bartlett reached over the front seat and tried to lay his hand on Kubis's shoulder, but Kubis brushed it aside.

"*Nothing* will help now!" he shouted. "I drank ale with men who will be six feet under after Heydrich has been killed by us. I was kissed by a beautiful woman who may be raped by her executioners before they murder her with their rifles. I was given a scarlet flower by a little girl—"

Bartlett and Gabcik shot a glance at one another.

"—whose body will follow her father's and her mother's into the rich earth. A few months from now, perhaps some fresh and quite beautiful flowers will have sprung up from that very spot and some child-monster already corrupted by Nazi doctrine will happen by, pick a few blossoms, and bring them home to her adoring fascist parents. *How can I cope with that? Tell me!*"

Jan Kubis drifted into silence after that, his mind tortured with images of the dying innocent.

Katrina joined Bartlett in the backyard of her home. Old friends Gabcik and Kubis had gone off by themselves to talk.

"This house is four hundred years old," she said with some wistfulness, indicating the two-story, white-washed building with a wave of her broad hand. "It has seen much, Stephen, much indeed."

"But nothing like the present," he remarked.

"That is right, that is right," she agreed as she sat in a much larger chair that just about accommodated her enormous frame. "And no man more evil than Reinhard Heydrich has slept here."

"Heydrich? Here?" Bartlett reacted with surprise.

"Months ago . . ." Katrina elaborated.

"Was he awful?"

"To be honest, he treated me with great courtesy."

"That's surprising."

"I felt that way, too; I surely did. But it was all on the surface. I could see that in his eyes."

"I've heard about those eyes."

"If they mirror his soul, then his soul is as bleak and cruel and cold as all the stories have said."

"Why did he stop here? Do you know?"

"Yes. He said it reminded him a bit of the house in which he had lived when he was a child."

"A sentimental streak in a madman!"

"I don't know about that. I heard Heydrich whisper, 'Ah, those were such simpler days.' For an instant, I thought I could see on that thin, sharp-nosed face of his some kind of feeling . . . regret possibly. Then the man with an iron heart came back into control and there was no more regret—or whatever it was a moment before—none that I saw during the entire week of his stay here."

"Anything else about him?"

"Oh yes, Stephen, there surely is. I learned that he loves to go for a ride early in the morning immediately after he has finished breakfast. I hear he does that even now, nearly a year later. Once he took over the estate his family occupies now, he settled on a different route than when he was here, but it has been the same ever since."

Bartlett picked up on that immediately.

"Heydrich never deviates?" he asked.

"I am not aware that he does, and I doubt it," Katrina replied.

"So Josef and Jan have made their plans accordingly."

She smiled as she nodded her head.

"In one week," she said, "Heydrich is going to Berlin for a major meeting with Hitler."

"What's that about?"

"No one except Heydrich and Gestapo chief Karl Hermann Frank have any grasp of the topic, not even the Führer himself."

"Ah, Frank, the man who declared, 'My goal is to humiliate and destroy the Czechs as a people.'"

"You stay up-to-date, Stephen," she complimented him.

"As much as I can be. Besides, Frank is as close to being a friend of Heydrich's as anybody has become. Judging by that statement, it's not difficult to see that they have the same brutal mind-set."

"I pray that Daluege is the one who goes on to assume Heydrich's command," Katrina said casually.

"How can you be serious?" Bartlett, startled, questioned her.

Katrina snapped her head around.

"Daluege is a barbaric fool, Stephen, but a fool nevertheless. You must remember that. Of those three evil musketeers—Heydrich, Frank, and Daluege—Kurt Daluege is the weakest. If my people and I cannot escape from devils, then may the least of them take the throne."

As he looked her straight in the eye for a moment, Bartlett was beginning to understand why Katrina was considered so valuable to the resistance movement.

"You seem surprised at what I have been saying," she commented, folding her huge arms and looking quite displeased. "Do you assume that, because I am a woman who weighs over two hundred and fifty pounds, I have a very small brain? Is that the case, my American friend?"

Bartlett realized his manner had sent her the wrong signal, and he started to protest that she was mistaken, his face flushed with embarrassment.

She threw her head back and started laughing a deep and wonderful laugh that seemed to shake her whole body.

"I am *playing* with you, Stephen!" Katrina said after a moment. "I should be the one who apologizes."

From her chair next to his she leaned over and hugged him around the neck.

"I want you to know that I am *glad* I have this body!" Katrina Hrdlicka declared. "Maybe the Nazis make the same mistake! Having everyone underestimate me may be my best weapon, don't you think?"

For his part, Bartlett was delighted that she released her hold on his neck a few seconds later.

Bartlett was appalled when he saw the cluster bombs Kubis and Gabcik had been planning to use. He told them that the way these had been constructed, it was likely that the two of them would be killed while Reinhard Heydrich was left unscathed.

Gently, aware that their egos could be trampled if he went about it the wrong way, Bartlett showed them what was wrong, starting with the firing mechanism and proceeding to the other components, including the actual explosives.

One problem was rust caused by too much moisture trapped inside. The rust was almost certain to make the bomb misfire, given the slightest miscalculation.

Rather than be offended, both men were grateful since they realized their mission was of such vast significance that it had to transcend personal feelings or they all were doomed. At the American's prodding, they switched from a cluster bomb to a fusion bomb, which Bartlett was convinced would serve them more reliably.

Providentially, they could get all the materials locally for the new bomb. The downside was that this meant increasing the circle of those who were aware that they happened to be in the vicinity, which in turn magnified the potential for betrayal.

The handmade fusion bombs were going to be similar to some of the armaments Bartlett had found in the camouflaged bunker, bombs and grenades that had not been purchased complete but were constructed by the partisans themselves.

"It is better, in a way, that it all had turned out this way," Kubis suggested and since he was going to be the one to throw the bombs, the other two were pleased that he felt this way.

"Why do you say that?" Bartlett asked as they sat in the basement of Katrina's house.

"Because the different pieces can be hidden in various places until we are ready to put them together. We don't have to have a complete bomb until the very last moment!"

Bartlett himself had disposed of their supply of cluster bombs, burying them under a bridge that had substantial Nazi military traffic on it.

"Someday, when tanks and troop vehicles are going over it, one of us or perhaps another partisan we have alerted may have the pleasure of blowing them all to damnation!" he said with some excitement over the prospect.

That was worth a combined cheer from the three of them.

A few minutes later, Bartlett asked them about their assassination plan. Contrary to what he had seen with their ill-advised work on the cluster bombs, their strategy for the assassination itself seemed as solid as anything he himself might have devised. After settling every detail, they decided to reconnoiter the site picked as the best place to assassinate Heydrich. Bartlett and Gabcik bicycled from Benesov to Prague, arriving prior to the time Heydrich would be driven past the attack point.

"I want to make sure I am familiar with every inch of that spot," Gabcik reasoned. "I don't want surprises."

Bartlett agreed, though his part of the mission would take him up the road to the estate where the Heydrich family had been living for some time.

Curiously, Jan Kubis declined to join them. Though Gabcik tried hard to persuade him, Kubis, behaving nervously, was adamant . . .

The grassy knoll overlooked the corner that Heydrich in his open-topped Mercedes would be turning. Just in front of it were tram tracks and the overhead cables that powered it.

"We must pray there is no tram coming along at precisely the moment the Butcher's car approaches that spot," Gabcik remarked.

"It is an ideal site," Bartlett told him as they took a "casual" walk across the knoll. "The driver will be slowing down, of course, for the *Obergruppenfuhrer* must never be seen to be in a hurry. To go into the curve fast, with tires squealing, would imply haste or nervousness or carelessness. If noticed by any strollers in the vicinity, that would be the wrong message to send to them."

"Business as usual," Gabcik agreed as he glanced at his watch. "We must not stay here too long. That, too, would make us stand out. *We* could be noticed then, and we cannot allow that to happen."

"Jan will be on the other side, with the bombs?"

"He will. At first, if I miss or if the wounds are only superficial, Heydrich will assume that there is only a single gunman . . . me. Whether I miss or hit the target, his back will be to Jan. Then our friend will leap out into the open for an instant and throw first one bomb, then two, unless something goes wrong."

"If we are fortunate, then," Bartlett spoke, "Heydrich and his driver both will be killed, no one will have seen Jan, and the investigation will center on a lone assassin."

"So much hinges on that," Gabcik said. "If the Gestapo can be made to believe such a deception as this . . . that I first shot the driver, then Heydrich, and threw at least one bomb to finish the job . . . Jan will have a far better chance to escape. I pray to God Almighty no one happens to see me on this knoll."

"It *is* a very good plan," Bartlett assured him. "When the two of you are safe, you can generate a leak that hints broadly at another assassin after all."

"Ah yes, Stephen, but only after the Nazis have gone on record that there was just one man involved. I think we can embarrass them before the world, shortly after we remove Heydrich!"

Gabcik glanced again at his watch: 9:30 A.M.

"Almost time," he said.

They were taking a chance by being there when Heydrich was driven by. But Gabcik felt the need to see the Butcher of Prague actually make the turn.

"I want everything to be the same," he said, "except for the outcome . . . I want to come up to the moment *now* and take it in my hand and *know* this is it! I must do this, Stephen, to prove to myself that this creature could have been destroyed that very moment if our weapons were in hand, that the only thing now separating us from the goal we seek is time. If I can do this, then I know we will gain the victory."

As they waited another two or three minutes, Bartlett thought of his part in the forthcoming drama. First, he would double-check the bombs, making sure the problems he had detected earlier with the cluster bombs would not flare up again with the fusion replacements.

Then, on the morning of the assassination attempt, after Heydrich had left home, Bartlett would drive up to Panenske Brezany, his estate, and gain entrance by posing as a Gestapo agent. He would use his best accent as he spoke and tell anyone inside that there had just been an alert about possible listening devices on the property. Katrina had already given him the necessary forged papers and procured a dark suit and a long, black trench coat, the usual garb of the Gestapo, together with a wide-brimmed hat. She was working on getting the right sort of car to use.

Security was extremely tight around Panenske Brezany, but curiously lax inside, possibly an outgrowth of the Gestapo and SS's collective mentality that they were infallible in such matters and no one on the face of the planet would be smart enough or strong enough to get inside in the first place.

But shortly after the bomb or bombs went off, there would be chaos outside the estate, as well as inside, particularly as far as several-months-pregnant Lina Heydrich and their two sons and daughter were concerned.

Bartlett knew he would have free rein for awhile. He hoped to have long enough to take photographs of whatever top-secret documents were at the estate, documents that could prove to be of incalculable value to the Allies and the partisans.

"He's coming!" Gabcik whispered.

Bartlett jerked his head in the direction the other man was nodding. A convertible Mercedes touring car was coming up the road to their right, about a quarter of a mile from the curve directly in front of them.

"Time how long it takes him to make the curve," Gabcik remarked.

Bartlett's gaze shifted down to his watch as inconspicuously as possible.

For a brief, strange moment, Heydrich saw the two of them. Both were compelled to smile pleasantly at him and tip their caps. Surprisingly, Heydrich returned the gesture; then the Mercedes was gone up the road.

Those eyes, those dark, soul-less eyes . . .

Both men thought they caught a glimpse of the evil quality often reported in those eyes, unsettling even to other dedicated Aryans like Heydrich. It was a cold, sinister glint that came across despite Heydrich's surface civility. Granted, anything like that might have been due to the power of suggestion, a moment of anticipation realized in their minds if not in fact. But later, when they discussed it, still trembling a bit as they recalled the moment, Bartlett and Gabcik continued to think, somehow, that what they had seen had been real, not just freakish imagination. And it could scarcely have been worse, this moment of contact, even from such a distance. Indeed, it could not have been worse if Satan himself had turned in their direction with an unspeakable list of mindless infamies revealed on his malevolent face.

"May God help us," Gabcik muttered, rubbing his left arm to rid it of the chill that had settled there momentarily as Bartlett and he turned from the knoll and walked down a slight incline to their bicycles.

In just over two hours, they had returned to the home of Katrina Hrdlicka, whose good food and knowing manner took their minds away, for a time, from the perverse and baleful feelings the Butcher of Prague had stirred within them.

The face had been partially covered by a wide-brimmed hat. Why did it seem familiar, despite so little of it being visible?

Reinhard Heydrich, dressed in his underwear, stood at the window in his bedroom, the boxer shorts a little tighter than he preferred over his large, feminine hips. A light mist hung over the grounds of the estate as he thought about the men who had drawn his attention during his ride yesterday morning.

"There is no heaven or hell, Lina," he said with some weariness. "I think we just go away, like that mist does when the sun hits it or a stiff wind carries it away."

He turned toward her, smiling, as she donned a pink cashmere robe, blushing a bit while she drew it over her bloated midriff. He held his left hand out in front of him, the fingers doubled over into a fist.

"We are here for awhile, and then we are not," he added, opening his hand wide. "Nothing is left. We cease, Lina, we cease altogether."

"But we leave behind those we love dearly," she reminded him. "We have that as a precious legacy. Look at the blond-haired, blue-eyed children you and I are sending out into the world, beautiful children, pure and strong."

He savored those words.

"I fear I do not do enough," he said.

Lina Heydrich walked up to her husband and kissed him on the cheek.

"You give everything you have," she told him. "Our children obey us. Someday, when they leave home, they will carry the ideas you and I have woven into the very fabric of their souls."

He winced a bit at that word.

"I meant it only figuratively," she was quick to add.

They could not allow themselves to take the primitive notion of a soul seriously. Both had learned to cling only to the reality of the present and whatever they could make of the future. Souls were nothing more than the fantasies of people too fragile to accept life as it was.

"The Jews seem to cling to the idea for one reason: If there are souls, then there is punishment for those who afflict them," he muttered. "They want *me* to have a soul for that very reason."

"If we are wrong, my darling," Lina remarked, "then it is the Jews who will be sorry when they find themselves in hell, and you and I walking the streets of heaven!"

They both laughed at the irony of that.

"An angel for you," he said, "an angel for me, and one for each of our children—and all Jews roasting in hell where they belong . . . the thing they pray for becoming the source of their torment forever. I like it, Lina, I like it very much."

"We must never talk like this in front of Hennie," she said, bringing her hand to her mouth to hide her smile. "Oh, really, I shouldn't refer to your mentor in that fashion, should I?"

"Hennie it is, Lina, but only between you and me. This man deserves no better. Some of the tattered remnants of his banal Catholicism still cling to him. He should be embarrassed ever to admit it. But he does, you know. There are moments when he signs a plea of clemency for some Jew or Gypsy."

"Himmler does *that?*" she remarked, quite surprised.

"I fail to understand his motivation. Very rarely is it a political figure or anyone with any influence at all. At least *that* could be rationalized; I mean, a 'friend' in the enemy camp, that sort of thing."

"He pardons ordinary Jews, you mean?"

He nodded puzzledly.

"The next moment, he will order the arrest of a hundred others. I find no consistency."

"Yes, darling, tell me what you think?" Lina asked teasingly as she ran a finger over his lips.

"I think he is a tormented man and therefore a weak man."

"And *you* are so strong."

"Do you not think so?"

"I said so."

"But are you merely humoring me?"

"I have *never* done that, my beloved."

He smiled.

"Let us go to breakfast now," he said. "The children are waiting."

"Your son has a present for you," she told him.

Heydrich was surprised.

"What is it?" he asked.

"He will give it to you after we eat."

"Tell me now, please."

"Can't you wait? You are like a child yourself."

"Now, Lina, tell me now."

In that large bedroom, furnished in the antiques they both adored, she saw the cold part of him, the demanding part. Even there he would have his way, he would make his demands. And he would expect obedience; oh, yes, he would expect that.

"Another of those lamp shades," she said, disguising her true feelings about the shades, as she had had to do so much during moments like this, as well as during those whispers about Heydrich's affairs.

"How thoughtful of him," he beamed.

"This one is quite special, I must admit."

"How so, Lina?"

"I think it must be quite fresh. There is a softness about it, like silk; it's not as brittle as the others. Oh yes, it has a nice little fringe around the top and the bottom. Very cute. Handwoven by some Jew seamstress at Flossenburg, I understand."

"I shall love it!" he declared.

"As your son loves you."

"Only my son?"

"As I love you . . . as I truly, truly do."

"We take our time today, Lina. I have earned that privilege for us and more. The plane simply will have to leave late. And that will be that!"

Katrina Hrdlicka awoke the men at dawn, but not before she spent the hour or so prior to that standing out in the middle of the field in back of her house. She stood silently or walked with slow, tired steps while occasionally looking up at the clear sky, stars gradually disappearing from sight as morning light began.

"Oh, Lord . . ." she prayed, her head bowed, her hands clasped tightly together. "This is a terrible day, this day You are giving us. There will be death, but a worthy death, a death You have ordained, the death of one of Satan's emissaries. If You will help, Lord, Heydrich *will* surely die in a few hours, Lord, and this world will have less evil as a result, for evil he is, spawned from the pit of hell."

She whispered "Amen," then turned toward the house, wondering why she suddenly felt so sad.

Katrina looked up at the heavens briefly, and asked, "Are You telling me something, Lord?"

In the distance she thought she heard the sound of gunfire.

"When will this land of my birth be at peace?" she spoke. "If it's not the Nazis, then it's a civil war between our peoples. When will it end, oh God? When will it end?"

She opened the creaking back door and walked inside the old house, its antiquity arising as odors from the past to confront her nostrils for the ten-thousandth time. She looked at the kitchen, a large place where meals had been cooked for kings and Gypsies and doctors and clergymen over the years.

"Katrina?"

The voice was Jan Kubis's. He had gotten up early, as she had, also unable to sleep well. He was standing in the kitchen, sipping a cup of tea.

"Where did you go yesterday?" she asked.

"I felt bad about not joining them," he replied. "So I went on into the city, perhaps an hour or so after Josef and the American left."

His hand was shaking.

"You're still scared, aren't you?" Katrina asked without scorn.

He nodded, knowing he could never deceive this woman.

"It's more than what you said yesterday, isn't it?" she continued. "Not seeing the monster face-to-face was only part of it."

He wanted to avoid answering but she wouldn't let him. He was essentially quite brave, but there was something so unsettling about Heydrich that the thought of confronting him soon and ripping his life from him was having an impact Jan Kubis could not have foreseen, Katrina reasoned as she thought back over the past twenty-four hours . . .

Josef Gabcik and Stephen Bartlett had looked so pale after returning from Prague, and they had spoken little at first. They had seen Heydrich, yes, but they said nothing more. Only after being warmed and nourished by Katrina's cooking did they relax a bit and tell her what it was like to come so close to the man, if *man* was what Reinhard Heydrich could be called in the final analysis.

They had looked up as Kubis walked into the room.

"Forgive me," he had said somewhat sheepishly. "I surveyed the site after you two did. I just couldn't face *seeing* Heydrich until it was time. I was an hour behind you. Not many people venture out at that time, I see. I think we can do what we have set out to do but we still need the providence of God Almighty on our side."

Then he had excused himself, gone upstairs, and slipped into bed without showering.

The next morning, as the depth of his fear came to the surface, Katrina knew she was facing someone who believed his manhood was on the line.

"Josef and the American are scared, too, you know," she told him. "They confessed some things to me after you went to sleep."

Kubis looked at her, wanting to believe what she was saying.

"But they *went*," he emphasized. "They faced up to their fears. Not me, Katrina, not me! I *retreated* from mine."

"So that makes you a coward and the two of them heroes?" she demanded. "Is that what you're saying?"

He turned away but she would not tolerate that. She reached out and swung him around to face her again.

"I have a friend confined at Birkenau," Katrina went on. "She fears each day. She fears being herded into one of the gas chambers along with hundreds of others. She has nightmares about stretching out on an operating table and having wicked men slobbering over her naked body before she is cut open in the name of their demonic 'medical' research. But, that fear hasn't stopped her. Still she has become a wonderful witness for Christ."

She grabbed his shoulders with surprising gentleness.

"My dear Jan, it was Saint Peter who had so much fear in his soul it drove him to deny his Lord three times. Yet even that was forgiven. Are you afraid it won't be the same for you?"

"It's the others!" he said, tears flowing. "I think Josef and Stephen have lost all respect for me."

"No, no," she said with some urgency. "Do you have any idea what they told me before we all tried to get some sleep last night?"

"I don't . . . please . . . tell me," he replied uncertainly.

"That they both love you very much. They, too, are so afraid they can hardly breathe at times. The only difference between you and the two of them is that they have been better at concealing it."

Kubis saw that Katrina was being truthful, saw the love in her eyes, and reached out to hug her but found his arms too short to wrap around her bulk. So he kissed her full on the mouth instead.

"Dear friend," he said, "dear friend. How deeply I feel for you!"

"And I know, as every partisan does, how deeply you feel for this country of ours, Jan, indeed for this precious land of our birth. That is why you are risking your life this day."

"It cannot be allowed to stay shrouded in darkness much longer."

Minutes later, Gabcik and Bartlett joined them. After a brief prayer, the three men took turns kissing her. Then they left in two cars, Gabcik and Kubis in one, the American in the second.

"Good-bye!" she yelled. "May the angels protect you!"

After they were gone, she retreated into the ancient house, its odors familiar, its history wrapping around her. It had been given to her by her parents and to them by their parents, generation after generation having lived in it since the first heavy wooden beam had been put in place centuries before.

So familiar, Katrina thought before a dizzy spell hit her.

For a moment, she had to lean against the wall to steady herself, chills gripping every inch of her body, the living room spinning in her vision.

"Precious Jesus," she whispered, holding one hand out before her as though reaching for someone to support her. "Oh, precious, precious Savior . . ."

In the deceptive quiet of that historic day's morning, Katrina Hrdlicka sensed—a flash of intuition or providence or whatever else was assailing her—that she would not see the three men together again.

12

After catching a tram to a nearby community, Josef Gabcik and Jan Kubis had to come the rest of the way on bicycles. Cars were in short supply and two ordinary citizens with a car and no apparent purpose for having it as they lounged at the site, would have invited official scrutiny. So they had to travel to Prague by tram, preferably one that was not packed with other passengers since they had to carry their bicycles on board. Their briefcases, one containing the bombs and the other carrying a disassembled Sten submachine gun, were strapped to the handlebars.

The two of them arrived just before 9:00 A.M. and waited as inconspicuously as possible for a few minutes before taking up their positions, Gabcik on the knoll across the wide street from Kubis, who waited inside of the U-shaped curve.

Two trams filled with passengers passed by.

Some may have to die, Kubis thought with great regret. *The tracks are in the middle of the street, Josef is across from me and Heydrich's car will be on my side. If my comrade cannot aim properly because of the tram, I shall have to act immediately, and there is every chance that I could, in my haste, miss the car and throw the bombs closer to all those helpless people, injuring or killing many of them.*

The hairpin curve bordered a dense, forestlike section of evergreen trees, a small area resembling a community park gone wild, the trees providing shadows in which Kubis could hide until the Mercedes was sighted.

He looked across the wide street and saw Gabcik bending down so that his coat covered the briefcase as he assembled the gun piece by piece. How many hours had he practiced this, putting a gun together without looking at what he was doing?

We used grass to cushion the gun and my bombs in the briefcases, Kubis reminded himself worriedly. *I hope none of it gets into the firing mechanism . . .*

Half an hour passed.

Heydrich *always* passed that curve at 9:30, give or take five minutes. Precision was at the center of his life, unlike Hitler who was always late for appointments and who knew little about a methodical approach to anything. That was a significant reason why Heydrich was so feared; his need for perfection carried over to everything he did, especially the killing of Jews, Gypsies, and anyone who opposed the Third Reich.

Fifteen more minutes went by yet Heydrich still had not arrived.

Kubis flashed a glance at Gabcik. Even across that distance, he could see—or did he merely sense?—the other man's expression, worried and fearful. If Heydrich had changed his plans and gone another route, the entire mission might be doomed since it was impossible to conjecture when there might be another opportunity as good as the present one.

Directly ahead of Kubis, with the knoll to his right and the trees in back of him, was a two-story cottage similar to others in that suburb of Prague. He saw a little blonde-haired girl in the second-floor window there. She was waving at him. He was tempted to return her gesture, but did not want to do anything to focus more attention on himself. Yet what if she turned away, and went to her mother or father and told them about the strange man in the raincoat who was hugging his briefcase so closely to his body?

Gabcik, in the meantime, now had the Sten gun fully assembled and so was in an even more awkward position than Kubis.

Jan's bombs are smaller, less cumbersome, Gabcik thought. *He could easily hide them in his pockets if necessary. But this gun is much too large. It's been put together now and here I am in the open, waiting . . .*

Ten o'clock passed. Then 10:15.

After fifteen more minutes, Gabcik was about to take the risk of waving a negative signal at Kubis, a signal that would spell the end of their work for that day.

At 10:32 a black Mercedes convertible appeared at the far end of the curve on Kubis's side of the street and to his left.

Heydrich! He hadn't canceled anything. He was merely tardy.

Gabcik's entire body was trembling, and he was sweating liberally under the heavy insulation of the raincoat.

A tram creaked along the rails down the middle of the street, not far behind the Mercedes. If the car and the tram ran parallel as Heydrich reached the center of the curve, Gabcik would have no clear shot, and the success of the mission would depend on Kubis's bombs.

The tram split in two like a toy train, people being thrown from it, hitting the hard street and dying on impact! Little children perhaps, life twisted from them!

Gabcik shook off this mental image and hoped it would never be more than that as he pulled out the Sten gun from under his raincoat and aimed it directly at the temple of the Butcher of Prague. He pulled the trigger.

Nothing. A misfire! Grass or dirt must have gotten into the gun.

In seconds the tram would come up beside the car and block Gabcik's view.

Not so.

The conductor apparently had seen the gun and Heydrich in the open car. Instantly he guessed what was going on; he slammed on the brakes of the tram, bringing it to a sudden halt that spilled virtually every passenger onto the floor, many on top of one another.

Gabcik could do little but stand helplessly watching as the Mercedes completed the curve.

Heydrich should have told his driver, *Oberscharführer* Klein, to speed up and pull away from that spot as quickly as possible. A moving target would be impossible to hit, given the circumstances.

But Heydrich did the opposite, ordering Klein to stop the car. His ego would not tolerate this attempt on his life. He jumped from the backseat and ran toward the fool who had thought *his* life would be so easily perishable!

A lone assassin.

Neither Heydrich or Klein had been able to glimpse Kubis, who remained hidden in the shadows of the tall, plentiful trees the corner half-circled.

Kubis threw a bomb at the Mercedes just as it came to a halt directly in front of him. Aimed at the interior of the car just as the two men were preparing to exit, it instead stopped short by three inches and bounced against the rear fender as it exploded.

Pieces of metal were ripped from the car and thrown in a dozen directions; the force of the explosion shattered the windshield of the Mercedes as well as the windows in the halted tram. Like Heydrich, the conductor had miscalculated; it would have been better if he had continued on past too. As it was, his passengers and he were trapped in the very center of the action.

Some of the shrapnel had broadsided Kubis's face, which was bleeding quite badly into his eyes, his nose, and his mouth. He could scarcely see the driver, Klein, coming after him while Heydrich, shouting obscenities, lurched after Gabcik.

When Kubis's vision cleared for an instant, he saw Klein aiming a pistol at him. The second bomb was now useless under the circumstances; a crowd had been gathered, and killing the driver while endangering the onlookers was not an acceptable combination for Kubis.

He managed to clamber onto his bicycle and push through the crowd.

"Stop that man!" Klein yelled futilely. "He's a traitor. Don't let him get away from here!"

No one heeded his demand.

Klein stood in front of the crowd of men and women and shouted demeaningly at them, but they ignored him, preferring to concentrate on what was happening on the grassy knoll across the street.

Deranged by mindless, livid anger, Klein slammed an elderly man across the cheek with the butt of his pistol. Already weak due to his age, the old one crumpled to the ground and started groaning.

Someone from the crowd grabbed Klein's wrist and snapped it back as he wrenched the weapon away. Klein could feel some bones breaking and screeched in sudden pain.

"I *will* remember what you look like!" he bellowed. "I will remember each and every one of you, and nobody will escape punishment, *nobody!*"

Reinhard Heydrich had been wounded by the blast and it was only adrenaline and his admittedly stoic resolve that allowed him to jump out of the Mercedes and pursue Josef Gabcik across the knoll.

Heydrich was walking like a man who had just consumed some drug that affected his sense of balance; his expression was one of maniacal determination. Gabcik froze for a moment, his Sten gun useless, as the tall, strong-looking Nazi came toward him. But Gabcik also had a standard pistol and whipped it out of his pocket as Heydrich reached the tram and used it for cover, then started firing at him. Gabcik ducked behind a tree on the knoll and returned the shots; at least two of his bullets entered the tram, accompanied by the screams of passengers and one loud, pain-filled cry.

Gabcik *had* to get to his bicycle at the bottom of the knoll. But he was pinned down by Heydrich and could see Klein running over to him.

Suddenly Heydrich fell away from the tram and staggered, for the briefest moment, into view. Gabcik aimed his pistol at the man's chest and pulled the trigger twice, emptying the weapon of all but its last two bullets. One of the shots missed Heydrich but the other catching him in the shoulder, and flinging him to the ground.

Klein reached his commander's side, and Heydrich, his voice harsh, painfully ordered Klein to "get the S.O.B. . . . He must not escape . . . Do it *now!*"

As Klein ran toward the knoll, Heydrich leaned against the Mercedes and managed to pull himself up to a tenuous standing position. He looked around at the bystanders, none of whom offered to help.

"I give you a better nation," he said, trying to control his voice, "and you give me nothing in return."

He fell again against the running-board of the Mercedes, a nauseous whirlpool beginning in his stomach. An instant before he passed out, he uttered a single name three times, "Lina . . . Lina . . . Lina . . ."

Klein had kicked the bicycle to one side at the bottom of the knoll, so Gabcik was forced to run uphill instead of down. Behind the knoll was an alleyway, and he hurried through it and out onto a side street.

Directly ahead was a butcher shop. Gabcik remembered meeting the owner some time earlier. What he did not know was that the short-but-broad, middle-aged man, Ernst Brauer, was a closet Nazi upon whom Heydrich and others had been depending for "secrets" about the resistance movement in that country; in addition, his brother was employed by the Gestapo.

Gabcik could hear Klein shouting, "Hold him! Kill him!" Brauer lurched at Gabcik and swung a large meat ax at the younger man's head. It came so close that its sharp edge grazed Gabcik's right ear. The action threw Brauer temporarily off balance and Gabcik kicked him against a freezer at the opposite end of the little shop, Brauer's head hitting the sharp end of a metal shelf just above the freezer.

Gabcik turned to run, thinking the shop had a rear exit, and collided with Klein, who burst inside, waving a pistol that jammed just as Kubis's Sten gun had done. Gabcik shot Klein through one leg and he collapsed onto the sawdust-strewn floor.

Another crowd had gathered, and as Gabcik ran from the shop, he waved his gun and purposefully shouted like someone deranged. This had the effect he intended. The people scattered in every direction, fearing for their own lives.

Gabcik fled down a side street to a safehouse two blocks east. For the moment, he could stop running, and he prayed that Kubis had likewise found shelter.

The two-story, castlelike house, complete with pseudo guard towers, was set back from the road quite a distance and surrounded by a spiked iron fence. Two SS troopers demanded Stephen Bartlett's papers when he arrived. They looked at them and at him in a cursory manner, then waved him past.

The Butcher of Prague is more careless than they say, he thought as he approached the building.

For an instant, a young child could be seen looking out at him from a second-floor window.

Lina Heydrich greeted him at the door.

He identified himself as a member of the Gestapo, then stood back for a moment, looking at her appreciatively.

"May I ask if you are part-Swedish?" he inquired as she invited him inside. He was impressed by her fresh, blonde-haired beauty.

"Quite so, Mr. . . ." she replied, fumbling with his name that she had already forgotten.

"Brimmer, Frau Heydrich, Hans Brimmer. I suspect my diction is not what it used to be," he said pleasantly, taking away her momentary embarrassment. "Interrogating too many Jews perhaps."

She found that amusing, as he had intended. "You are very . . . large," she said.

"But your husband is tall, is he not?"

"To a midget, yes!" she said, trying some humor of her own.

Bartlett chuckled politely.

"I meant," she continued, "that you are broad, muscular. So many of the Gestapo look like little weasels."

"There are many who would agree with you."

She looked at him intently for a moment. "You seem so . . . so . . ." she said, fumbling her thought.

"Young?"

"Yes, yes, that's it! I wondered if you are so young as you appear," she said.

"I am not."

"What is your age?"

"Must I?"

"If I tell mine, will you tell yours?"

"Surely, Frau Heydrich."

"Well, I'm not going to do so!" She smiled broadly.

Bartlett found her personality to be the opposite of his perceptions. He never expected someone with such a light-hearted, rather flirtatious manner.

"Have you been driving long?" she asked.

"Yes, I am afraid that is the case."

"May I get you some tea?"

"I have something to tell you, Frau Heydrich."

"Has . . . has something happened to my husband?" she blurted out, then realized that he would not have been so conversational if that were the reason for his visit. She added, "Sorry to be so apprehensive. You see, Reinhard and I are still very much in love even after all these years."

She spoke as someone who understood the need to keep up appearances, at least to a degree, and her remark fit squarely into that category.

"I would like to check over this beautiful house for—" he started to say.

"A bomb?" she asked. "Do you think—?"

"Not that," he assured her.

She was greatly relieved.

"Termites perhaps?" she said mischievously.

"We would have sent a guard from Auschwitz for that purpose," he said, finding it difficult to be facetious.

She threw her head back and roared with laughter.

"Listening devices," he added. "Sometimes they can be quite small, and hard to uncover."

"Go anywhere you like," she assured him. "Our house is yours. Perhaps you will find one in the bedroom. Bedrooms are logical places, I understand."

"Indeed they are," he agreed.

She paused just long enough to send him a message with her eyes and her body language that was unmistakable, then she walked off. Bartlett hesitated, grateful for how easily everything had gone thus far. He pretended to be looking downstairs first, behind furniture and picture frames and in the foliage of potted plants. Then he walked up the curved stairway to the second floor.

The Heydrichs' bedroom was nearly as large as the small house where he had met Otto Brunner earlier.

"There's a fortune in antiques," Bartlett muttered.

That was when he saw the first of the lamp shades. They seemed made of thin, nearly transparent swatches of parchment. He started to sweat as he remembered what the material was. It was resting on a leather-topped desk at the opposite end of the room from the high-postered, canopy bed. Another was on a nighttable next to the bed.

Oh God, keep me from doing something I'll regret, he prayed silently.

He went through dresser drawers and a large walk-in closet and found nothing more than odds and ends of letters written from one Heydrich to the other. After leaving the bedroom, he approached the room next to it, opened the door, and found their young son sleeping.

The next bedroom was empty. The final room upstairs served as Reinhard Heydrich's den. It was kept so neatly it seemed never to have been used at all. Three walls were covered from floor to ceiling with bookcases. Just behind Heydrich's cherry-wood desk was a very large window.

Bartlett sat down at that desk. On top of it was a Luger, loaded and ready to fire.

Heydrich doesn't seem concerned that one of his own children might get this, Bartlett thought. *I suppose he's ordered them to stay out of here—and expects perfect compliance, as always.*

At first glance the heavily constructed desk seemed to hold nothing other than routine communiques, photos of Hitler, Göring, and others, including a few shots of starving Jews from various concentration camps and scores of bodies in a ditch, plus some cablegrams of little importance.

He was about to leave and look elsewhere when he saw that the top of the desk was quite thick, but had no center drawer. Knocking it briefly with his knuckles, he found what he had guessed: It was hollow.

If it opened only with a key, he was out of luck.

Which was the case.

He dropped to his knees and glanced up at the underside of the thick portion of the desk, spotting a keyhole. Exasperated, he found a lever to the left of it, and as he wistfully tried to slide it to one side, expecting nothing to happen, the top started to lift upward.

Heydrich must have forgotten to lock it. Even the brilliant damned make stupid mistakes.

He slammed the desktop shut and removed a lamp with one of the parchment-like shades, a battered old phone, and a photograph of the entire Heydrich family, along with a large notepad and a pen-and-pencil set with a black onyx base.

Then, under the desk again, he slid the lever to one side and the desktop opened to reveal exactly what Bartlett had been seeking.

Maps rolled tightly together . . . envelopes marked TOP SECRET . . . diagrams . . . folders.

Bartlett stood back away from the desk for a moment, stunned at his discovery, which could prove to be far more valuable for the Allies than anyone had dared to hope.

His hands shaking with excitement rather than nervousness, he took out his Minox spy camera and started snapping shots of the more crucial items, stowing the used film canisters in a special hem at the bottom of his trench coat.

Then he examined as much of the material as possible, in case the film were lost.

Just then he heard a voice . . . Heydrich's young daughter was standing in the doorway, watching him.

"Who are you?" she asked. "Why are you here?"

"I'm trying to help your daddy keep some secrets," he told her.

"You *shouldn't* be going through his desk like that," she said sternly. "No one's allowed in here but Daddy."

"Darling, I—"

She ran screaming into the hallway. He managed to catch her before anyone could hear her and clamped his hand over her mouth, making the mistake of using his still-mending one. She bit it as hard as she could, forcing him to do something he thought he would never be driven to commit against a child. As he yelped in pain, he knocked her unconscious, careful not to apply too much force, but hating the fact that he had to use any force against one so helpless.

Then Bartlett hurried back into the den, resting the limp little body on a surprisingly threadbare sofa opposite the desk. He took her pulse to make sure it was normal, then returned to the pile of documents and examined the final few pages.

There could be no doubt that the find was a striking one; it showed even more of Heydrich's arrogance. No truly sensible military officer would have kept so many documents of such caliber together in one spot. With Heydrich, though, prudence invariably gave way to his godlike view of himself and the protective powers he had over his family and his possessions, military or otherwise. He lived under the assumption that no one would *dare* get as close to him as his private den, for they knew what would happen when—not *if*—they were caught.

Plans for future maneuvers were included. Since only Heydrich knew where these were kept, it might be weeks or months before their loss was discovered, enough time for some of the battlefield tactics to have been executed. With the Allies knowing in advance what the Nazis were planning, countermeasures could be taken to neutralize any tactical effectiveness.

After closing the top, he placed everything back where he had found it, and proceeded to walk out of the room, ignoring the child.

He shouldn't have.

She regained consciousness just as he was leaving and sprang off the sofa, grabbing his leg and biting it.

"You must be a dirty Jew," she shrieked. "My daddy *hates* you!"

Bartlett tried to shake her loose but she was clinging tightly. He bent down and grabbed her, wrenching her loose, but as he did so, he could hear some of her bones snap and she cried in pain, tears instantly welling up in her eyes and trickling down her cheeks. She stumbled away from him and fell back hard against the edge of a long, low table next to the sofa, her body going limp as it hit the tongue-and-groove wood floor.

The noise upstairs had finally attracted attention. Lina Heydrich came running up the stairs, her eyes widening as she stood in the doorway and saw him bending over her daughter.

"Herr Brimmer, what has happened here?" she demanded, shedding her previous manner.

"Your daughter—" he started to say, thinking the child remained unconscious.

Wrong.

Groaning with pain, the girl opened her eyes, saw her mother, and started screaming, her voice trembling as she spoke, "Mother, Mother, watch out! He's with those dirty Jews. He—"

Lina Heydrich's mouth dropped open and she started backing away, out into the hall.

Bartlett drew his pistol and told her to stop.

But she didn't listen; instead she turned and ran toward the steps. He caught up with her at the third step, grabbed her by the hair, and dragged her back to the hall and toward the den.

"My baby!" she cried. "My baby!"

Instinctively he reacted by releasing his hold. She used the opportunity to jam a fist into his crotch. As he dropped the pistol and doubled over she started toward the stairs again but noticed the dropped weapon and dashed for it, then slipped and fell on her stomach.

"Oh, my G—" she started to say, reacting to what was going on in her body.

The pistol was just inches from her hand. She pulled herself to it, closing her fingers around the handle, and started to lift it.

Bartlett, bolts of pain lancing through him, stumbled toward Lina Heydrich and grabbed her hand. Considering her own plight, the strength she showed proved to be astonishing. She was growling as she fought him like a wounded beast that had somehow regained strength, an older version of the daughter who also had attacked him.

But he got the gun away from her. While still training it on her, he sat on the hallway floor for a minute or so, trying to catch his breath, and ignore the lingering pain in his hand.

"Why do you . . . work for . . . the . . . Jews?" she gasped, now on her side, looking at him.

"Because people like your husband are slaughtering them," Bartlett spat out the words.

"They are animals, and animals end up where they should—in slaughterhouses."

"They are *not* animals. They are as human as you, as your husband."

She eyed him curiously, as though about to say something, but passed out, spittle dribbling from the corners of her mouth.

Bartlett straightened uncertainly. In the background, he heard loud voices, the screeching of tires. He glanced at his watch: 10:45 A.M.

They've done it, he thought. *Praise God above, they've done it!*

Yet there was another possibility. The confusion upstairs could have been heard outside or by someone else in the house. He grabbed the pistol again and put it in the right pocket of his coat, keeping his hand on it just in case.

After dragging Lina Heydrich's body into the den, Bartlett started to shut the door but stopped, momentarily, as he heard the little girl moaning.

How can I leave her there? How can I?

But he had no choice. He had to get out of the house and as far away from it as possible. He was tempted to rationalize that, after all, she would simply grow up to be another Nazi. Though he resisted that very cynical thought, he still reached his hand around the side of the door, turned the lock counterclockwise, and closed the door, securing both mother and daughter inside. If neither of them were conscious by the time their absence was noticed, someone would have to break down the door to get to them—all of which bought him some precious time.

Bartlett walked cautiously toward the steps. He could hear someone on the first floor shouting upstairs, "Frau Heydrich, are you—?"

Bartlett showed himself then.

"She is not here," he replied. "Frankly I am very concerned for her safety. There is the distinct possibility of suicide."

The man below was an SS trooper.

"There has been an attempt on the life of Herr Heydrich," the trooper, quite young, and ashen-faced from what had happened minutes before, seemed confused, not expecting someone from the Gestapo to be in the house.

"How badly has he been hurt?" Bartlett asked, exhibiting his most imperious manner as he walked down the stairs.

"I do not know sir," the nervous trooper replied. "There were some shots and—"

"Yes?"

"An explosion."

"Stay inside, at the front entrance to this house," Bartlett ordered, without opportunity for debate on the matter. "Do not let anyone in until I return. Understood?"

"Understood, sir? I will guard it with my life."

"You may have to do exactly that."

"Sir?" the trooper asked.

"If partisan or Allied intruders are the ones who staged this attempt, they may not be at all content to stop at Herr Heydrich, you know. Access to this house must be restricted. It has, shall we say, strategic importance, quite apart from safety considerations for the rest of the family. Let no one in unless you get orders from Berlin."

"I will serve the fatherland with everything I have."

"May—" Bartlett started to say, "May God bless you!" But he caught himself and said, "May the Führer himself learn of your splendid willingness to sacrifice."

The trooper clicked his heels together and saluted. Bartlett marveled at how really callow he seemed.

Yet how many innocent lives have you taken, young man? he thought sadly. *How many children have dangled on the tip of your bayonet? When will such horrors start to be etched on that youthful face of yours in deep lines and haunted eyes?*

"I am not a soldier," Bartlett commented.

"But you serve our holy cause," the young trooper said, "and I must salute you for that!"

Bartlett recoiled at the use of "holy" but thanked him anyway, and walked outside. The front door slammed shut behind him.

Praise Jesus, he whispered to himself, *praise Your blessed name!*

Bartlett hurried to his car, which was parked at the front door, and climbed inside. He forced himself to drive at an unhurried speed as he left the estate conspicuously through the front entrance so as not to generate suspicion from the guards.

Then he headed out of Prague and in the direction of Katrina Hrdlicka's home—the rendezvous point for Josef Gabcik, Jan Kubis, and himself . . . if any of them could manage to escape the net that surely must have been falling over the assassination site and for miles in every direction.

13

After Reinhard Heydrich was taken to Bulkova Hospital and examined by a staff physician, the initial prognosis was encouraging. The *Obergruppenführer* seemed to have sustained only moderate flesh wounds. But later x-rays showed that Heydrich had actually suffered far more damage and his survival was in question. He had a broken rib, a ruptured diaphragm, and shreds of metal in his spleen. The Czech chief surgeon recommended an immediate operation, but Heydrich demanded that someone be flown in from Berlin to perform it.

"That would require too much time," pleaded the surgeon, Dr. Klaus Dick. "You could be dead by the time he gets here."

Heydrich was not one to be dissuaded by lesser men, yet he read the sense of urgency on the doctor's face. Grimacing, pain challenging his well-known iron will, he agreed to have Professor Hollbaum from the nearby German Clinic supervise the operation.

Less than three hours after the attempt on his life, Heydrich was in surgery.

The hospital was put under tight SS and Gestapo guard, machine guns mounted on the roof, and barbed wire strung around its perimeter. No Czechs were allowed anywhere near Heydrich. Armed troopers were on every floor and several stood directly outside his private room. The irony of such tight security after he was shot was not lost on those familiar with his disdain for the caution that could have avoided the incident altogether or else mitigated its seriousness.

Once again, the early prognosis after surgery was upbeat. Both Dick and Hollbaum had done so well it seemed Heydrich was out of danger. After only a few days, though, he developed peritonitis, which led to septicemia. The Nazis did not possess penicillin, and used instead a primitive form of sulfonamide, which was not strong enough to alleviate the poisons that were spreading throughout Heydrich's body. The logical next step would have been to remove his damaged spleen, but Himmler's personal physician and Surgeon-General of the SS, Professor Gebhart, who had been flown to Prague by order of Himmler himself, deemed this too dangerous in view of how weak Heydrich had become.

On June 2, Himmler, after calling hourly for news during the preceding days, finally flew to Prague and spent several hours by Heydrich's bedside.

They talked of little but death and the potential of life afterward. Himmler instigated the discussion, fascinated by what Heydrich told him. Despite ordering actions that resulted in the slaughter of millions on the battlefield, in the extermination camps, and elsewhere, Heinrich Himmler had never probed the subject of death with anyone close to him, and whatever he might have felt about the other man's ambitions, he still regarded Heydrich as an equal.

"Reinhard, I wish to heaven we could do something," Himmler told him earnestly.

"There *is* something," Heydrich said, his voice stronger than it had any reason to be.

"Whatever you say, whatever you ask, my comrade."

"Do not speak of heaven."

"It was just an expression."

"It is not for me."

"You do not believe in heaven?"

"Do *you?*"

Himmler hesitated. Even so close to death, Heydrich was capable of playing mind games.

"If you say yes," Heydrich added, "you will be showing that you are a slave to a belief system I thought you had rejected many years ago."

"And if my answer is no?"

"Then you are admitting we all end up where the Jews and Gypsies and other scum—"

Pain robbed Heydrich of his voice for a number of minutes.

"But I could never envision that, Reinhard," Himmler continued in the interim. "I could never accept that such a fate is ours. If God is real and just—"

"If God *is,* you mean," Heydrich managed to say finally.

"Oh, He is, He is. That is why I believe heaven does exist. That is why I believe hell exists. The Jews were consigned to hell the moment they betrayed their own Messiah."

"But there is no Savior, there is no heaven, there is no hell. We are gone forever, like the early-morning mists after the noon-day sun."

"Aryans are His chosen people, not the Jews."

"Elementary. We all know that."

"But if we know it, why do you dispute the facts?"

"What we *know* is only, finally, a delusion, Heinrich. I slip away into nothingness."

Indeed, Heydrich then lapsed into unconsciousness. Himmler yelled for Gebhart, who had learned to come running whenever his superior needed him.

After examining Heydrich, Dr. Gebhart looked at Himmler and said, "He may come out of this, and he may not. It is impossible to say, Herr Himmler."

Half an hour passed. Heydrich regained consciousness briefly and started to cry. This was such an extraordinary sight from someone dubbed "The Man with the Iron Heart" that Himmler turned away in embarrassment until Heydrich reached up and grabbed the sleeve of his uniform.

"Are you in pain?" Himmler asked, deeply concerned.

"I have known nothing *but* pain of one sort or another so much of my life," Heydrich replied. "And now I go on to . . . to . . ."

Himmler could see an unaccustomed expression of fear on the other man's face. He took a tissue from the table next to Heydrich's bed and wiped his cheeks dry.

"I will get Gebhart," Himmler said, alarmed. "I—"

"A doctor will not help, nor a priest. Even now, I would demand that a priest leave."

He raised himself up on his elbows, his eyes darting from side to side.

Suddenly, with abrupt clarity, he said, "There *is* more beyond the veil. I have heard just now, oh, how clearly, Heinrich, I have heard ten thousand upon ten thousand voices rising up around me, like the sirens urging Ulysses to his doom before his odyssey could be completed. They were Jews, these sirens with their hook noses and their foul, lower-class, cackling voices; how I hate the very sound! How it has filled me with revulsion from my youth to this moment. They screamed something about 'Judgment! Judgment! Judgment!' Over and over I heard that one cold and foul word, Heinrich, as they beckoned me with their fleshless hands and eyeless sockets and brainless skulls."

Himmler could not cope with what Heydrich had become. He pulled away from the man's grasp.

"I shall return in a short while," he said as warmly as he could manage.

"No, that is not so, Heinrich, not so at all. I shall never see you again in this life."

When Himmler reached the corridor outside Heydrich's room, he was determined not to seem affected by anything that had been said between himself and Heydrich. He set his jaw firmly in place, held himself straight, saluted the two troopers stationed at the door, and clicked his heels together as he marched from Bulkova Hospital into the bright sunlight of the June afternoon.

The death of Reinhard Heydrich was treated as a tragedy of historic proportions for the Third Reich. A state funeral was held for him, with Himmler and other top Nazis gathered together for the occasion. Words of praise such as "hero" and "martyr for the cause of the fatherland" spewed out of even those who had come to distrust the man.

And then Lidice was destroyed less than two weeks after the assassination.

Another Czech village, Lezaky, was included as a last-minute add-on . . .

June 9, 1942. Just before 10:00 P.M.

Rumors had been passed from house to house. People knew something was happening as the SS presence grew larger and travel became more restricted for the citizens. Fear of the intangible was a weapon the Nazis had long ago learned to use, and it was one of the most effective in their arsenal.

The women and children were separated from their husbands and fathers and sent off to destinations unknown; in fact, most went to concentration camps, with a handful of the children adopted into Nazi homes for the process of indoctrination as proud children of the Third Reich.

That was the first stage . . . families that had been together for generations were split apart forever.

The second stage involved the men.

They were rounded up in groups of ten and murdered under the scrutiny of a human monster named SS *Hauptsturmführer* Max Rostock. All were shot. A few survived, only to suffocate in a mass grave as their bodies were covered by the very earth they had claimed as their own, the land that had supported them for so very long a time.

Their homes were set ablaze and the ruins were bulldozed over a period of months until nothing remained to show that the community ever existed. Corn was planted where families once lived.

It was worse, if such could be imagined, for the people of Lezaky. Not a single adult man or woman was allowed even the living hell of one of the death camps. They were murdered on the spot—shot, stabbed, or hanged.

Only two of the children escaped the most terrible of fates; these two were turned over to Nazi families. Some of the others were raped then murdered, or inducted into one of the Third Reich's anonymous child pornography rings, anonymous because the official government stance expressed great abhorrence over any kind of pornography, calling it the evil brain child of the craven Jewish elements. But as with so much of German life, a double standard allowed high officials to indulge whatever personal predilections they wished, so long as they did it secretly. Thus, the porn rings thrived. If ever exposed, the participants would be dealt with harshly.

Lidice and Lezaky were the most notable of the specific promises of retribution that were carried out. But what happened there was duplicated in other forms all over Czechoslovakia, in random, often quite spontaneous, killings, the numbers reaching into the thousands. People even suspected of partisan sympathies were picked up willy-nilly and murdered.

But, in addition to these monstrous acts, two final tragedies enhanced all the others.

The first tragedy was not that Hitler would be succeeded by someone more dangerous, more demonic than himself. That part of Benes's planning had fallen into place, but the second half of the scheme had failed.

"If we do this," Benes had told the men in his "shadow" cabinet early on, "if we take the life of this evil creature, we send the Czech people a message, a message that tells them the Nazis are *not* invulnerable and even the mightiest of the devils can be brought down."

That was the aim, the prayer.

But the opposite happened, and this was where the first tragedy occurred.

As a result of the harsh retribution for Heydrich's murder, Czechs all over that occupied land were driven to terrified subservience, not knowing when another town would be destroyed. It was not the death of Heydrich that determined these actions but the slaughter at Lidice and Lezaky.

Thus, the rallying point Benes had planned became instead the bludgeon that shattered much of the effectiveness of the resistance movements in Czechoslovakia, Germany, and elsewhere. After Heydrich's assassination they could exist only as covert, very loosely structured organizations with great dependence upon the support of the people they were trying to liberate. That support withered to a mockery of what it once was as a direct aftermath of the death of the Butcher of Prague.

That was one of the two final tragedies.

The other was the fate of Josef Gabcik and Jan Kubis . . .

As safehouses became unavailable due to the campaign of terror instituted by the Nazis, the two partisans ended up in the crypt of the famed old Karel Boromejsky Church in Prague. They hid in a section with a secret entrance. It was thought that no one could possibly learn their whereabouts; church officials were pledged to silence at the risk of their lives.

Gabcik and Kubis were given as much food as possible, so they did not have to deal with hunger. But their surroundings proved depressing, and the atmosphere and the odor of centuries of the dead ate away at their spirits. Like Reinhard Heydrich during the final day of his life, they came to discuss what it would be like at the time of their deaths, and it was altogether a different moment from what Himmler and Heydrich shared. For Gabcik and Kubis, there was a sense of expectancy, not fear.

"I have been ready for a long time now," Gabcik remarked, shivering in the dampness of that place.

"I, too," Kubis agreed. "For me, I think, well, it began the moment the Germans invaded."

Gabcik turned to his friend as they sat on a marble bench.

"That was *exactly* the way it was with me, Jan," he said. "How fascinating!"

"I knew my destiny was to help in some way," Kubis continued. "I knew the Lord God would not have me sit by and do little or nothing."

He looked up at the ceiling of the crypt.

"We are in the very center of Prague," he commented. "If the Nazis find out about us being here, their actions will be observed by a large percentage of the population. That may put some constraints on them."

"I don't think so, Jan," Gabcik disagreed. "At this point, it is more important to them that we do not live much longer. Whatever accomplishes that goal transcends all other considerations, I'm afraid. Every day we remain alive sends a message of the Nazis' vulnerability to our countrymen. Karl Hermann Frank, Kurt Daluege, and their gang cannot allow that to spread. While we remain alive they seem ineffectual in the eyes of the very people they seek to subjugate. If they cannot bring to 'justice' a mere two men, then many more men—and women—are encouraged to acts of defiance."

"Well spoken!" Kubis said, clapping his hands. "You have a gift of words. I pray that at least *you* escape because you are so well equipped to tell the world the story of what has happened to this land of ours."

"I appreciate your kind words, Jan, and . . . well, while you've been sleeping, I went so far as to scribble down some thoughts. Would you like to read them?"

Kubis nodded eagerly and took the crumpled sheets of paper the other man handed him. Occasionally, because Gabcik had hand-written everything, Kubis had to ask him what a certain word was, but overall he could get through the scrawled material quite well.

When Kubis was finished, he could not speak for a while. He had read of his friend's devotion to a country whose origins dated back many centuries. But there was more—he had been exposed vividly to Josef Gabcik's pervasive religious faith. And he also learned how much the bond between them meant to Gabcik.

"We shall be walking the golden streets together, shall we not?" Kubis said, still enveloped by the truths the other man had put on paper.

"Oh yes, I believe that. It may be tomorrow or it may be fifty years from now, but it *will* happen."

"Whatever the promise of redemption does bring us in time, I hope in *this* life we . . ." Kubis's words suddenly caught in his throat for a few seconds before he could continue. "I hope we live to see Czechoslovakia free."

Neither of them talked for a long time after that.

Until the sound of an explosion rocked the hard ground beneath them.

The Gestapo had found the partisans' location after interrogating one of their comrades. The man, Ata Moravec, had been captured and taken to Pecek Palace, where he was subjected to various forms of "persuasion." He resisted valiantly, refusing to betray Josef Gabcik and Jan Kubis . . . until they filled him with liquor and while he was in a drunken stupor, showed him the severed head of his mother that had been dropped in a tank of carnivorous fish.

Moravec snapped then, unable to deal with the shock, and blurted out where Gabcik and Kubis could be found. Gestapo agents and SS troopers were immediately dispatched to the church and surrounded it.

Prevented from joining the two partisans in the crypt, other resistance members had taken up positions inside the church and on its roof, determined to take a stand for their country and for the men below who had rid Czechoslovakia of its worst human monster.

"We will die for those two if we have to!" one exclaimed. "But they can never know what we are doing before it is too late because they would never allow me this sacrifice if they could prevent it."

And sacrifice—total, bloody sacrifice—was what their stand against the Waffen SS proved to be. Not a single one survived the Nazi attack.

The troopers used grenades effectively and their massive numbers doomed the defenders, yet still, it took two hours for a vastly superior force to overwhelm and destroy a pathetically inferior one. The last moments took place on the roof, where hand-to-hand combat was especially ferocious.

Among the bodies found later was that of Jan Kubis. Both he and Gabcik had decided to leave the crypt after hearing the chaos above and guessing the cause; they wanted to join the other partisans, preferring to die with their comrades rather than hide like cornered rats where they had been.

Gabcik never made it. He slipped as he was climbing the steep stairs out of the narrow crypt entrance and fell back down, momentarily unconscious. Kubis did not notice that Gabcik wasn't with him until he reached the sanctuary.

"Josef?" he said then, turning and seeing no one behind him.

For a moment he was torn between finding out what had happened and making his way through the debris-littered sanctuary to the steps leading to the roof. He chose, with some misgiving, the roof.

When they found Kubis's body, the troopers rejoiced it was that of one of the two culprits responsible for the death of Reinhard Heydrich. They were even happier when they discovered he was still alive.

He was rushed to the same hospital where Heydrich had been confined during the final week of his life. Surgeons fought to save him so he could stand trial and be used as an example throughout the Third Reich, but they failed. Twenty minutes after the start of an operation to remove bullets and shrapnel from him, Kubis died.

They thought only Gabcik could have remained alive.

A vent was discovered leading into the crypt. The grill over it was knocked out and water hoses were jammed into it, then huge amounts of water were pumped into the catacombs under Karel Boromejsky. But each hose was mysteriously sliced open, cutting down the pressure, or the hoses were pushed back through the vent.

The Waffen SS commander was astounded.

"How can this happen?" he screamed. "How can one man do this?"

Finally the commander decided to order his men to attack en masse, using an age-old offensive weapon, a battering ram, to break through the concrete entrance to the crypt. The troopers entered with no particular caution, prepared to encounter just one man. What they didn't know was that three other partisans, retreating from the battle on the roof, had found their way to the catacombs to join Josef Gabcik.

A battle ensued, with more than a dozen troopers dead by the time a retreat became necessary for the survival of the remaining soldiers.

"We could see no one," the commander was told over and over by a number of his men. "Shots came from the darkness, there were screams of pain, and our comrades fell at our feet."

More than one man after all!

The commander decided to smother the catacombs with tear gas. Canisters were tossed down the vent, one after the other, but still there was no surrender; in fact, many of the canisters were tossed right back out, falling at the feet of the commander and several

Gestapo agents standing with him, all of whom had to pull back temporarily, rubbing their irritated eyes.

An even greater force was assembled, armed with flamethrowers, grenades, and machine guns. They stood before the crypt, the secret entrance blown away by explosives. The order to attack was given, and the troopers waded into knee-deep water and the lingering stench of whatever remained of the tear gas.

Some movement was perceived directly ahead of them.

Three troopers with flamethrowers turned on their jets of roaring fire, and much of the crypt area became an inferno. Previously the partisans had tossed the contents of two newly discovered cans of gasoline onto the water, which ignited instantly, engulfing the forward part of the force of Waffen SS troopers and sending them from the catacombs in a frenzy!

The commander, embarrassed by the thudding failure of his troopers, including the deaths of four of them, was prepared to bomb the historic church into rubble but was required to phone back to Berlin headquarters for any such authorization.

Initially Himmler resisted this, perhaps due to some residue of his early adherence to Catholicism, more than likely mixed with ample insight into the political consequences. But he was worn down by an undeniable fact, hammered at him by one of his most trusted commanders: If they could not either kill or capture Gabcik and the others soon, the public in Prague and elsewhere would be emboldened to join the resistance after having seen the ineptitude of the "elite" Waffen SS.

"Only the catacombs," Himmler ordered finally, his voice sounding unusually strained. "Spare the rest of the church."

The commander directed his troopers to prepare the explosives. Then, as they were about to enter the catacombs again, four shots rang out.

Gabcik was not alone after all. Three other men had managed to make their way to his side. They all had decided to take their own lives rather than be captured and tortured into giving the Nazis a Pandora's box of information about the resistance movement in that country and elsewhere.

After the four bodies were dragged out into the street, one of the troopers found, clutched in Gabcik's hand, a water-soaked page from a small bible. One passage, Isaiah 49:26, now barely discernible, had been circled:

And I will feed them that oppress thee with their own flesh; and they shall be drunken with their own blood, as with sweet wine: and all flesh shall know that I the Lord *am thy Saviour and thy Redeemer, the mighty One of Jacob.*

Himmler was told about this some hours later by Josef Goebbels, who handed the communique to him and stood with a smirk on his face as he waited for the other man to finish reading it.

"Stupid swine," Goebbels sneered. "They cling to their moronic faith like the idiots they are. Do you not agree, Heinrich?"

He was surprised when Himmler turned away from him and said nothing.

14

Stephen Bartlett had remained hidden at Katrina Hrdlicka's house since leaving the Heydrich estate. A few weeks passed. He didn't want to leave before finding out what had happened to Gabcik and Kubis. The plan had been for the three of them to leave the country together and head back to London. When they hadn't followed him to the house half a day later, he knew something had gone wrong.

"Within an hour, the patriotic citizens of Prague cooperated with the forces of the Third Reich to seal off the city." The radio announcer's voice provided the answer.

"They're still inside," Bartlett said as Katrina and he sat before the old radio that crackled with static, listening to the unfortunate news. "They were never able to leave . . . the Nazis acted far faster than we could have guessed!"

Katrina's normally jovial manner had changed. Wearing a dark blue dress instead of her customary floral patterns and lace fringes, she seemed more like a widow in mourning over the death of her husband.

He told her this.

"It is the way I feel," she replied somberly. "My clothes reflect my mood, and my mood now is one of despair for Josef and Jan and the hundreds, perhaps the thousands, who have become tacit Nazis out of fear for their lives."

"Eduard Benes predicted the opposite would happen, that—"

"Benes is a puppet of his own ego," she blurted. "The man has allowed his *image* to stand in the way of his dedication to freeing this country from the domination that is strangling it. He sees himself as a messiah come to rescue the enslaved."

"And as a messiah, he is infallible?"

"That is, I suspect, *exactly* the way he allowed himself to feel, Stephen."

Katrina's massive shoulders slumped and she seemed at once devastated and hopeless.

Bartlett walked over to the stuffed and worn couch and sat beside her, resting his hand on her shoulder. When she looked at him, he could see that her eyes were filled with tears.

"What hope do we have?" she pleaded. "The people are *not* going to rally around the cause of independence, as Benes had thought. The murder of Heydrich, I suspect, will have the *opposite* effect, Stephen. It will freeze the resistance in its tracks, and fear will chip away at them until there is nothing left. Safehouses for partisans will quickly become a thing of the past. It was a risk before, but now the chances of being caught are so much greater."

"But you wanted his death as much as the rest of us," Bartlett reminded her.

"I did, I know that, *I did!*" she agreed. "And . . . now . . . now . . ."

"You're ashamed, aren't you?"

He could hear Katrina catch her breath.

"You're ashamed of the people for their cowardice. All of *us* have been willing to sacrifice our lives for them, yet they aren't willing to do the same for *us!*"

Katrina jumped to her feet, the couch and a small square table in front of it shaking as she did.

"*You* are an American," she said, at nearly a shout. "Yet you came thousands of miles to die here if necessary, so that *they* could be free. Josef and Jan were safe in London, away from the front lines, but they loved this land enough to come back and expose themselves to the most awful suffering *because they wanted to be citizens of a liberated Czechoslovakia!*"

Her heart beating dangerously fast, her face a sudden red, Katrina brought her hand to her chest as she fought against the constricted breathing that filled her with rare panic.

"Please, dear lady, please calm down!" he begged her.

"How can I do that when—?" she replied, then fell silent as the news came over the radio, news that froze her words in her mouth.

"The parachutists could not endure the prospect of justice," the announcer declared, "so they committed suicide. By direct order of the Führer, their heads have been separated from their bodies and—"

Katrina put the palms of her hands to her ears and let out a single shriek of despair before collapsing on the floor. Bartlett couldn't move her. As strong as he was, her great weight made getting her into bed impossible. So he went upstairs and got a pillow and a blanket, then helped her to be as comfortable as he could on the living-room floor.

For quite awhile he sat beside her, holding her hand, his own two hands needed to wrap around one of hers.

"I've seen photographs here when you were younger," he said, not certain she could hear him. "You've always been very pretty, Katrina."

He leaned over, kissed her on the forehead, then lay down on the floor next to her, pressing his body close to hers, thinking that, even though unconscious, she would somehow *feel* him.

Katrina mumbled fragments of phrases every so often.

"Stefan . . . you wanted to dance the first time we met . . . so kind . . . You accepted me, my love . . . Don't die . . . I can't let you . . . Take my life, Father, let this man live . . . Your blood's all over me, beloved . . . I shall never be able to wash it off, never wash it off . . . always there . . . reminding me . . ."

She regained consciousness when moonlight shone through the large window in the living room, touching her now-moving form.

"How long have I been like this, Stephen?" she asked weakly.

"For hours," he replied.

"I felt your hands," she told him. "I felt your body next to mine. You are a kind, sensitive man, Stephen."

"And you are a remarkable woman, Katrina. It is possible that I will never meet anyone like you as long as I live."

"You would have liked Stefan. Stefan and Stephen, isn't that a funny thing?"

He agreed it was.

"We used to dance together, my love and I," she recalled, "dance in the moonlight, its glow covering us from head to foot. I was a little less heavy in those days but still big, make no mistake about that. Yet Stefan made me feel like a gazelle instead of an elephant. To him, the weight didn't matter."

She asked Bartlett if he would help her to her feet. With some effort on both their parts, she was able to stand.

"I remember a little waltz Stefan taught me," she said. "May I show it to you?"

Bartlett nodded, prepared to help her if she started to fall.

That didn't happen. But something else did, something remarkable.

She seemed almost to shed her enormous bulk and her age, and she became as a young girl, small, lithe, dancing with grace, even as the floor creaked, the furniture shook, and Bartlett held his breath, captivated by the waltz she was performing but fearful that she would stumble and hurt herself.

Finally, the illusion of youth gone, she stopped, gasping for air, but not falling, and turned to him. She smiled a nervous smile of pride and some embarrassment.

"How wonderful it was then, Stephen," she said. "Stefan and I were so in love. And our country was free. The butchers hadn't descended upon us yet."

She was still a little wobbly and reached out for him.

"Stephen, would you help me?" she asked pitiably. "I need to lean on you a bit."

He stood beside her. She rested her head on his shoulder.

"I felt a chill then," she remarked. "It seems to announce death, you know. I don't think it will be long, Stephen," she said, "not long before my beloved and I are dancing together again."

"It doesn't have to be that way," he tried to reassure her, "not yet, anyway."

"You think I'm sad, don't you?" she whispered. "Oh, how can it be sad for me to imagine Stefan and I no longer apart but dancing together with the angels? How can that be anything but joyous, dear friend?"

He must have felt the same chill she had; he rubbed his arm as it filled his entire body, wondering, in a moment of panic, what the morning would bring.

The two friends had their last breakfast together, Polish sausage, scrambled eggs, and toasted bread Katrina had made, along with freshly ground coffee. Minutes after they had finished, the approaching sound of a car's motor could be heard, and they both saw the telltale black Mercedes coming up the narrow, winding road leading to her house.

Bartlett fled through the back entrance into the nearby woods, pausing for a moment to turn and wave to Katrina, but she had returned to the house, preparing for the intruders . . .

Katrina saw the two stern-faced Gestapo agents walking up the path to her home and thought, *they all look the same with their long leather coats and their wide-brimmed hats and the devil himself about them.*

She went to the back window to make sure the American was gone.

He needs as much time as he can get. Partisans will be waiting for him. He will make it safely to France, then across the English Channel and into the arms of his loved ones.

Katrina held out her own arms for a moment, remembering her husband, remembering that cold day two years before when she had buried his body in the backyard so the Nazis wouldn't know whether he was dead or alive.

He came to me in the middle of the night, poor Stefan . . . all covered with blood, banging on the door and falling into my arms when I opened it, but not before he smiled and said, "Thank God for you, Katrina, thank God!"

Stefan had lost too much blood. A partisan doctor could not save him. He died holding her big hand with a feather touch because of his weakness, whispering something to her as she bent down, trying to hear what it was; just three words, spoken ten thousand times before during the course of their marriage, but never richer, sweeter, finer than now . . . *I love you.*

The ground had been hard as she dug into it with an old shovel. But she was strong, stronger than Stefan, stronger than any of the men she had met in the resistance. That's why she was nicknamed "Tough Mama." How many male egos had she bruised by besting them at arm wrestling? Stefan lifted weights, did other exercises and put on a few pounds of solid muscle, but still, she won—and not because he *let* her.

"They will have to send an army after me," she said, chuckling, as she turned from the window. Her thoughts were interrupted by insistent banging on the front door.

She answered it with a smile on her face.

The two men tried to push their way past her, but she would not let them, a massive presence blocking the doorway.

Both drew pistols.

Katrina grabbed one man's gun hand and bent it back, breaking it at the wrist. The other, backing up a foot or two, got off a shot that caught her in the shoulder. She winced, then lunged for him, wrapping both large hands around his neck, and lifting him bodily from the ground. He was screaming for his partner to help. The other man stumbled to his feet after retrieving his gun and aimed it at her, but when he pulled the trigger nothing happened. He was out of bullets. Instead, he used it as a club, hitting her half a dozen times over the head.

Katrina fell back against the door frame, then threw the agent she had been holding to one side, his body crumpling to the ground. She turned to the one who had been hitting her, and ripped the pistol from his grasp, grabbed his head like a melon, twisted it, and broke his neck in one swift movement. She strode over to the second man, who lay moaning on the ground, bent down and finished him off in the same manner. Finally she dragged each one to the rear of the house and dumped the bodies down the storm-cellar steps, then lifted the heavy wood doors and let them slam shut.

When she was back inside the house, Katrina concentrated on getting the bullet out of her shoulder. After running steaming-hot water over a short-bladed hunting knife, she drank down two shots of whiskey and cut open the flesh around her wound. The bullet had been cushioned by a mound of fat and she managed to dig it out, and bind up the incision.

Katrina stood in the middle of the kitchen, every inch of her body covered with perspiration. She glanced around at the familiar surroundings, though never before had she felt as completely isolated and alone as then. No one could help her. Gabcik and Kubis were gone. So was the American. She dared not contact any other partisans for fear of leading the Gestapo to them.

And surely the demons running this country will descend with all the screeching of hell once two of their kind fail to return, she thought, shivering at the notion.

Dusk would be along soon.

Katrina decided to gather together all the weapons at her command, but found that her mind was befuddled a bit in the aftermath of the surgery she had had to perform on herself.

I will not let them come here and take me to one of the camps or a torture chamber in some basement and tear from me the truth about good men who have trusted me with their lives, she told herself.

I will not let them come, uninvited, into this home of mine and rob it of the security and the peace it has provided for so long.

There were fifty sticks of dynamite and several grenades in the house, plus three small land mines, two cluster bombs, a shotgun as well as a rifle, three pistols, and an assortment of knives plus an ax.

"For one fat lady!" she exclaimed out loud.

She planted two mines near the front entrance, another at the back door. Next she rigged the grenades to tripwires at intervals on the first floor; then she dismantled the electrical system so any intruders would have to walk around in the darkness, with only flashlights to guide them.

In the course of all the activity, her shoulder had started bleeding again, but she decided not to patch it up, for she saw, seconds later, a parade of headlights winding up the twisting road that led to her house.

She aimed one of the rifles as best she could and managed to blast out two sets of headlights before the caravan stopped. She could hear car doors being slammed shut as agents hurriedly jumped out and prepared to go the rest of the way on foot.

Katrina had already decided she wanted to die in the bedroom she and Stefan had shared for twenty years, so she hurried upstairs as fast as her bulk and blood loss would permit, then locked the bedroom door behind her.

She picked her steps carefully and approached the large, strong bed Stefan had built for the two of them.

How could you make love to someone like me? she marveled. *How could you do that, dear one?*

She climbed in under the covers, her blood pressure shooting upward as she waited for the sounds that were certain to come in rapid succession.

One of the land mines was triggered, with screams of shock and pain following. The one at the back of the house also exploded, shaking the structure as though it had been hit by an earthquake. Cautionary shots were fired, followed by—

Footsteps on the stairway. Down the corridor, to her bedroom door.

"Your little game is over!" a harsh voice yelled. "We are here to take you with us. There is no point in resisting any longer."

A shape appeared in the darkness, framed by the doorway, then a second one and a third moved in behind it. The beam of a flashlight caught the upper part of her body, now blood-soaked along with much of the bed.

"Do not resist us!" the first man demanded.

"I shall not, you can be assured of that!" she said, feigning a Prague high-society accent. "No need, sir, to hesitate as you enter."

The door opened slowly. One man stepped into the bedroom, followed by the other two; the three of them approached her bed without noticing the tiny, nearly invisible wire stretched tautly from beneath a concealing pile of boxes in one corner of the room up to the bed and under a goose-down comforter. The end was wrapped around her thumb.

"Welcome to hell!" Katrina said as she smiled at them.

"What are you telling us?" the first agent asked dumbly, pointing his Luger directly at her temple.

The smile gone, a look of revulsion on her face, she screamed an obscenity about the Führer at him. He fired twice, the second shot blowing away the top part of her head.

The one who had shot her bent over the bed, looking at the massive body in the darkness. Then, mumbling the words, "Slovak pig," he contemptuously gave Katrina's body a viscious shove.

Payback time for Tough Mama.

15

Bartlett soon met the partisans who would accompany him to the German border. In so short a period of time, he had become a symbol to them, even more so in view of the deaths of Josef Gabcik and Jan Kubis. As they approached Germany, one of them told him what had happened to Katrina Hrdlicka. Despite the grim news the man laughed with great affection for Katrina and remarked that in the Slovak language, her last name meant "gentle as a turtle dove."

They stood, briefly, in prayer for Tough Mama, then the American thanked his new friends for their help and began the brief return journey . . .

The bunker was directly ahead, the familiar discreet bulk in the mountainside visible despite the intensity of the storm. As Stephen Bartlett approached, he knew if Franz Kallenborn or anyone else could see him at all, they would open the massive front entrance immediately.

Nothing. No response whatsoever.

Heavenly Father, what has happened? he prayed.

Bartlett could not wait any longer, with the rain beating at him, driven as it was by a high wind; he pushed through the thick gathering of trees and bushes to the left of the bunker and around the side of the mountain to the back, his breath coming in uneven spurts by the time he made it.

The door stood wide open. As heavy as it was, there was little likelihood that it had been *blown* open, despite the heavy wind that day. He took out his Colt and walked slowly up to the doorway.

"Franz?" he asked. "Franz, what has—?"

As soon as Bartlett stepped inside, he saw the bodies. In the corridor leading from the rear entrance, in doorways along either side. Some had been shot. Others had been bayoneted. A few, it seemed, had been strangled to death with a thin wire; deep cuts and bruises appeared on half a dozen necks.

Sheets of paper were scattered everywhere, chairs were turned over, coffee cups had been smashed on the floor.

"How could the Nazis have found this place?" he said out loud. "Who tipped them off?"

But, of course, the answer had been obvious for a long time, however much the resistance fighters tried not to let it concern them. All that was necessary to doom them was for someone to stumble upon the original plans for the bunker. Though these would be some thirty years old, they undoubtedly still existed somewhere, available to an especially attentive assistant of Goebbels, perhaps.

Or there could have been a traitor, another Emil Kleist who had led the SS to the spot! Yet somehow, that seemed the least likely eventuality. If it had been a traitor, why hadn't the bunker been raided before then? Every month of safety for the partisans meant another month of sabotage, ambushes, and whatever else the resistance was capable of throwing against the Third Reich.

He thought he would find no one alive. Those who had survived undoubtedly were taken to a concentration camp or a Nazi prison.

Franz Kallenborn proved him wrong.

The man lay prostrate on the floor of his quarters. Bartlett assumed he was dead, like the others, and started to turn away.

"The troopers made the same mistake," came the nearly inaudible mutter, accompanied by a slight chuckle and then a deep cough.

Bartlett rushed to his side, cradling the man's head in his lap.

"How long have you been like this?" Bartlett asked.

"A day, perhaps a few hours longer than that. I don't know."

Vulf! What had happened to Vulf?

He asked Kallenborn that question.

"I . . . I . . . saw him take down a trooper. Vulf tore away his throat. There may have been others, too. I think the poor thing did his best, like everybody else. That animal stood with us, Stephen, every step of the way. I heard him snarling again and again. I could hear screams coming from people who were being attacked by him. I . . . don't . . . know where Vulf is now. He might be dead . . . our poor friend might have been shot."

Suddenly Kallenborn's eyes widened.

"I think it's time," he whispered, with no evident fear. "I've prayed for a very long while now that the Lord would take me to be with Him . . . I'm so weak, Stephen . . . I haven't eaten since—"

His face contorted with pain. His eyes closed, then opened again, wide this time. He grabbed Bartlett's coat and pulled himself up slightly.

"I shall wait for you past the gates; you must believe that," he said, then dropped back against the American's lap, his arms falling, his head turning to one side, his body now limp.

Bartlett managed to get the body outside, toward the rear of the bunker. Finding a shovel was not difficult. Within twenty minutes, he had dug a hole for the body and found a tablecloth to wrap around it.

"There should be a procession, Franz," he said, "with twenty-one guns going off. Churchill, Casey, de Gaulle, and the others giving speeches in your honor. It should never be the way it is now, my friend, in the middle of a Bavarian wilderness, with only one mourner standing by."

What about the bodies of the other men? How could he bury every single one? He had gotten to know quite a number of them. He had thought, foolishly, that some of the friendships begun during those weeks in the bunker would last a lifetime.

Bartlett bowed his head, overcome by everything that had happened. A moment or so later, he thought he heard footsteps, but ignored them as he surrendered to his grief.

"We were sure it would work," an emotionless voice broke the silence. "And we were right. Swine like you are so *predictable!*"

In an instant, Bartlett's head was jolted backward, wrenching his neck, and he was looking up into the face of an SS officer.

"I am Major Wilhelm Glagau," the rather pudgy German said, spit from his mouth settling in a few tiny beads on Bartlett's cheeks and forehead. "We have been waiting, how shall I say, in the woods; oh yes, we have been waiting here ever since my men cleared this place of its vermin.

"Intelligence reports suggested you might be headed in this direction. Since there is no other possible destination *here* but *this* bunker, I simply assumed it was where you would end up."

The round face, almost cherubic in appearance, seemed at odds with the heavy, dark circles under Glagau's small, rat-like eyes, rouge-ruddy cheeks, and visible veins near the surface of the skin, all of which pointed to someone who had been drinking far too many alcoholic beverages.

"How did you find them?" Bartlett asked.

"A chap named Bruno Vetters proved more than a little helpful to us," Glagau told him, chuckling at the revelation, "oh, indeed he did. You know this splendid individual, do you not, Stephen Bartlett?"

He slapped the American hard across his face, nearly breaking his jaw.

"You should realize something else," Glagau said, beaming. "We were delighted to uncover such a nerve center for the resistance movement, make no mistake about that. But *you* are the real prize, my American gutter rat. If you had not been involved, I doubt we would have tried so hard."

The German stood back and sneered, then added, "What should be on your conscience for as long as you live—which will be only another day, I might add—is that you are, shall we say, in part *responsible* for all those bodies in there. You, Stephen Bartlett, are not the frosting on the cake. *They are!*"

The Nazi mentality was such that avenging the Allied resistance's successful attempt to assassinate Reinhard Heydrich assumed crusade-like proportions. The top leaders had drawn around themselves grandiose illusions of godlike invincibility. They were convinced that they were protected by forces that went beyond the physical. But only Heydrich had gone so far as to carry that notion to extremes by having lax security around himself—while Himmler and others kept a pragmatic edge to their mysticism by "assisting" the supernatural through heavily armed escorts.

The fact that Heydrich had been attacked and had ultimately died of wounds inflicted by partisans proved to be a threat to an important underpinning of the Nazi belief system, the precept that they would be absolutely impenetrable to any such attempts, that they could do whatever they wanted, to whatever country they wished in whatever manner they chose and never be punished by the devil-gods of the dark and terrifying netherworld who supported them—or the people they oppressed. Since these gods were far more powerful, they supposed, than the Judeo-Christian deity, they literally could act with impunity twenty-four hours every day for the rest of their lives and die as very old, very powerful men.

Reinhard Heydrich's death changed an important aspect of that doctrine. There indeed was a price to be paid; if they were careless, one or more of them would have to forfeit their lives, their mystical "connections" not withstanding . . .

Bartlett was incarcerated in the basement of an old building on the outskirts of Stuttgart, Germany. That city showed its bleak, industrial face more than ever in an era of war, with smoke, black or gray or soiled white, pouring into the atmosphere, its buildings dirtied by layer upon layer of soot and other airborne debris. From a small window set high in the south wall of the basement he could see the outlines of factories, hulking structures within which were manufactured machine tools, ball bearings, and internal-combustion engines.

Perhaps the Allies will bomb tonight, he thought, while realizing any such desire stemmed from a streak of vengeance he was feeling, vengeance over what had been done to those within the bunker but, even more so, to the innocent citizens of Lidice, a ghost town now. Most of its buildings had been leveled and no one was left to live within any that might have been still standing.

He pictured Bruno Vetters in his mind and faced the same corrosive rage. But there were questions this time: Why were the man's hands nearly destroyed? Was this a bizarre kind of continuing cover? Or had signals been crossed and the pilot of the plane not aware that Vetters was a double agent?

The next thought was perhaps the most puzzling of all: Why had the plane been sent in the first place on a mission to track down a rumored resistance command center? If Vetters had managed to get out reports to the Gestapo, then anything else seemed superfluous.

Bartlett was weary. His bad hand was throbbing again, though not nearly as painfully as at the beginning. He looked around the basement. It reminded him somewhat of the Marmatine Prison in Rome, the supposed final place of imprisonment for Paul the apostle; it was a place he had visited just before the fascists under Mussolini had taken over . . . small, damp, dark, cold.

He had no bench to sit on, no toilet facilities, no water. The place held the lingering scents of other prisoners, still so strong he had to make a conscious effort to ignore them or he would surely gag.

They will take me out, when it suits them, and stand me up against a wall or a backdrop of trees, and their troopers will open fire.

Strangely, the thought didn't terrify him. Strangely, he felt at peace about what would surely happen to him within the next day or two. What *saddened* him was thinking of his family and how any such news would affect them. They would survive, yes, for they were strong and they were faithful, yet the pain would be monstrous. Picturing them in the midst of it sent him into a torrent of misery. He slid down the cold, dirty wall and held his head in his hands.

"I love them so much," he whispered. "I can almost feel them by my side now. I can imagine running my fingers through Natalie's hair and feel Andrew trying to wrap his little arms around my waist."

Bartlett fell asleep like that, thinking about his wife and son, imagining the three of them hugging one another in the midst of an English meadow under a bright afternoon sun . . .

He awoke to the sounds of a heavy wooden door being opened, a man's cry of pain, then the door being shut. Groggy, momentarily disorganized, he opened his eyes and saw a body lying on the damp floor a few inches from his feet. As his vision cleared, the man turned over, groaning as he did so, a man with bandaged stumps where his hands should have been . . . *Bruno Vetters!*

Bartlett's immediate reaction made him want to jump to his feet and pounce on the traitor, strangle him, beat him, do something to punish him. But he restrained himself for the moment, sitting still, waiting to see if Vetters would notice him, and if he did, how the German would react.

Several minutes passed.

Vetters was finally able to raise himself to a sitting position. At first he seemed unaware of anything. He went through a series of racking coughs, spitting up blood several times, then he sat in that one position, breathing heavily and staring at his surroundings as though he was convinced he was trapped in the worst nightmare of his life and soon, quite soon, he would awaken from it and be grateful.

"Who's there?" he said. "It's so dark . . . Who are you?"

"Stephen Bartlett," came the cold, stern reply.

"Thank God!" Vetters replied weakly. "I wondered . . . what would happen . . . when you made it back . . . to the bunker."

"So many are dead, Bruno."

"Franz, my dear Franz . . . and the others . . . Stephen, Stephen, what is going to happen now? How . . . can the resistance function . . . with such a loss?"

"You accomplished a great deal, Bruno."

"I . . . don't know what . . . you mean."

"Even now you play with the truth," Bartlett said harshly. "How can you do that? Look at yourself, Bruno. You have no hands. That is the extent of their gratitude."

Vetters held his arms out in front of him.

"We concentrated so much on munitions, Stephen, and so little on the proper medicines. Even you paid no attention to that area. You were sent with a singular purpose and you, like us, gave short shrift to everything else. We had rifles, bazookas, grenades, and many, many bullets; we could destroy any enemy we met. But we cut corners on antibiotics. Any money we had, any petitions for help, concentrated on the hardware.

"My hands became infected; the pain was unbearable. There were times when I was delirious, when I would rant and scream and beg Franz to kill me. One night, I didn't know what I was doing. I wandered outside. I kept on walking, stumbling, getting up, walking some more. An SS patrol found me eventually in a ditch a long distance from the bunker. I was close to death."

"But I'm sure the men in the bunker looked for you," Bartlett told him. "I'm sure they looked for quite a distance."

"The SS got to me before the others could. After I had regained consciousness and some strength, I was taken to a lab. Someone who looked like Mengele said my hands would never heal, so they had to be amputated. He personally performed the surgery. There was no anesthesia. I blacked out several times but he made me regain consciousness again and again. I felt this beast snap off my fingers first, Stephen, one by one, like branches from an old tree.

"Then he stopped and smiled, demanding that I say where the bunker was. I said I wouldn't betray anyone! But he told me if I did not cooperate, he would peel the skin from what was left of my hands, and then he would chop my hands off at the wrist. That was when he showed me a common ax, used to chop wood for a fireplace. I knew he meant it."

Vetters struggled backward to the wall and braced himself against it.

"I gave in!" he cried. "God help me, I did give in, Stephen. I told those devils everything. And . . . and this man, whoever he was, Mengele or somebody else just as maniacal, took the ax anyway and hacked off my hands. Then he patched up the stumps . . . and sent me here. I . . . I . . . want to die, Stephen. My life is over. I have betrayed my comrades and I want so much to be dead!"

Bartlett understood what Major Glagau had been trying to do by telling him Vetters had betrayed the bunker. It was yet another step in the process of intimidation and eventual collapse of all moral and other restrictions.

"Bruno?" he said.

"I am worthy of nothing but disgust," the other man sobbed. "There is no requirement that you pay any attention to me."

"I knew nothing of what you've just told me. I thought you were on their payroll from the start."

"Oh, Stephen, I know, I know. They have the cleverness of Lucifer himself . . . I just wish I had been strong enough. I just wish—"

Bartlett crawled over to him and cradled Vetters's head against his chest.

"When will they execute us?" the German asked, sounding more like a frightened child. "Can you guess?"

"I think in a day or two, Bruno."

"My wife and two daughters are in Switzerland . . . safe."

"My own dear Natalie and Andrew are back in England . . . well guarded."

"They shall get a taste of hell when they find out. It will be agony for them, yours and mine."

"Stay with me now . . . please," Vetters begged.

"No need to worry. I'm not going anywhere," Bartlett said with a wry chuckle.

Vetters tried to chuckle, too, but it hurt too much, and he stopped.

"God bless you, Stephen."

The two were silent for awhile, then Vetters said, "Do you think they will simply shoot us? Or will they try to prolong . . . things?"

Bartlett could see fear in the man's eyes.

"I don't know. I hope it *is* quick for you, for me. I never did like the thought of lingering."

"Yes, that would be the best . . . quickly."

They fell asleep like that, one man holding the other. Bartlett was awakened only once, just after midnight . . . by the distant sound of wolves.

"What should be on your conscience for as long as you live—which will be only another day, I might add—is that you are, shall we say, in

part responsible for all those bodies in there. You, Stephen Bartlett, are not the frosting on the cake. They are!"

In the midst of a sleep riddled again and again with those words, accusing him, he saw so clearly that he had become more of an immediate target for the Nazis than any of the GRM members. The Nazis undoubtedly considered Franz Kallenborn, Bruno Vetters, and the others dangerous, but they were rather anonymous, and if disposed of, more were ready to take their place. But Stephen Bartlett was a special case. It was one thing to have Germans or Czechs involved. It was quite another for an American to be part of it. Stephen Bartlett represented everything the Nazis had been conditioning the German people to loathe. Though not Jewish, he was captive to their interests and serving their will, and had to be eradicated along with the rest of them. If he was not caught, and punished, he would serve as a symbol, a symbol that the very heart of Deutschland could be penetrated with impunity.

Bartlett knew his death would be heralded throughout the fatherland. Josef Paul Goebbels's Ministry of Information would be working day and night, grinding out self-congratulatory "news" releases to every sector of Germanic society and every conquered country now controlled by the Third Reich.

What will happen when Natalie and Andrew find out? he thought in the midst of his strange and wrenching dreams that night. *Bruno is right—they will experience a taste of what hell is like.*

Every so often, he would skitter on the edges of consciousness, the odors of the basement assailing his nostrils, the moaning of Bruno Vetters reaching his ears, as well as other sounds in the near and far darkness, trucks traveling under its cover, distant indications of battle, voices outside, a dog barking—and those wolves.

Vulf . . .

He could not reasonably believe that any of the howling he heard vaguely through his sleep came from Vulf. That creature surely had disappeared, reabsorbed into the life he was meant to live. Or he had been wounded by the intruding troopers and had gone off to die under the tall Bavarian trees.

My son would have adored you, Vulf. You two would have been friends for life, Bartlett thought, awakening for an instant, then falling asleep again just as quickly.

A hand grabbed his shoulder, shaking him.

"Stephen! Stephen!" the familiar voice whispered frantically. "Von Tresckow here. Please wake up. We have to leave *now!*"

Bartlett opened his eyes slowly and focused on the patrician features directly in front of him, the long, thin nose, the sharp chin, the piercing eyes.

"Henning!" he exclaimed. "You—"

"It *is* I," the other assured him. "I have tried what you Americans would call a con game. But we must leave before it is discovered."

Still disoriented, Bartlett felt the weight of Vetters's body continuing to press against his own.

"Wake up, Bruno," he said. "We have a chance now. We—"

He saw von Tresckow's expression.

"Bruno!" Bartlett started to say but was unable to finish.

Von Tresckow nodded sadly.

"For hours now, I suspect," he said.

Von Tresckow lifted the limp body and gently laid it out on the cold floor, then helped Bartlett get to his feet.

"We must leave him like that?" the American asked.

"We have no choice. He is dead. You are alive. There is nothing more to say, I am afraid."

Bartlett hesitated at the doorway.

"He seems so cold, so lost . . . abandoned," he mumbled.

"Only the physical suit that hung over his spirit. That spirit now is free, Stephen; remember that!"

Bartlett leaned on his friend's strong shoulders and they walked as quickly as possible down the long corridor to the flight of stairs that led up to the ground floor of the ancient building.

An SS trooper met them at the top.

"Papers!" he demanded.

"I am Major General von Tresckow," he retorted. "I need no papers."

"Major Glagau has ordered us to—"

"Glagau be damned!" von Tresckow said with great anger. "Must the dog be allowed to dominate his master?"

The trooper hesitated, confronted as he was with the older man's intimidating manner.

"But what do I tell the major?" he asked, obviously very concerned. "He won't accept—"

"Tell him to go to—" von Tresckow started, but he caught himself, adding instead, "Tell him anything you want, young man.

Now, step aside or I shall be your accuser at a court martial hearing!"

The trooper did precisely that.

They made it away from the building and onto a country road.

"We have to act quickly," von Tresckow said. "We can't pull the same trick as before, so you won't have to beat me up."

"What's the alternative?" Bartlett asked.

"I will take you to a prison near Rastenburg."

"What?"

"I will throw you into prison, my American comrade. But this will be a prison run by an officer who is part of our group."

"Who will allow me to escape when the timing is right?"

"What is it you Americans say?"

"Right on the money?"

"Yes! You hit it right on the money, Stephen. Partisans will be waiting nearby to take you through a GRM route to the English Channel, where a boat will be waiting for you."

Von Tresckow's expression wasn't one of great jubilation, though.

"What is it, Henning?" Bartlett asked.

"You are far from being safe even when you get on that boat. German submarines are more than plentiful throughout the channel. It could be a form of running the gauntlet, I'm afraid."

"But it hasn't been much different since I parachuted in six months ago. At least I will be within sight of a friendly nation."

"There's more," von Tresckow spoke slowly. "England itself may not prove a safe haven for you."

"I don't understand."

"Hitler is furious. So is Himmler. Destroying Lidice did not entirely satisfy them. They want *you,* Stephen; they want you very much. If it came to a choice right now between you and, say, de Gaulle I half-suspect they would pick you."

Bartlett wasn't prepared for that. He felt the blood drain from his face.

"I must look like I feel," he said nervously.

"And for good reason, Stephen: They have many hired guns, each waiting for a command. Some have been imported for purposes such as this. Others were born and raised in England and became closet Nazis during the last decade for one reason or another."

Bartlett was trembling as he replied, "They could get to me here or on English soil or back in the United States."

"You are not safe anywhere until the Nazis are defeated, and even then some loose cannons may still try to do the deed out of some selfless loyalty to Deutschland!"

"Aren't you in similar danger, Henning?"

"No doubt I soon will be. But *for the moment* they don't suspect me with sufficient conviction or logic to keep me under some kind of observation. It's not that way with you, though. They now know all they need to know to have issued a call for your extermination."

Bartlett's face reflected his feelings.

"I know what it must be like, Stephen," remarked von Tresckow. "It is something *I* anticipate happening in my regard tomorrow or the next day or perhaps a month from now—soon, my friend, soon. I have no illusions that I and others like me will be alive at the end of this war, waiting at the doors to the *Reichstag* for the victorious Allies to enter and hug us with great gratitude for our help in bringing the infamies to a halt!"

He slowed down and pulled over to the side of the road, surrounded then by Bavarian forest.

"It will not be by a firing squad or a knife in the back or poison in my tea or bare piano wire around my neck," he said earnestly. "I can say that much, Stephen."

Von Tresckow had been looking straight ahead through the jeep's windshield but, now, he turned and faced the American.

"I will leave a note, that I do know," he added, "a brief one, to be sure. And it will go something like this: 'In a few hours I shall stand before my God, responsible for my actions. I believe I shall be able to say that I have done my best in the struggle against Hitler. God once promised Abraham to spare Sodom should there be ten just men in the city. He will, I hope, spare Germany because of what we have done, and not destroy her . . . The worth of a man is certain only if he is prepared to sacrifice his life for what he believes.'"

"You sound as though you've already written that note, Henning," Bartlett spoke knowingly.

As he started to steer the jeep back onto the road, von Tresckow answered, "I have, Stephen, I have . . . in the very center of my soul."

Abruptly, his eyes widened as he came out of a curve. Directly ahead, the road was blocked by a canvas-covered transport truck, two jeeps, and a dozen SS troopers. Standing in front of them was Major Wilhelm Glagau, his arms folded with exaggerated defiance.

"Say nothing, Stephen," von Tresckow muttered. "This has to be my show."

The American nodded.

Von Tresckow stopped the jeep less than a two feet away from Glagau, climbed out, and walked quickly to him.

"What are you doing?" von Tresckow demanded.

"Retrieving a prisoner," Glagau told him.

"That prisoner is *my* responsibility. He will be confined near Rastenburg."

"Oh, yes, I know the place. Some call it the country club."

"It is a prison. The American will be confined to a cell while awaiting word from Berlin."

"I already have word," Glagau sneered as he walked past the other man toward Bartlett, who had stepped out of the jeep.

Von Tresckow drew his Luger and aimed it at the back of Glagau's head. The troopers immediately aimed their rifles at von Tresckow.

"Do you want to be tried for the murder of someone of my rank?" von Tresckow shouted. "That *is* what will happen, you know, and each one of you will face the consequences. Even in these times, justice can still be found."

Abruptly Glagau stopped walking and reached into his pocket. Von Tresckow aimed the pistol to one side and pulled the trigger, deliberately missing him.

Beads of perspiration on Glagau's forehead showed that, though reined in, his emotions were playing havoc with him. As he handed von Tresckow a sheet of paper, his hand shook.

"*That* is word from Berlin, as you put it," Glagau said, turning around and glowering.

Von Tresckow read what had been sent by teletype. Then he crumbled up the sheet and threw it contemptuously to one side.

"I shall get the order for execution overturned," he said.

"Can you be so sure?" Glagau asked. "Are you willing to risk your career to try it? Questions have been raised already about you. Are you certain you can handle what develops if others are brought to the surface?"

Von Tresckow, with Luger in hand, continued aiming it at the confident Glagau, who now turned to the troopers and said, "Lower your weapons. This man will not shoot me. He has too much to lose."

Now it was von Tresckow's turn to sweat. His gaze drifted from the major to Bartlett. After a few seconds that seemed far longer, he lowered his arm, his shoulders slumping.

"That *is* a good move!" Glagau beamed.

Von Tresckow reholstered his gun, strode up to the other man, and punched him in the jaw with such force that the sound of bones breaking was audible before Glagau crumpled to the ground.

For an instant, von Tresckow seemed about to say something to the American but didn't. He turned toward his own vehicle. Casting a sideward glance at the astonished troopers, he barked, "In my report, I will call my action the reprimanding of an insubordinate junior officer. *Is that clear?*"

Everyone nodded.

"Good!" he said. "Now take your prisoner and your injured back where they came from."

Von Tresckow slid into his jeep, wanting to turn, however briefly, and shout back to Stephen Bartlett what he was feeling at that moment, the regret, the pain, and the other emotions that were devastating him. But he knew he could not, he dared not; he must show no one what was behind the hard, cold mask he had to wear.

As forsaken a thought as it was, von Tresckow knew that the American was one man and one man only, and there were many others who had to be considered in and out of the military, any number of whom could be subjected to the same impending fate if any true Nazi, especially someone like Wilhelm Glagau, were handed further reasons to suspect the fervor of his own allegiance to the Third Reich.

It will not be by a firing squad or a knife in the back or poison in my tea or bare piano wire around my neck. I can say that much . . .

"No man can take from me that which I and I alone will one day hand to my Creator," he said out loud, enjoying a surge of exaltation that he knew would not last very long, but grateful for it nevertheless.

Ahead, slicing brazenly through the ancient Bavarian woods, that long and frequently curving road continued, now deserted except for himself. His fingers tightened around the steering wheel of the jeep and Major General Henning von Tresckow drove on a bit faster now, the third stanza of "Deutschland-Lied" playing over and over in the troubled recesses of his mind.

16

They kept Stephen Bartlett alone for nearly a week in the same dungeonlike room as earlier. Bruno Vetters's body had been removed but Bartlett's memory of holding the corpse in his arms stayed on, awakening Bartlett several times each night. Sleep or prayer or simple contemplation was all that he could do with the rest of the hours that stretched out before him.

He was given a simple bedpan, water that filled a medium-sized urn, and a loaf of stale bread each day.

Nothing else.

No one came near the room except to give him the bread each day, empty the pan and refill the urn. He occasionally heard voices outside but that was all. Mostly there was only the bleakest silence, except for the occasional scampering sound of rats . . . part of the process of debilitation the Nazis had been perfecting for more than a decade.

This is the way I will die, he thought, *with my loved ones a thousand miles away.*

On the sixth day, just after dusk, two SS troopers dragged him from that dank and black confinement, his eyes getting no time to adjust to the bright daylight outside. One of the troopers noticed his reaction and laughed coarsely.

"It takes an animal to enjoy treating other human beings like one!" Bartlett screamed in anger, regretting the outburst in an instant.

The men understood what he had said and as they reached a small stairway leading to an old, oblong, cobblestoned courtyard, both of them let go. Too weak to stand, he tumbled down the half-dozen steps, bumping his side and his head, and yelling out.

"We have no ovens here, Jew-lover," the taller of the troopers sneered. "You will be shot down like a rabid dog! And I will be pulling one of the triggers myself!"

As they bent over Bartlett and started to pick him up and carry him to a canvas-topped military truck at the opposite end of the courtyard, he was tempted to spit in their faces, but he knew they would cause him as much pain as possible in response, so he pretended to pass out, closing his eyes and letting his head flop to one side, forcing them to carry his dead weight.

When they reached the truck, they lifted him up, threw him into the rear, and slammed shut the tailgate.

"It's the American!" he heard someone mutter.

Bartlett opened his eyes and saw nearly a dozen men, most of whom he recognized. They all wore only torn and ragged clothes, some smeared with blood, all quite dirty and smelling of sweat.

Men from the bunker!

"We lived together," one of them said, "we die together."

The man nearest Bartlett helped him to a sitting position.

"Heydrich is getting revenge even after he's dead," this one said.

Bartlett glanced at them and saw that none were better off than he was. A few seemed even worse, those who had been severely beaten, with bruises on their faces and necks, black eyes, and cuts.

"Where are they taking us?" he asked.

"To the woods," replied a short, middle-aged, completely bald resistance member whom he recalled was Dimitri Radick.

"Why there? Why not in the courtyard?"

"Too close to the city. No one must see what is happening. We will be buried in the middle of the forest . . . gone and forgotten except by our loved ones!"

"They really are that concerned about secrecy?"

"Very much so," Radick replied. "They want the outside world to know as little as possible until they have conquered all of it. News of atrocities tends to harden the hearts of even the most dedicated pacifists."

"That's why the average European has heard only the vaguest of rumors about the camps!"

"Even the Jews aren't yet *fully* aware."

"That's astonishing," another man put in. "No wonder there's been so little resistance on their part."

"But it's changing," added Radick. "These people cannot hide in their blindness forever. They must surely see *reality* when their neighbors disappear in the night, when whispered truths about atrocities can no longer be ignored."

He turned to Bartlett and said, "The shame of it is that the Allies are not doing more to educate their own people. It seems to some of us if all the known facts were spread throughout the network of media at their command, even the German people would have little choice but to stand up against the Führer."

His face was red with emotion.

"The United States entered the war six months ago," he went on, "yet American troops have just now landed in England. What was happening during the interim?"

The discussion was cut short as the truck came to a stop and they were ordered outside.

A roughly cut path snaked through the dense woods.

"It's invisible from the road," Radick whispered. "God help us!"

"No one tries to run away," a trooper yelled. "He will not be shot down and die so easily. He will linger, he will linger in much pain. That is a warning to everybody!"

Nighttime sounds joined their labored breathing as the walk continued. Owls could be heard and other night birds. Rustling sounds stirred the dark woods as unknown creatures resented the human intrusion and scampered elsewhere.

And something else. Shapes.

"There is activity out there tonight," Bartlett said, rubbing his arms.

"I sense the same," Radick assured him. "Or we are going crazy before they kill us. Maybe that's what they want. They can tell the world they had to shoot a group of madmen!"

"Look!" Bartlett said as he pointed into the woods on the right side of the truck.

"Fireflies!" the other man offered. "Fireflies ready to dance in the air over our graves! What do you think about that?"

"I don't believe they're—" the American commented, cut off by his own astonishment over the number of them.

"More than I've ever seen before," Radick admitted. "Dozens of them!"

"Little angels in the dark," spoke a sad, hoarse voice inside the truck, "ready to welcome our souls into the kingdom . . . "

Bartlett and Radick glanced at one another, not sure what to believe.

Finally, they approached the edge of a clearing.

"That odor!" Bartlett spoke what they all sensed.

The ground had a strange coloring to it, not a healthy rich-brown but more of a pale, parched green.

"Lime!" somebody whispered. "I see lime. God in heaven, this is—!"

They started murmuring among themselves as they were pushed into the clearing and told to form a circle in the center.

The odor filled their nostrils more and more, a sick odor, like the inside of a crypt centuries old, mixing with a chemical-like scent.

"Look!" Radick said, nodding toward a spot just in front of them.

Something bleached white amidst the dirt, something that looked like—

"They've buried the dead here!" Radick shouted. "They're going to shoot us down and pour lime over our bodies and—"

He broke away from the others and walked quickly toward the surrounding trees.

"Shoot me now!" he said. "Shoot me as I reach for the freedom that all of our peoples will enjoy again one day!"

They did just that as he started to run, one of the SS troopers using a machine gun. There was little left of Dimitri Radick's head as his body hit the ground.

"No more!" a trooper yelled.

Twenty-four soldiers lined up around the dozen prisoners, blocking any escape exit. Then they waited.

"What are they doing?" Bartlett asked.

"Tormenting us like the devils they are," the man next to him replied. "The longer we wait, the worse it becomes."

"I think it's more than that, another purpose. Any anguish we experience is a bonus."

A number of minutes passed.

The troopers seemed like frozen blocks of granite, betraying no movement, no emotion. After perhaps half an hour, they heard the motor of another vehicle. Minutes later, two more men entered the clearing. One of them was Major Wilhelm Glagau, his jaw set in a wire frame. He could not speak, so he scribbled orders on a white pad of paper.

The troopers raised their rifles and aimed at their prisoners.

"We sing!" Bartlett shouted to his comrades. "We show them no fear. We sing until their bullets take the life from our bodies!"

He had no idea what songs the others knew, so he launched into the first one that entered his mind.

"When Johnny comes marching home again, hurrah, hurrah . . . " he began, his heart beating faster as his voice sang out with gusto.

Haltingly, the others picked up the words as he went along. They sang in perfect rhythm, smiles on their faces, their eyes shining in the moonlit darkness, more than one man weeping.

Glagau stamped his foot on the ground in frustration as he tried to scream out his rage but he emitted only a hoarse series of almost comical noises instead. Finally he rushed up to one of the troopers and started to wrench a rifle from his hands.

Growls . . . deep, chilling growls seemingly from all around the clearing. Even Glagau was startled. And then glowing, bobbing pinpoints of light, *reflected light* as dozens of pairs of—

"Eyes!" Bartlett shouted. "It wasn't fireflies we saw earlier."

"We're surrounded by wolves," another man gasped. *"Holy Mother of God!"*

Their black shapes were scarcely visible in the darkness. But enough could be seen to indicate the large number of them prowling the woods just beyond the clearing.

Recovering from the initial shock and scribbling another note, Glagau then took the rifle the unnerved and pale-faced SS trooper now handed over and aimed it directly at Bartlett. The same trooper walked solemnly up to the American and gave him the note, which read: GO TO HELL, STEPHEN BARTLETT, WITH THE REST OF THE JEW-LOVERS!

The first shot grazed Bartlett's ear. Glagau, cackling, pointed the rifle directly at his forehead but never got to pull the trigger again.

A large dark-gray male wolf leapt out of the surrounding darkness and clamped its strong jaws onto Glagau's arm, cracking the bone into splinters. Glagau dropped the rifle and staggered, falling to his knees, and screeching in agony, blood coming past his lips, down his chin, and onto the front of his uniform.

Before the troopers could act, more wolves sprang into the clearing, a dozen of them, two dozen, sometimes three or four attacking each soldier. All around them, the prisoners saw terrifying scenes of men being torn to pieces within minutes.

"They leave *us* alone!" Bartlett could hear someone saying disbelievingly.

"Don't be too sure," another remarked. "Look!"

Nearly all of the troopers had been slaughtered. Only two had managed to escape into the woods. Now the wolves were turning their attention to the prisoners.

"We have no chance!" someone screamed. "We have no bloody chance!"

One by one the animals advanced on the panicky men, ringing them in more and more tightly.

"On your knees!" Bartlett shouted at the others.

"The American's touched in the head," mumbled one of them.

"Now! Please . . . trust me!" Bartlett pleaded.

In seconds, they did what he asked while collectively doubting his sanity.

"Blessed Mary . . . full of grace," rose the beginning of one nervous prayer.

"Father," Bartlett said, his head bowed, "deliver us from the power of—"

He was interrupted by a large, wet, very rough tongue licking his left cheek, then his nose, his forehead, and finally a heavy, firm body block that knocked him over.

As the other men looked in astonishment, Stephen Bartlett wrapped his arms around the biggest of the wolves and kissed it directly on the mouth as he cried out, "Vulf! Vulf! *Praise God it's you!*"

A brief period of rest followed, with men and wolves mingling in extraordinary harmony. In some rare and beautiful fashion, Vulf had transmitted knowledge of his experiences to the rest of the pack, which seemed to consist of magnificent thoroughbred show dogs more than wild beasts of the forests and mountains.

The other men could scarcely believe what was happening. At first apprehensive, then quickly falling in with the way Stephen Bartlett treated the wolves and was treated by them in return, they later seemed like children romping with their pets.

Until, in the middle of the night, rifle fire tore through the air, and wolves and men fell dead one after the other.

Apparently the two troopers who had escaped came in contact with an SS patrol, which radioed to Stuttgart for reinforcements. Though Bartlett and the others had not been foolish enough to remain in the same spot, they did lose track of time, reveling in an almost surreal world of camaraderie with the wolves, and they did not flee the area as fast as they might have otherwise. The wolves who saved them earlier now unwittingly brought all but Bartlett to their deaths. After retrieving a Luger that had been dropped by a trooper, he fled . . .

Behind him, he could hear rifle fire, then a machine gun. Running wasn't a comfortable option for him but he saw no other way. There were too many SS troopers now in the clearing. Partisans who could do so fled, but most were shot down.

Vulf . . .

As before, the animal had saved his life. When a trooper aimed at him as he started to run, Vulf had knocked the man off his feet, his rifle falling from his grip.

That was the last image Bartlett glimpsed before he plunged into the forest, away from the carnage. He expected to be followed but wasn't. Apparently, as the chaos escalated, no one but that one trooper had spotted him.

He kept on running until he had no strength, no energy left, and he collapsed, his lungs heaving as pain ripped through them.

Then, after resting several minutes, he got to his feet and ran farther, but soon he knew he had to stop for more than just a short while. For weeks, he had not eaten properly except at Katrina Hrdlicka's home. He felt very weak. Spots danced before his eyes.

Something nudged his hand. He looked down.

Vulf . . . there was blood on the wolf's side.

"You've taken a bullet!" Bartlett said, in shock. "I don't know what to do. I don't know where we are, where we can go."

Vulf seemed to be trying to understand his words, that large, beautiful head cocked slightly to one side. Then Vulf started to run directly ahead, stopped, turned, and called to Bartlett in his own fashion.

"You know a place, don't you?" Bartlett yelled at him. "You want me to follow you!"

He gathered together whatever strength he had left and trailed Vulf. After what seemed like a mile or two, the land changed from flat forestland to more mountainous terrace, and he saw a cave opening in the side of a small but steep cliff.

Vulf stood there for a moment, then scampered inside.

Bartlett approached cautiously, then followed him inside.

Vulf was still alive by morning but had spent the night in agony. Bartlett found an underground stream a bit farther back in the cave; he tore off part of the sleeve of his shirt, soaked it in the clear water, and returned to Vulf to wipe his face and snout with it, hoping the coolness would help him.

As dawn's light filtered into the lair, Vulf was deteriorating badly, coughing up green-tinged fluids and burning with a high temperature.

Vulf moaned continuously and began to jerk with awful spasms. Bartlett settled down on the rock floor and wrapped his body around Vulf's as much as possible, hugging him gently. This seemed to help but only for a short while.

That animal stood with us, Stephen, every step of the way. I could hear him snarling again and again. I could hear screams coming from people who were being attacked by him.

Franz Kallenborn's words surfaced.

It's almost over, Bartlett thought. *You gave so much to me, to the others, and now I can't give to you what you need the most.*

The spasms had stopped, but Vulf's moaning intensified.

Bartlett's hand fell on the Luger he had managed to retrieve. He started to sob as he closed his hand around it and slipped his finger over the trigger. Then he whispered into Vulf's ear, "Good-bye, dear friend, good-bye . . ." He placed the barrel against the back of the animal's head.

Only a single shot was needed.

Vulf let out one whimper, then slumped immediately in his arms.

Bartlett screamed with deepest anguish, the sound echoing off the walls of the cave.

Suddenly . . . voices shouting. Flashlight beams sliced through the low light in the cave.

Bartlett grabbed the Luger and jumped to his feet.

Three men stormed into the cave, aiming rifles at him.

"We heard a shot!" the shortest and youngest one demanded. "And some terrible screaming!"

He looked at the wolf's body, then at Bartlett, aiming his flashlight at the American's face.

"Are you . . . Stephen Bartlett?" the man asked cautiously, also noticing the raised Luger.

Bartlett wavered, realizing this could be a typical Gestapo gambit. But, whatever the case, the intruders were armed with rifles as well as pistols.

"I am," he replied, sucking in his breath. "How did you know?"

"We have been looking for you for some time now. We heard reports that you escaped and had probably made it to this general area."

"Thank God we found you!" another man exclaimed. "Hurry! We've got to get you into France and then up to Cherbourg. A boat will be waiting to take you across the English Channel."

Bartlett hesitated, looking down at the body next to him.

"Leave the wolf and come with us!" the young man hollered.

"No!" Bartlett said, walking toward the three of them like a man possessed. "I will go nowhere until you promise me you will bury my friend Vulf!"

The three men glanced at one another

"Vulf?" the first one repeated. "That is Vulf?"

After Bartlett nodded, they chattered briefly among themselves.

"We have heard much about this animal and what he meant to our comrades at the bunker," one man said with sad urgency. "Of course we will bury this valiant one. But we must do so quickly and not squander the gift of life that Vulf bought for you with his own."

17

Bartlett's journey from Bavaria to the northern coast of France was not a quick one. The assassination of Heydrich and the almost immediate cowardice of a majority of the Czech populace occurred in an unfortunate and unanticipated chain. Partisans had been increasing their activities until the Butcher of Prague was dispatched. Then, as the days, weeks, and months passed, more and more Czechs, Poles, and others drew back, not wanting to add further misery to the stinking pile of anguish that already threatened to destroy them.

So Bartlett's travels were slowed not inconsiderably as one safehouse after another, the owners previously unwavering in their willingness to help, became off-limits to the American and the three partisans accompanying him.

Finally, after delays that bordered on the maddening, they arrived at Cherbourg after passing through Rouen, Lisieux, and Caen. Bartlett and his companions embraced, their closeness forged by a bonding few other men would ever know.

"Someday we will get together again," one of the partisans told him, "after the war . . . we will break bread and drink some vintage wine and share what happened from this moment until then."

"I would like that," Bartlett answered. "I would like that very much."

"And some good cheese," another added fondly.

They talked a bit longer and embraced a final time, the partisans kissing Stephen Bartlett on each cheek, then stepping back as he boarded the waiting vessel, a simple fishing boat.

"After the war, Stephen," the three men said in unison.

"We will learn to sing 'The Star-Spangled Banner,' as though we had been born in Milwaukee," one of them promised.

"And I shall learn 'La Marseillaise' as though Charles de Gaulle were standing next to me, ready to exile me to Saint Helena if I make a mistake," he shouted as the boat's motor started up, glad that his friends could still laugh, glad he could make them.

In minutes, they had faded into the fog of that warm July evening . . .

Stephen Bartlett thought wistfully of the pleasant little community of Cherbourg he had just left behind, its building and streets and friendly people seemingly suspended in an untroubled time capsule. It would be nice to spend a few days there with Natalie and Andrew. Even with what had been happening all around them, the people of Cherbourg seemed so calm. He was lost in images of Natalie, Andrew, and himself walking a pure white beach or swimming in the unpolluted water, no more war, no more death or dying or pain, at least for the time being, a respite from what the past few years had brought.

"Stephen! Stephen!" the frantic voice brought him back to the present.

Guiding the boat was Marcel Archambault, in his mid-sixties, looking perpetually unshaved but not quite sporting a beard, dressed in modest fisherman's clothes and wearing a battered old dark-blue beret.

"What is it?" Bartlett asked, trying to see through the gathering fog.

"I thought I saw a shape out there."

"What was it?"

"Perhaps nothing more than another vessel like this one, just passing in the night."

"But you think it was more than that, don't you?"

"I worry so much, Stephen. You are so close to home. I pray that nothing stops you now."

Bartlett was touched.

"Why are you so concerned?" he asked kindly.

"Because of what you have done."

"I have *done* so little, Marcel."

Archambault looked at him disbelievingly.

"Even if it were only getting rid of that scum Heydrich, you would deserve the help of *every* European."

"But *I* didn't do it," Bartlett protested.

"Oh, but you did, more than you realize. Without that new bomb, the beast would still be alive."

He saw that the American wasn't quite aware of all the details. "You don't know what happened, do you?"

"Only that the attack succeeded but Gabcik and Kubis were forced to sacrifice their lives afterward. What more could there be?"

"Kubis's gun jammed!" Archambault told him. "If the bomb hadn't worked properly, both men still would have died, but Heydrich would be alive—and pursuing a course of vengeance right from the bowels of hell itself!"

"But they seemed capable enough to have—"

"Do not insult me with pretense," the Frenchman interrupted. "Yes, they were brave, and we all should honor them till the end of our days, but they mistook dedication to a righteous cause for a thorough knowledge of explosives. That was part of what you provided, Stephen."

"Part? I don't understand."

"You managed to survive even the excesses of Eduard Benes, a man with such a messianic complex he assumes any decision he makes must come directly from the Almighty Himself!"

Archambault was chuckling.

"Stephen, Stephen, you still don't see, do you?"

Bartlett had to admit he didn't.

"You scored a victory for every resistance member, every partisan," the Frenchman added. "By bringing Benes down to size by your very survival, you proved that if his so-called wisdom had prevailed, a very real chance existed that the mission against Heydrich could have failed. It may not have failed, of course, but the truth is that with you involved it *did* succeed."

His manner changed abruptly.

"Except for poor Josef and Jan," Archambault remarked.

"You were close to them?"

"They were my very best friends."

Neither of them talked again for a number of minutes. And when Archambault did, it was with more than a trace of fear in his voice.

"I think we are being followed," he said intuitively.

"Another boat?"

Archambault's eyes abruptly widened and he fell back, sliding off his seat and tumbling onto the floor of the boat.

When the fog cleared momentarily, the American saw a Nazi gunboat heading for them.

"We don't *know* it's here because of me," Bartlett said.

"And we don't know it isn't," Archambault replied. "Take the wheel! I'm going to radio for help."

He went below deck as Bartlett steered the boat.

The other vessel was less than a quarter of a mile away. There was no possibility that the gunboat could be outrun, for Bartlett knew he would be fortunate if the fishing boat made it to Dover at normal speed, given its apparent age and condition, let alone attempt a fast getaway.

Archambault came above deck again.

"They've been alerted," he said.

"They? Who are *they,* my friend?"

"You'll see. I planned for something like this."

"You *anticipated* running into a Nazi ship!"

"This Channel has become a rat's nest of enemy activity. If this gunboat is the only one we encounter, we should thank God!"

"But how are we going to—?"

"Quiet, Stephen, ye of little faith," the Frenchman said, shushing him.

He stopped the boat as the Nazi vessel came up to its side and a rope was thrown on-board.

"Secure it!" a helmeted trooper demanded.

Archambault obeyed, and two men from the gunboat jumped over to the deck of the fishing boat.

"I am Major Wilhelm Kolbe and this is Lieutenant Hans Shilling," declared a tall, thin-faced man with pockmarked cheeks. "Explain what you are doing here."

"These are international waters," Bartlett told him. "No explanation is necessary."

Kolbe viciously slapped him across the face with a leather-gloved hand.

"You are an American," he said. "You have earned no right to be insolent."

He turned, clicking his heels as he ordered Shilling to bring them onboard the gunboat.

Bartlett was about to lunge for Shilling when Archambault grabbed his arm, stopping him.

"No, Stephen!" he said. "Wait, it is not as you think."

Shilling walked over to them and gave Archambault a shove.

"No talking!" he said. "Move!"

Already back on the gunboat, Kolbe spun around.

"Stephen!" he repeated. "I heard the name Stephen."

He focused his attention on Bartlett.

"I see we have found you," he observed triumphantly.

"I'm sorry," the Frenchman said softly to Bartlett. "Forgive me . . ."

Shilling pulled out a pistol and aimed it at Bartlett.

"You are to be shot on sight," he said. "At first they wanted you alive. Now it no longer matters."

He closed his finger around the trigger.

"No," Kolbe told him. "We need to question him first."

"What could he tell us? Their bunker has been raided, the other two are dead. What could he possibly know?"

Kolbe drew his own weapon.

"Do not kill the American!" he ordered.

"Only *you,* the real traitor!" Shilling shouted as he turned and aimed at Kolbe instead, managing to get off one shot that hit the other man in the shoulder.

Kolbe fired more accurately, catching Shilling directly in the heart and flinging him backward.

The rest of the crew, which had been watching, started to draw their weapons.

"I would not do that," Kolbe told them coldly.

"You are just one man," one of them shouted, "we are a dozen. What chance do you have?"

"Until now . . . I would have said . . . very little."

None of them noticed the vague forms of boats that appeared in the midst of the fog, half a dozen of them, each filled with fishermen like Archambault, each armed with a rifle or a machine gun.

The Frenchman stepped forward.

"Throw your weapons overboard," he told the Germans.

The crew members obeyed without hesitation.

Kolbe was barely able to stand.

"We will get help for you," Archambault said, ready to jump back to his own boat.

"No good now," Kolbe responded. "I am of no value now. Sink this ship. That is the only way. Not one of them can be left alive."

"If we do that—" the Frenchman protested.

A crew member bolted, ramming into Kolbe and knocking him overboard. A shot rang out. The bullet hit Kolbe in the temple as he struggled in the waves, and he died immediately.

As he raised defiantly the pistol he had wrenched from Kolbe, the crew member was immediately fired upon by several of the fishermen.

Archambault leaned over and whispered to Bartlett, "They must be done away with, you know."

"Even with Kolbe dead?" the American asked.

"Anyone associated with the man is now suspect. Lines of communication to him from others in the resistance movement could be traced. We cannot permit any of them to live."

Bartlett nodded, unable to dispute the cruel truth Archambault had just told him. As the small fishing vessel pulled away from the larger gunboat, the other fishermen opened fire from their own vessels. Then several men boarded it and made sure every German was dead. Two were not. Their throats were cut.

Marcel Archambault was able to land his boat just to the east of the white cliffs of Dover. After an emotional parting, Stephen Bartlett watched him push off into the English Channel and begin the uncertain journey back to his homeland.

It was not long before Bartlett made contact with a land patrol at Dover and was taken by military truck first to Charing Cross Hospital and then on to No. 10 Downing Street.

Halfway to London, he heard over the truck's radio a report about a German gunboat being sunk minutes earlier, apparently quite close to the area where he had been picked up.

18

Stephen Bartlett phoned his wife and son immediately after reaching his private, heavily guarded quarters at Charing Cross Hospital in London. Natalie wanted to come right away, but he asked her to wait. He would come to her, he said, since it would be much safer for them to stay away from the city, which had become infested with Nazi spies intent on sabotage.

"Please be patient, my beloved," he urged. "We can talk frequently by phone. I ache to be with you right now, but I don't want any harm to come to you or Andy. Your location continues to remain a secret. No spot can be guaranteed, I admit, but I just feel the chances are better if you remain where you are and don't come to the city. It has become a target for undercover Nazis."

Finally, just after sunrise on the morning of the third day, Winston Churchill personally put through a call to Natalie Bartlett to say that her husband would be home by noon.

"We are proud of him," that now-famous voice told her. "We are very, very proud of this man whom you love."

"As I am," she replied. "As our son will be when he is old enough to understand."

A short while later, Charles de Gaulle, to everyone's surprise, asked to accompany Bartlett with only a driver along with them so they could have as much privacy as possible.

"It's warm this year," Bartlett said idly as he glanced out the back window at the familiar countryside, with small villages and green fields often bordered by trees, not unlike what he had seen in Czechoslovakia.

"Indeed," de Gaulle said.

Well, there goes that attempt at conversation, Bartlett thought as he sank back against the soft seat, understanding why the Rolls Royce was considered such a comfortable car.

Several minutes passed, the two men dealing with separate and private thoughts. Less than twenty miles from the cottage, the Frenchman touched Bartlett's shoulder and said, "You must not think of me as an unfriendly man, the way the press seems to enjoy depicting me."

Bartlett was surprised but pleased.

"I judge no one in such matters," he commented honestly. "Besides, I think I may understand something about you."

At first de Gaulle seemed miffed by that, his expression a customary one of contempt for anyone who wasn't French, especially for an American who claimed to ***understand*** a Frenchman!

"Forgive me," de Gaulle said. "I have lived so long feeling so superior that it is difficult for me to behave any other way. I am afraid all that showed on my face just now."

"It did," Bartlett acknowledged with a warm smile.

"Someone like you has begun to change my impressions."

"Me? How?"

"Too often, Americans come to my country and spend their tourist dollars and act in the manner *I* am accused of."

"Arrogantly?"

"Yes, arrogantly. They flash their wealth, in comparison to what we have, and it is offensive."

"But it's also more than that, isn't it?"

De Gaulle's eyes widened slightly in surprise.

"It is, yes, but how did you know?"

"Before you go to another country as a spy, you must study their culture and a great deal else."

De Gaulle was smiling.

"Why do you look at me in that manner?" Bartlett asked.

"You are a very big man. You are very broad, muscular. You have a strong face. I expected you not to be interested in such matters."

"You are very tall. You are very straight. You look rather disdainful much of the time. I expected you not to be interested in the kind of dialogue we are having now, nor be willing to communicate at all."

De Gaulle's cheeks reddened.

"There was a time when I would have slapped you for that," he admitted. "But now it *is* you who are speaking in this manner."

"And that makes a difference?"

"More than you know."

They were less than five minutes from the cottage.

"You love your wife and son so deeply," de Gaulle said.

"I do. Is it that obvious?"

"To me, yes, and to others along the way. You talked about them to most of the people you have met over the past six months."

"You have very clear lines of communication, it seems."

"I am *French*. We are clear about everything," de Gaulle said self-importantly.

And then he started laughing, deep inside his gut, a laugh so loud and infectious that the driver, an RAF pilot, after initially being quite startled, joined in along with Bartlett. The three of them became so wrapped up in the moment that the car had to be stopped at the side of the road for everyone to regain control.

Three miles later, Bartlett saw the cottage on top of a small hill with a pathway leading to it that was now lined with flowers.

"Natalie has it all looking so pretty," he muttered.

"Madame Bartlett must be quite a woman," de Gaulle observed.

"She is. We shall want you to be our guest for dinner."

"A great honor, friend Stephen."

The driver stopped the car and Bartlett got out while the other two men waited inside.

Bartlett started to walk toward the two figures standing at the front door, holding his arms out.

He saw Harrison Cowles standing in back of them. It would be good to spend time with—

Abruptly, Cowles pushed Natalie and Andrew to one side and took aim at Bartlett, firing three shots, all of them direct hits. Then he trained the pistol on the driver, who had started to draw his own weapon, but had not yet been able to fire; the bullet hit him in the arm.

Cowles dashed for Bartlett's fallen body and aimed the gun at his head, but in a sudden, astonishing display of speed, de Gaulle leapt from the car and jumped at Cowles, knocking him over. The two men struggled and the Frenchman managed to wrest the gun out of Cowles's hand then grab his neck and squeeze it while the other man flailed at him, trying to break the suffocating hold.

"*You!* A traitor!" de Gaulle screamed.

"I serve the only hope any of us have . . . the immortal Führer!" Cowles gasped. "Reinhard Heydrich has now been fully avenged."

De Gaulle smashed him across the bridge of his nose and kept hitting him until Cowles was unconscious.

The Frenchman then staggered toward Bartlett. Kneeling beside the American were his wife and his son.

"Get help!" de Gaulle shouted at the driver, who was able to drive, despite the bullet in his arm. "For the love of God, hurry!"

Then he joined Natalie and Andrew Bartlett.

"Sir, he can't be allowed to die like this!" she sobbed.

De Gaulle touched her hand with his lips and whispered, "Soon, Madame, soon. We'll get help here soon and—"

Bartlett attempted to talk but succeeded only in coughing up blood. Natalie tried to wipe it from his mouth with the lower part of her dress but there was too much, too much.

He looked up at her and smiled, reaching out his hand. Natalie, in shock, didn't see it, and de Gaulle grabbed it instead, wrapping both his own hands around Bartlett's with great tenderness, whispering, "Why are you smiling, Stephen? How can you be smiling *now?*"

Bartlett's eyes started to roll up in their sockets.

"Dad, Dad, no, please, please, don't go, don't die like this," Andrew begged hysterically.

De Gaulle bent down over Bartlett, and spoke directly into his left ear.

"You shall not die just yet!" the Frenchman ordered sternly. "I pray to Almighty God that you be given more time!"

Bartlett's eyes closed again, and his body went visibly limp.

"Reach up for me, Stephen!" de Gaulle demanded. "Put your arms around me. Let my strength be your own."

Bartlett was too weak to do that, so de Gaulle placed his arms under the American's body and lifted him up less than an inch with great and tender care. He whispered directly into his ear some words that no one else could hear, then rested his friend gently back on the ground.

It seemed a very long while that this scene was suspended, like a moment in a motion picture that had been freeze-framed. Moans came from Stephen Bartlett, then ceased. Finally, one hand again reached out blindly for whoever would take it. This time it was Andrew, as he snuggled closer to his father.

Minutes later, dispatched from a nearby Army base, an ambulance pulled up, accompanied by a transport vehicle filled with troops. The medics took over, pumping a painkiller into Stephen Bartlett, then rushing him back to the base, where a week-long fight for life would be fought . . . and won.

July 21, 1944

Major General Henning von Tresckow tore that page from the desk calendar in front of him, crumpled it up, and threw it into a nearby wastebasket.

The very last day of my life, he thought grimly.

From an open file on his desk, he picked up a *London Times* clipping that told of the recovery of an American munitions expert and counterespionage agent named Stephen Bartlett. He put the clipping aside, then examined a strip of microfilm using a special hand-held viewer. It contained a letter to all three Bartletts. He told them that he was not a poor man. After taking care of his own loved ones as much as he could, he had arranged for money to be deposited in a special bank account in Switzerland. It would be quite enough so that none of them would face financial worries for the rest of their lives.

I am so sorry I could not do more, Stephen, he prayed. *I have reached the end of my ability to help anyone.*

Except by his very death.

Von Tresckow had decided to take his own life in order to avoid any possibility of serving as a link to other members of the continuing conspiracy to assassinate the Führer. The latest effort had been at Rastenburg just days earlier in what would come to be known as the July Plot. Hitler had been injured and others had died, but that was all.

If only the attaché case had been placed on the opposite side of the table's concrete leg. If only . . .

For such if onlys, the maniac who had been unleashed upon the world survived again and again!

Rastenburg . . . translated Wolf's Lair.

The Nazis had indeed taken the bait and assumed that the Führer was the target two years earlier. The guard around him was tripled, while Reinhard Heydrich did nothing to protect himself, just in case. When the Butcher of Prague was attacked and later died, the assumption was that naming the plot WOLF'S LAIR was nothing more than a gambit by the Allies, and no one in the Nazi hierarchy gave further thought to Rastenburg ever becoming the actual site for *another* strike at Hitler.

So, we succeeded as far as we went, von Tresckow reminded himself. *Heydrich is long dead, and Hitler has been hurt. It is said that he is now partially deaf and his mind is just not the same. He is more paranoid than ever, his judgments increasingly erratic.*

Von Tresckow sighed.

Perhaps we did achieve some form of success. A greater threat, Heydrich, never survived, and an already neurotic Hitler could be counted on to conduct the rest of the war in a decreasingly coherent fashion.

He bowed his head and whispered a simple prayer: *O Father, forgive me for now embarking on the journey I feel I must take. I pray that I do not meet Your condemnation at its very end.*

Then von Tresckow stood, making sure his uniform was straight and his medals polished, and left the command tent, walking outside toward the front lines less than a mile away. He nodded to soldiers who had served with him for a number of years. Most were oblivious to what he had planned for himself. A few, co-conspirators with him, sensed what he was about to do. He did not tell them directly but they knew by his manner; they could have objected but they understood that he would not be dissuaded.

"Good-bye . . ." one SS trooper said simply.

"Perhaps I will see you in the kingdom," von Tresckow replied.

"It shall be my wish until the end of my days," the man told him.

The trooper saluted, somewhat stiffly, awkwardly, then von Tresckow continued on his way.

The trenches . . . he had fought in them often over the many years of his service to Deutschland. Now he was to leave them behind, never again turning back to whatever security they offered. He jumped over one, then another.

Ahead a lull had developed. The big guns fell silent, rifle fire pausing, no grenades in evidence.

After walking a few hundred feet beyond the trenches, von Tresckow stood quietly for a moment, looking up at the sky, the stars sparkling clearer, he thought, than ever before. He reached up toward them.

What will it be like, Lord, he prayed, *soaring beyond even the many stars of Your handiwork?*

He took out his Luger, looking at it for a moment, and started firing until the weapon was empty of shots. He reloaded and spent those bullets as well, shooting ahead, to his left, to his right.

No one responds. Do they think I am mad? Is a madman not a trophy of war?

Silence . . . total. He patted the bulge at his side, hesitating briefly.

I do not relish the pain, Lord. I do not relish the pain at all.

Finally he delayed no longer, and took out the grenade.

"Unto Thy hands I give my unworthy soul, O Father," he prayed out loud, "with this my final act."

For a long time afterward, the sounds of battle were still abated . . . until two SS troopers retrieved what was left of Major General Henning von Tresckow's body and took it back behind German lines. It was not more than a short while later that the big guns on both sides sent their fury into the clear July night.

Back in his tent, those same young men found a note that began, "We have done the right thing. None can doubt that. And now, in a few hours, I shall stand before my God . . ."

They wept quietly, careful that others might not find them out.

Afterword

By the end of World War II, Eduard Benes managed to eradicate the names of Josef Gabcik and Jan Kubis from the records of his resistance organization as well as from the Czech government records. He also did his best to persuade the Allies to make sure the two partisans were never officially mentioned by them as well.

Benes had been widely criticized for allowing the mission to kill Reinhard Heydrich and for the slaughter of hundreds of innocent Czechs during the wave of reprisals that followed. While the memory of the Butcher of Prague faded, accusations of "bloodthirsty egotist" were being leveled with greater stridency at Benes himself. He decided the only way to keep the matter from being a perpetual shame was to insist he had never heard of the two men. If questioned about them, his response was a simple: "Well, whoever they were, they must have acted on their own."

Human nature is willing to believe a lie repeated by men of stature, including, in this case, Winston Churchill, Charles de Gaulle, and William Casey. The British cooperated with Benes the most zealously of all the governments. Certain high-placed "former" fascists, more than one residing at Buckingham Palace, feared they would be exposed as some of the individuals who tried to terminate the WOLF'S LAIR mission before the two partisans could even leave England for Czechoslovakia. Though they were at opposite ends of the political arena, Benes accepted the cooperation of this element in British society that he despised, did so because of common interests that made a temporary association between them useful.

Ultimately the machinations of officials in four countries resulted in success for what Eduard Benes wanted to accomplish, and a kind of sanctioned oblivion descended over the partisans as well as

Stephen Bartlett, the American who aided them. The only crack in the official wall of silence came many years later, ironically from Charles de Gaulle a short time before his fatal heart attack on November 9, 1970. He confided to an aide about his cooperation with "the group of cowards," as he called them, who caused Bartlett, as well as the partisans, to be denied the recognition they deserved. On his deathbed, he was heard to say in a voice as strong as ever, "I pray that, if I am to be in the same eternal place as this good man, Stephen Bartlett, that I can look him in the face and not have to turn away because of the shame I have carried with me for so long. If I could do that, I would know it was heaven indeed."

Only a little stone memorial in a tiny and isolated English park, many miles away from the nation for which they sacrificed themselves, pays any continuing tribute to Josef Gabcik and Jan Kubis. Against the most strident Allied protests, it was put there by their families and friends as well as other partisans who, though they had not met the two men, respected what Gabcik and Kubis had done for their cause.

The words on the front of that memorial have said it all for a very long time: "These two men laid down their lives for freedom." Yet, for the next fifty years Czechoslovakia had to exchange one oppressor for quite another, with more atrocities piling up at the hands of the Communists instead of Nazis.

It was only in the early part of the final decade of the twentieth century that the dream of Josef Gabcik and Jan Kubis became a reality as marching millions finally celebrated the emergence of this freedom throughout that ancient land.